SCOUT

THE TALE OF BILLY THE KID AND THE DEADWOOD DWARVES

EDWARD J. KNIGHT

MYTHIC WESTERN PRESS LLC

INTRODUCTION

Eight years after the Jotunheim giants destroyed the Confederacy and most of the Union, the Army of the West stopped their last advance into what was left of the United States. Now the Army polices the borders while rebuilding its strength.

Billy McCarty hates army life. He loathes the daily regiments and rules. Strange sightings in the Black Hills offer him the chance to leave it all behind and lead his own small scout team to investigate.

But Billy's never led a team before. As they head into the wilderness, where only the rules of survival matter, his every decision could mean serious injury or death.

For him or his friends.

Or both.

In the Mythic West, where gunslingers battle monsters of myth, *Scout* continues the epic adventures of the hero, Billy the Kid.

Date	Event
April 12, 1861	United States Civil War begins.
April 9, 1865	Robert E. Lee surrenders the Army of Northern Virginia to Ulysses S. Grant.
April 14, 1865	President Lincoln is assassinated.
April 21, 1865	The Rift to Jotunheim is opened at Andersonville Prison, Georgia. Specific details are unknown as there are no human survivors.
April 27, 1865	General Wilson and his Union Army raiders become the first humans to encounter an army of Jotun giants in Georgia and have survivors. The human army is soundly defeated but is able to dispatch reports to Washington and Richmond.
August 6, 1865	A combined Union/Confederate Army under the command of Ulysses S. Grant, with Robert E. Lee as his second, fights a large Jotun army outside of Lynchburg, Virginia. The humans are defeated, but "Grant's Last Charge" kills the Jotun commander, temporarily halting the Jotun army advance.
July 13, 1866	Richmond, Virginia, falls to a Jotun army.
September 2, 1866	Washington, D.C., falls to a Jotun army.
December 25, 1866	The Christmas Miracle. General Lee defeats a Jotun army attempting to cross the Hudson River into New York City. The Jotun make no further attempts to invade New England or upstate New York.
June - July 1867	Jotun cross the Ohio River in multiple locations. Fighting rages throughout lower Illinois, Indiana, and Ohio. The area becomes known as the Contested Lands.
August 10, 1867	The First Battle of St. Louis. Believing he has superior numbers, General Custer crosses the Mississippi from St. Louis and attacks a Jotun army. General Custer and his army are annihilated.
August 31, 1867	The Second Battle of St. Louis. A Jotun army crosses the Mississippi and sacks the under-garrisoned city of St. Louis.
September 1867 - May 1868	The Long Retreat. The Army of the West under General Sanborn makes multiple raids on St. Louis. The Jotun assemble a force to crush the Army of the West. The human army begins a long retreat along the Platte River. The Jotun pursue, as they believe that the Army of the West is the last capable human resistance.
May 24, 1868	The Battle of Golden City. The Army of the West lures the Jotun army into a trap between the Table Mesas outside of Golden City, Colorado. In a Pyrrhic victory, the Jotun army is destroyed.
1873	Plague sweeps New England and Europe.
June 1875	Giant Killer Cassidy returns to Golden City. Billy McCarty's adventures with him, as described in *Sidekick*, occur.
August 1875	Billy McCarty joins the Tennessee Raid, as described in *Sharpshooter*.
March 1876	Billy McCarty sets out for the Black Hills, as described in *Scout*.

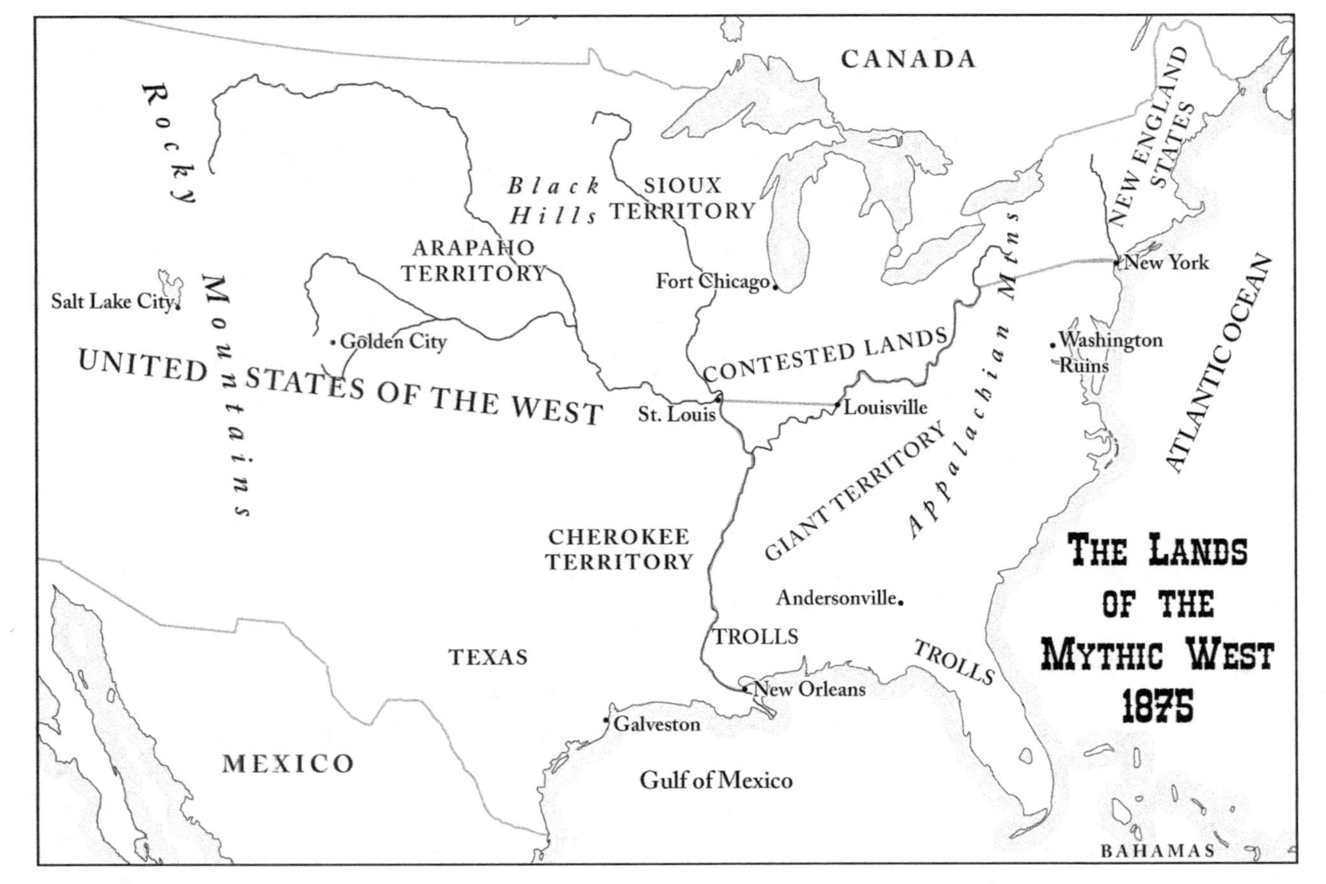
CANADA
Rocky Mountains
Black Hills
SIOUX TERRITORY
NEW ENGLAND STATES
ARAPAHO TERRITORY
Fort Chicago
New York
Salt Lake City
CONTESTED LANDS
Washington Ruins
Golden City
ATLANTIC OCEAN
UNITED STATES OF THE WEST
St. Louis
Louisville
Appalachian Mtns
GIANT TERRITORY
CHEROKEE TERRITORY
THE LANDS OF THE MYTHIC WEST 1875
Andersonville
TROLLS
TROLLS
TEXAS
New Orleans
Galveston
MEXICO
Gulf of Mexico
BAHAMAS

ONE

WE SPOTTED the Indians about an hour before dusk. They were a ways off, down one of the dirt roads that led northwest from Fort Chicago to places I'd never been. At the distance, they were little more than sticks on horses, but I could see raised spears, so I knew who it had to be. As for why they were here, I hadn't a clue.

I raised my hand and brought my scout patrol to a halt. The six of us had been riding the western loop on what had been a beautiful spring day. A gentle breeze balanced the warmth of the slowly sinking sun. Even the horses had enjoyed being out of the fort. Mine shuffled and shifted beneath me, eager for another run down the road.

I almost gave in. I didn't want to go back to the fort and stables any more than he did. As much as I hated the army, I loved being out on the trail. I could do things that needed to be done, without worrying about all the rules I was supposed to follow.

Fortunately, my superiors had figured that out. They'd promoted me to lieutenant in the autumn because of my bravery in battle. Then over the winter, we'd all realized how bad a leader I was.

It wasn't that I didn't take care of the men in my platoon. I did. I was good at taking care of them. It was that I didn't see the need for all the army's rigamarole. Salute, don't salute. Say "sir," don't say "sir." And all the rest of the rules that didn't involve fighting. Who cared?

Well, the army did. But they didn't want to court-martial "the Hero of Louisville." It would've been too embarrassing to give me the Army of the West's Medal of Valor and then kick me out.

But, I was warned, that wouldn't stop them from putting me in the stockade for a night or two. That would've been just a clear reminder to the troops "about the value of good discipline."

And I didn't really want to spend any time behind bars. The food was horrible. Far worse than the mess hall, I'd heard.

So… my friend McNab suggested a scout unit. It was close to what my hero Cassidy had done, and what I'd dreamed of when I was younger. I wanted to ride where there was trouble, just like in the dime novels I'd read repeatedly until they'd fallen apart. An army scout patrol wasn't quite the same thing, but it was at least halfway there. I was sure it was the right thing for me.

And, fortunately, the army agreed. At least until they were ready to march again. Then it was almost certainly back into the thick of things. But until then… I scouted the side of Fort Chicago away from any likely attacks from the giants or trolls. Where there was nothing but farms and fields as far as one could see.

It was beautiful.

But now there were Indians. Who shouldn't have been anywhere near the fort.

As they grew closer, I realized it wasn't just Indians. Four of the eight riders wore army blue. When they saw us, they spurred their horses to a canter. The two soldiers in front pulled ahead by a couple of lengths before settling in to a steady pace.

I looked over my own unit. Only Zeke sat straight at attention on his horse. The big Negro trained his eyes forward as he lightly held the reins. Of the lot of us, his uniform was the only one close to crisply neat and clean. The hilt of his saber glinted in the sun, and I briefly wondered if he'd been polishing it again before dismissing the thought. We'd been riding the entire day, so I knew he hadn't had the time. At our mid-day break, he'd broken out his Bible instead of his polishing rag and sat quietly, his lips moving as he read.

The other four men in my unit were unkempt but not quite on their way to slovenly. An undone button here and there or a stubble-covered chin. Slouching in the saddle. Things I didn't care about when we were on the trail.

But, I realized, the incoming soldiers might.

"Attention!" I ordered.

My startled men shifted into position except for Zeke, who already sat upright. He let a thin smile appear as he watched the others adjust themselves, but didn't say anything.

The two lead riders slowed as they approached. The one on the right, with a full brown beard and wavy hair, raised one arm and hailed us. The one on the left, a somewhat plump dark-haired soldier with glasses, seemed to be hanging onto his reins too tightly to raise his hand. I returned the hail and waited until they'd stopped in front of us.

Both soldiers saluted, even though Brown Beard was a lieutenant like me. He had a large pointed nose and bushy eyebrows under his broad-brimmed hat. Sweat stained the armpits of his uniform, but his buttons still gleamed in the sun. He nodded at me, and then turned to take in my soldiers. His eyes widened when he realized they were all Negroes.

Fortunately, he recovered quickly. "Lieutenant Caldwell, from Fort Randall, with an emissary from the Sioux to General Sanborn." He gestured to the soldier next to him. "Private Brody." Then he reached inside the breast of his jacket. "Our orders," he said as he withdrew a folded sheet of paper.

He brought his horse close enough to pass it to me. I unfolded the paper and started to skim it.

Zeke gently cleared his throat.

"Um, sorry," I said without looking up. "Lieutenant McCarty, Fort Chicago, western patrol."

The tight cursive was easy to read. The orders from Captain Logan, the Fort Randall commander, were to escort the four Sioux warriors to Fort Chicago and General Sanborn. Then they were to await the General's orders.

"Umm… uhh…" Private Brody stammered.

I looked up from the orders. "Yes?"

"Umm.. sir, are you… uhh… *Billy* McCarty? The Hero of Louisville?"

His eyes were wide with eagerness. I hadn't seen that look in months, mostly because the starry-eyed in Fort Chicago had long run out of excuses to talk to me.

"Yes…," I said.

"Oh my gosh, oh my gosh! You're Billy the Kid!" He turned to Lieutenant Caldwell. "From the book!"

"What book?" I asked warily.

"Lemme get it!" Private Brody hopped off his horse so he could rummage in his saddlebags more easily. Then he passed me the book I'd both expected and dreaded.

Jeremiah had told me he'd written a book about our adventures in Colorado, but I'd tried to put it out of my head. I'd read all the dime novels he'd written about Cassidy the Giant Killer before I'd met either him or Cassidy so I knew he could do it, but I just didn't think much of it. Besides, books take a long time to write, don't they?

Except here it was. A book with my name on the cover. *Billy the Kid and the Giants of Colorado.*

I held it in both hands and stared at it. I'd told Jeremiah to call it *Cassidy's Last Ride*, but he'd chosen to write about me instead.

My heart raced, but not from excitement. More like anxiety. Yeah, I'd wanted to be a hero back then. But I'd learned too well since then how often heroics were just luck. I'd been lucky. I wasn't sure that made me a hero.

But I'd also learned that people sometimes needed the idea of a hero more than the actual person.

I forced a casual grin and handed the book back.

"Yeah, that's me," I said as calmly and as casually as I could, "but don't believe everything in it. The writer took a lot of liberties."

"But…," Private Brody stammered. "But… it's you!"

I shrugged because I didn't know what to say.

About then, the rest of their party caught up to us. The Indians drew my attention. They looked regal in their buckskin shirts with their long black hair pulled back. The first was small and wiry—not much bigger than me. The second was more muscled and larger with a hooked nose and high cheekbones. I glanced at the other two, but my eyes kept drifting back to the second.

He had a dangerous presence about him as his eyes flicked over my patrol. He sat tall, but looked ready to spring. His gaze settled on me and then met my eyes. His were cold and steady. We both broke away when Lieutenant Caldwell spoke.

"This is Otaktay," Lieutenant Caldwell said with a gesture toward the Indian. "He leads the Sioux." Then, "Otaktay, this is Lieutenant McCarty, also known as Billy the Kid."

Otaktay nodded without recognition of the name.

Caldwell then introduced the rest of the Indians and his other two soldiers, but most of the names went in one ear and out the other. I remembered Private O'Fallon's, though, because he reminded me of my old friend Tom O'Folliard back in Golden City.

With a pang, I realized I hadn't received a letter from Tom in several months. Which was probably because I hadn't written myself. I needed to change that.

After the introductions, Lieutenant Caldwell cleared his throat and held out his hand. With his eyes, he indicated the orders that I was still holding. After I handed them back, he tucked them into his jacket.

This time I knew what to say. "Let me take you to the general. I know the fastest route."

Since our horses were rested and the road flat, I decided we'd canter. I told Zeke to take charge of the patrol and bring up the rear while Lieutenant Caldwell rode up front with me. The Sioux didn't balk at being surrounded by more soldiers, but I guessed they were used to it after their journey. My memory of Fort Randall's location was a bit fuzzy, but I knew it wasn't close by. I thought about asking, but we were riding just a bit too hard to talk.

Instead, I enjoyed the wind on my face and the way my heart beat as we rode. I was still only a fair horseman, but I'd come to appreciate riding. There was an exhilaration I just couldn't get from walking.

But all too soon we were back at the Fort's western gate. The sprawling complex was almost as large as the city of Chicago itself. It actually had several western gates, but only one was close to General Sanborn's headquarters. That was part of my problem with the army—the fort was just too dang large. It wasn't open like the road.

The gate guards eyed the Indians warily and kept their hands on their guns, but waved us through after Lieutenant Caldwell showed them his orders. We drew a few more stares as we rode at a more relaxed pace to the headquarters building, but I still felt happy to just ride without speaking. When we finally arrived, I turned to Lieutenant Caldwell.

"We can take your horses," I said. "There's some stables not far from here." Then I glanced at the Sioux. "If they're okay with it, of course."

Otaktay was close enough to overhear my offer. He shook his head vehemently. Private Brody had a pained look on his face.

Lieutenant Caldwell looked at the two of them and then at me. "Can you, at least, stay?"

"Sure," I said. I looked at Zeke. "You, too." Then I turned to the rest of my patrol. "Take the evening off. Be at the barracks at reveille."

Some of them immediately perked up, but none immediately left. After a moment, I realized why.

"Dismissed," I ordered, and they quickly dispersed.

I sucked my breath in frustration. This was the army. They knew what I'd wanted, but the rules meant they had to wait for the order. It was stupid. Another advantage of being on the road. Less stupidity.

After we'd all dismounted, Lieutenant Caldwell, Private Brody, and most of the Sioux headed into the headquarters building. Lieutenant Caldwell's other two privates and the remaining Indian tied their horses to nearby hitching posts and began rubbing their horses down. Zeke dug into one of his saddlebags and pulled out a small sack of grain for his own mount.

He gave me a big amused grin. "Never thought I'd see Indians."

I shrugged. "The Arapaho used to visit Golden City from time to time. They're not much different than us."

"Dunno about that." He pointed at their horses. "No saddles."

I chuckled. Trust Zeke to notice the details.

I watched the remaining Sioux warrior care for the Indians' horses. He didn't do much different than we did, which made sense when I thought about it. Horses were horses.

The headquarters door opened. To my surprise, my old friend Sergeant-Major McNab, one of the army's top quartermasters, stood there. His uniform was clean and pressed and the ring of grey hair around his bald top had been recently trimmed. It'd been several weeks since I'd seen him, and he looked more worn and tired, but he didn't slouch. He had an amused smirk as he registered my surprise.

"Billy," he said, "the general wants you inside."

TWO

I STARED at McNab for a few seconds. For some reason, I realized his face looked more lined and ragged than I'd ever seen, though now was a strange time to notice.

"What're you doing here?" I asked.

"Reports," he said. He nodded toward the building. "At least until the general stepped out of his meeting to tell me to get you."

"Do you know what he wants?" I asked.

"Does it matter?"

My face flushed. Of course it didn't. If General Sanborn, the commander of the entire Army of the West, wanted me inside, I was gonna be there. I was still a soldier under his command.

I glanced over at Zeke, who nodded. He'd keep an eye on the horses and the Indian. So I followed McNab into the Headquarters foyer.

The general's aide immediately ushered us into the briefing room. General Sanborn himself stood in front of the map of the West. His thick, grey hair set off the wrinkles in his face and made him look old and serious. His uniform hung loosely and I guessed that, like many of us, he'd lost weight over the winter. He was talking quietly with my direct commander, Captain Mercer, as well as Lieutenant Caldwell.

The Sioux had stood in a cluster at the far end of the long table that filled the rest of the room.

Captain Mercer also looked more worn than I'd seen him recently. We hadn't crossed paths much once I'd been assigned to scout patrol. Still, his uniform, wavy hair, and mustache were all impeccably groomed. But his eyes seemed sadder than usual. He gave me a small smile.

McNab and I took three steps into the room, came to attention, and saluted.

"At ease, Lieutenant, Sergeant-Major," General Sanborn said. After we'd dropped our salutes, he continued, "I understand you speak Arapaho."

"Sir, yes sir," I said.

"You speak it well?" he asked.

"Not too well, sir," I said. "Just enough to get by."

"That'll be enough," he said.

"Sir?" I said. I glanced over at the Sioux. Arapaho territory was beyond theirs and the two tribes didn't get along.

"We have an urgent mission for you," General Sanborn said. "To the Black Hills."

I glanced at Captain Mercer, who nodded gravely.

"The future of the West," he said, "may be at stake."

I stood there in shock. The corners of General Sanborn's mouth quirked up as he regarded me. My eyes darted to Captain Mercer but his hard expression told me nothing.

"Excuse me, sir?" I finally said. "The entire West?"

"The Captain is exaggerating," General Sanborn said with a wry smile.

"Perhaps not, sir," Captain Mercer retorted.

The general waved his hand in dismissal. "We don't know." Then he turned to Lieutenant Caldwell. "Please fill Lieutenant McCarty in on the situation."

"The Sioux," he nodded in their direction, "arrived at the gates of Fort Randall five weeks ago. They said a new town had appeared in the Black Hills, consisting of well over three dozen buildings. They also said it was not there last autumn, and so must've been built over the winter."

"That's fast," I murmured before remembering I was with the General and clamped my jaw shut. I needed to listen, not talk.

"Indeed," Lieutenant Caldwell continued. "When the Sioux tried to approach, horsemen rode out and fired arrows at them. They decided to meet with us before engaging further."

"To make sure the town wasn't ours," Captain Mercer added. "It is not."

"We sent a patrol to investigate," Lieutenant Caldwell said. His face tightened as he chose his words. "They did not return."

"Didn't return?" I blurted. "They were killed?"

"The Sioux think so," he said with another nod toward the Indians. "But it's possible they were caught in a snowstorm as well. Captain Logan dispatched a patrol to look for them at the same time he sent me here."

"The Indians," Captain Mercer said with a glance in their direction, "wanted to talk with someone with more authority than Captain Logan. He won't promise to help them destroy the town."

"I won't either," General Sanborn said. "But I did say we'd help." He looked at me.

I swallowed hard. "So what do you want me to do, sir?"

"We're only a few weeks away from launching our next attack on the Jotun. We can't afford to send a sizable force into what is, for all intents and purposes, our rear area. However, the Captain," he nodded toward Mercer, "believes an elite team could investigate and perhaps resolve this problem."

"The town shouldn't be there," Captain Mercer said. "We don't know who they are, we don't know where they came from, and we absolutely cannot have a hostile force arrayed behind us."

"And both the Crow and Sioux claim the Black Hills," General Sanborn said. "These intruders could trigger a war between the tribes."

"Worse," Captain Mercer said, "these newcomers might just be the start. What if it's a new invasion from another realm?"

I tried to calm my racing pulse.

"You will lead the reconnaissance team," General Sanborn said.

I blinked in surprise. Then I realized he was waiting for a reply.

"Sir, yes sir."

"I'm leading the raid on Knoxville," Captain Mercer said with a sour smile. "I'm sorry you won't be along."

"You want me to take my current squadron, sir?" I asked.

"No," General Sanborn said. "When I said elite, I meant elite. I want your team to return, do you understand?"

"Sir, yes sir."

"These are your orders, Lieutenant. Assemble an elite team. Accompany the Sioux to the Black Hills. Investigate the new town. If you determine there is a threat to the United States of the West, eliminate it."

I sucked in my breath. Those were *big* orders.

"And do *not* start a war with either the Sioux or the Crow," he added. "Any questions?"

"Sir, no sir," I said.

"Good," he said. "You'll receive those orders in writing shortly." The corners of his lips turned up as he looked at McNab.

"I'm assigning Sergeant-Major McNab to you," General Sanborn continued. "His orders are to make sure you return to us alive. We can't have the Hero of Louisville getting himself killed out there, now can we, Sergeant-Major?"

"No, sir!" McNab said.

"I suggest you make plans with Lieutenant Caldwell as soon as his team has rested," General Sanborn said with a nod toward Caldwell. Then he turned back to McNab and me.

"We've been discussing your role in the army, Captain Mercer and I," General Sanborn said. "We think that if you do well on this mission, we could make it your permanent assignment."

I blinked in surprise and then looked at Captain Mercer.

"Troubleshooter at large," he said, "like Captain Cassidy."

My heart raced, but I forced myself to nod calmly.

"Dismissed," General Sanborn said.

McNab and I both saluted, turned, and marched out.

In the foyer, I realized my gut was churning, as much with excitement as nerves. My heart raced as we trod across the wooden floor.

"Did you hear that?" I exclaimed. "Troubleshooter at large. Did you hear it?"

McNab chuckled. "He spoke pretty clearly."

"Like Cassidy! I could be like Cassidy! I could set my own rules!"

"I wouldn't go that far," he said. "Even Cassidy had to follow the rules when he was in the fort."

I snorted. Who cared? Cassidy was barely ever at the forts, at least according to the books.

Of course, the books weren't wholly true. That brought me up short. Cassidy had also died on his last mission. The memories of that took the wind out of my sails. At least it didn't send me into a sad spiral like so often before.

McNab seemed to know what I was thinking. He shook his head with a grin.

"We're going to The Black Hills," he said. "We'll miss the attack on the Jotun."

"We won't be there," I corrected. "We won't miss it. At least I won't."

McNab ruefully chuckled. "There was a time you couldn't wait to kill giants."

"Yeah." I pulled up short before we went outside and glanced back toward the conference room. It was closed, so the general and the others couldn't hear me.

"I killed plenty," I said quietly. "How many more do I hafta kill?"

McNab snorted but didn't otherwise reply.

"Besides," I added, "too many of our men died last time."

"That's war." From the tone in his voice, I knew that was his rote response. It wasn't particularly comforting.

Before I could say anything else, the conference room door opened and Lieutenant Caldwell, Private Brody, and the Sioux came out. Brody's eyes lit up when he saw me and his pace quickened.

"You're coming with us!" Brody exclaimed.

I nodded. Then I caught Lieutenant Caldwell's gaze as he approached. "Your doing?"

"Suggestion," he said. "The general liked it, though." His eyes darted to Brody, and when I raised my eyebrows, Lieutenant Caldwell nodded. No need to ask who the suggestion had *really* come from.

"I'll show you to your barracks and the mess hall," McNab said to Lieutenant Caldwell.

The Sioux had come up behind the lieutenant. Otaktay's jaw was set. His eyes darted everywhere.

"Horses," he said.

McNab furrowed his brow, but Lieutenant Caldwell nodded knowingly.

"Are the barracks near the stables?" he asked me. "The Indians aren't going to let their horses out of their sight."

McNab muttered something but forced a smile. "I'm sure we can make something work. Come on."

<hr>

I kept thinking about what the general had said as we got the horses stabled and quarters assigned for the Sioux. Troubleshooter at large. My own team.

Part of me wanted it more than anything. But I knew how much work it was. How hard it could be. And part of me was scared to death.

I knew the books weren't true, but people still died in them. Only the witch Maria had been with Cassidy from the start. And sometimes a lot of innocent people died. People that Cassidy couldn't save. In the books, their entire life got reduced to a sentence: "We found the bodies."

Except I'd be the one doing the finding. I'd be the one wondering if they'd still be alive if I'd just done a little more.

Before he'd died, Cassidy told me not to be a hero. He'd said it was an awful life. Better to be a sharpshooter in the army, he'd said. Well, I'd been a sharpshooter in the army. It stank.

I didn't want to be a hero. Not anymore. I knew that so clearly now. I hated the hero worshippers like Private Brody. No, hate was too strong a word. I just seriously disliked their naivety. Mine had been burned off in blood.

But I wanted, oh I wanted, to be on the road. And if I succeeded at this assignment, I could have that.

———

McNab and I huddled with Lieutenant Caldwell and Otaktay in the mess hall after dinner. It was a filling meal—goat stew and some winter potatoes. We'd picked the end of one of the long tables away from the door for our conference. Lieutenant Caldwell clutched both hands around his mug of coffee and occasionally shot grateful looks at McNab. In his role as quartermaster, McNab had somehow wrangled up some of the precious drink. With Galveston the only good port left for shipping from the south, coffee was hard to come by. I had my own mug, which I sipped slowly.

We sat close, but despite my full stomach, I didn't feel at all relaxed. "So what are we facing?"

Lieutenant Caldwell shrugged and looked at Otaktay. The Sioux warrior crossed his arms across his chest and his lip curled into a frown before he spoke.

"Big town," he said. "Many buildings. In hills. Has wall."

"It has a wall?" I asked.

"Yes. Like your forts, but stone."

"They put up a stone wall in six months?" I said incredulously. I looked to Lieutenant Caldwell for confirmation.

"I haven't seen it," he said with a shrug.

"What about soldiers?" I said to Otaktay. "The general mentioned some riders?"

"Many," he said. "Two hands worth. More."

"With bows," McNab said. Otaktay nodded in confirmation.

"Not guns," I said. "So they're probably not ours."

"That was Captain Logan's thinking," Lieutenant Caldwell said. He took another sip of his coffee.

"How far are you accompanying us?" McNab asked Lieutenant Caldwell.

"To Fort Randall," he said. "From there Otaktay and his men will lead you to the new town."

I frowned. I didn't like the idea of having the Indians as my only guides. It wasn't that I didn't trust them, but…

Well, I didn't trust them. Not because they were evil or anything, but because we weren't on the same side all the time. There'd been too much blood spilt between the Sioux and the army before the Jotun had arrived and forced a necessary truce. I had a sneaky sense that Otaktay wouldn't hesitate to leave us lost in the wilderness if it suited him. I wanted my own guides.

"Do you know the Black Hills?" I asked McNab. "Ever travel there with Cassidy?"

"No. We never had any reason to go into Sioux Territory," he said with a shrug. "Cassidy's orders always kept us near Jotun lands."

I frowned and looked over at Otaktay. He kept his arms crossed and his stare flat. I definitely did not like this Indian being the only thing between me and trouble.

"Jeremiah might know someone who's been there," McNab said.

"Yes," I said. "We need to talk to Jeremiah. About the book as well."

THREE

WE AGREED to meet Lieutenant Caldwell and the Sioux at noon at their barracks. I figured I could get most of my team recruited that night and McNab thought he'd be able to get us provisioned in the morning. I already knew I was taking Zeke if he wanted to go, and I was sure he would. He was the best man in the army with a sword, even if he was a lousy shot. I wanted him at my back.

Which meant the next stop was Jeremiah. Him, I knew where to find. He'd been assigned to train some green recruits as their squadron sergeant. The smartest man I knew, the best writer I knew, and the army had him instructing fresh fish on how to salute and stand in line.

Because he was a Negro.

It rankled me. When we'd fought the Battle of Golden City, we'd all been the same—White, Negro, Mexican, Indian. The only thing that mattered was stopping the monsters.

But the army forgot that the very next day.

Jeremiah seemed to make the best of it. At least he never complained to me.

So McNab and I walked through the night toward a barracks that was the farthest from the well and closest to the latrines. We could smell the faint stench in the still air. We could also hear a guitar from one of the barracks we'd passed, but none from Jeremiah's. Only a thin beam of light leaking out from under the door gave hint of anyone's presence.

As we got closer, I noted more light coming from numerous cracks between the wallboards. They'd been sealed with mud instead of plaster over the winter, and some of it had washed away in the spring rains. We could now hear the sounds of low conversation.

We stepped up to the door and knocked twice. The talking paused and, after some shuffling, the door opened a crack. A Negro private I didn't recognize stuck his head out.

"Lieutenant McCarty and Sergeant-Major McNab to see Sergeant Freeman," I said.

"Yes, sir," the private said. He disappeared and a minute later the door swung wide. Jeremiah stood straight in the entryway.

"Lieutenant McCarty," he said after a quick salute. "Sergeant-Major McNab."

"It's me," I said. "You don't have to salute."

Jeremiah's eyes darted back toward the busy barracks. "Sir, we are in the middle of the fort."

"How'd you like to hit the trail instead?" McNab said.

Jeremiah cocked an eyebrow and looked at me.

"We're going to the Black Hills," I said. "We want you to join us." I quickly explained our orders.

Jeremiah nodded as he listened and his grin grew.

"It's a small team?" he asked. "Just us?"

"Just like old times," McNab said with a broad grin.

"Then I'd be delighted to come," Jeremiah said. "Who else is part of the team?"

"Zeke," I said. "Maria. After that, I don't know."

"I don't know if they'll let Maria go," McNab said. "They'll need a good witch when they head east."

I nodded. They'd need her, but we might need her more.

"She's not the only witch in the army," I said. Well, there weren't that many, but still. "The general said he wanted an elite squad. I want her."

"I know someone else we might want," Jeremiah said. "He's from the Black Hills, but it's too late tonight. When are we leaving?"

"At noon," I said, "but we can go meet this soldier mid-morning."

He nodded and started to salute, but I waved him off.

"One other thing," I said. I gestured for him to step further away from the barracks. "The book."

"Ah. Just a minute." Jeremiah stepped back inside and said something. When he returned, he closed the door behind him. "Let's go for a walk."

"I think this is between you two," McNab said. "I'll wait here."

Jeremiah and I headed away from the barracks, past the latrines, and toward the garbage dump. Slowly, the sounds of the barracks faded and were replaced by the chirps of crickets. I'd been thinking about what to say for a while, and in the end I decided to go with the question I cared about most.

"So," I said, "one of the men from Fort Randall had the book. About me. How come you never showed it to me?"

He slowed his pace and let out a sigh. "You said you didn't want to see it."

I blinked. "When?" I honestly couldn't remember.

"The night after I finished it. We were sitting outside the shooting range, talking about Cassidy."

That I remembered. Not him mentioning the book, but the evening. It'd been cold, but clear. I'd shivered a lot as we talked. I'd been having bad dreams about Cassidy, and so Jeremiah and I'd slipped off to talk. The conversation had meandered and I'd wished for some alcohol to drown my sorrows. Instead I'd gotten all wrapped up in my memories and worries. The pit in my stomach had felt immense.

"I don't remember."

"You just shook your head when I offered to have you read it."

I shrugged. I still didn't remember.

"You started talking about Cassidy again and how sometimes you wished you didn't think about him. I figured that was your way of saying you didn't want to see the book."

I sighed, but Jeremiah didn't push. We walked in silence for a while.

"I…," I finally said. "I dunno. I kinda wanna read it, but I kinda don't. I mean, I know you lied in it."

"No lies," Jeremiah objected with a smile. "Just some… storyteller liberties."

"Do you have a copy?"

"A couple," he said. "They also sell them in town."

I nodded and we walked further. My mind was awhirl. Did I really want to read it? I kind of wanted to see my name in print. But then my gut tightened when I remembered what had actually happened, and I wanted to vomit.

"You don't have to decide now," he said. "I'll bring a copy with us."

I nodded at that. "Plenty of time on the road."

"There always is."

"I just don't know if I want to read your 'liberties.'"

He paused in our walk and looked up at the stars for a minute. I stopped beside him as the stillness descended once again.

"The thing is, Billy," he said without turning his head. "The world's a difficult place right now. We've got the Jotun trying to conquer us and the trolls trying to eat us. We've barely avoided wars with the Indians. All over the place, there are people starving and being cruel to each other and too many of our politicians aren't looking out for the people they should."

He looked down and shuffled his feet, and then kicked a small rock, sending it flying. When he looked at me, his face was firm.

"The world needs heroes, Billy," he said. "It needs hope. And if we have to take liberties to give it to them, by God we will."

I stepped back in surprise at the forcefulness of his voice. Jeremiah had always been the calm one, the voice of reason.

"The world needs heroes," he repeated.

I nodded, unsure of what to say.

"That's why I'm going with you." Jeremiah turned and gave me the most serious look I think I'd ever seen from him. "My job—my calling, so to speak—is to write the stories about the heroes. And right now, that's you."

I stared at him, completely at a loss of words.

"I'll bring the book," He turned and led the way back to the barracks.

———

I thought about what Jeremiah had said as McNab and I made our way to the hospital to look for Maria. I'd devoured those books about Cassidy and Hickok and the others when I was growing up. I wanted to be like them. I didn't quite want to *be* them—that was too far. But I wanted to be on their teams.

But I hadn't known what it was really like, and now I did.

I still didn't know if I wanted to read the book.

But I knew I wanted Maria along, and I hoped she'd be eager. As an unmarried Mexican woman, she'd faced some of the same prejudices as Jeremiah, perhaps a little less since she was a healer. People expected healers to be different. Still, I suspected she'd be happy to be out of the hospital. She'd never said so, but I sensed that was the case.

We found Maria mixing medicines in the apothecary just off the main hospital wing. Tables, shelves, and benches filled the crowded room. They were all covered with books, beakers, bags, scales, and even a handful of lit candles. They flickered and created multiple weak shadows that danced with the stronger ones from the lamps on the wall. Two large open windows kept it from being too stuffy, but foul, sour smells still lingered.

Maria hunched over one of the tables sorting piles of tiny leaves and dried flowers. She wore a faded brown apron over her nurse's uniform and had braided her long black hair into a single queue down her back. Her light brown hands were covered in the golden dust of dried leaves. She seemed to be meticulously counting little yellow flowers and didn't break off and look up until she'd finished.

"Billy," she said with a smile. "McNab." She straightened up and wiped her hands on a towel.

"Maria," I said. Her smile was infectious and I grinned back.

She gave us a questioning look. "Yes?"

"We have orders to investigate something strange in the Black Hills," I said. "We'd like you to come with us."

"Oh?" She pursed her lips and glanced at McNab.

"Jeremiah's coming too," he said. "Just like old times."

"No," she said. She looked me straight in the eyes. "It is not."

I stared at Maria for two heartbeats. Her eyes bored into mine but they were firm instead of fiery. I heard McNab shuffle his feet next to me. He cleared his throat, but neither Maria nor I looked over.

"It is not like it was," she said. "You are not Cassidy."

I broke eye contact and looked down at my feet.

"No one's asking him to be," McNab said.

She turned to him. "But that's what you want."

"No… no," he said. I looked up to see his frown. "No, I… I just want one last ride." He gave me a sheepish look. "I'm tired, Billy. Tired of the army, tired of the fight. But I want one more ride before I call it quits."

"You can quit the army?" I had a hard time believing that.

"When you're my age, with my service, they'll let you." His frown turned to an ironic smile. "They don't want to, but they will."

"Better," Maria said. "More honest." Then she turned to me.

"I'll go," she said.

I let out a deep breath I hadn't realized I'd been holding.

"When do we leave?" she asked.

"Tomorrow afternoon. Do we need to talk to your commander?" I wasn't sure exactly who that was, since nurses had a different chain of command.

"Yes. He's in the main ward."

The head doctor was indeed treating patients personally despite the late hour. The ward itself was mercifully near empty. Most soldiers wounded in the fall campaign had either recovered or died. Accidents over the winter had added a few patients, but for once the room didn't smell like gangrene and death.

We found the doctor changing bandages on a soldier with a nasty slice in his arm that'd gone to the bone. Fortunately for the patient, he'd gotten plenty of opium juice and now lolled his head and babbled quietly.

McNab and I stopped a respectful distance away. McNab saluted, and I belatedly remembered that the doctor outranked us and followed suit. The doctor acknowledged us with a nod and finished his work. Then he gestured for us to follow him into a more deserted part of the ward.

"Lieutenant McCarty," he said, "Sergeant-Major. What can I do for you?"

"We have orders directly from General Sanborn," I said, "to assemble an elite team for an investigation. I'd like Maria on that team."

He frowned and then slowly looked me up and down.

"She's one of my best nurses," he eventually said, "and perhaps the finest witch in the army."

"I know, sir," I said. "That's why we want her."

He regarded me closely, and I could see the war of emotions on his face. He didn't want to say no, but he didn't want her to go, either.

"Please, sir," I said.

Something seemed to break and he nodded.

"You did a good thing, Lieutenant McCarty," he said, "when you kept coming around to visit the wounded over the winter. Some of them said it was the best part of the day, and I know you gave them hope."

I tried not to blush.

"So for you," he continued, "she can go."

I let out a relieved breath. "Thank you, sir!" I probably could've had General Sanborn order the doctor to let her go, but this was much better.

The doctor turned to McNab. "And you, Sergeant-Major. Please tell General Sanborn that we need that opium I ordered a month ago, and we need it before we muster. That is, if he wants our supplies to last the campaign."

"Sir, yes sir."

"See to it." He gave us a wave that might've passed for a salute and turned to go back to his patient.

We headed for the hospital door. McNab chuckled when the doctor was out of earshot.

"What?" I asked.

"I thought he'd ask for a lot more than opium," he said.

"For Maria?" Somehow I wasn't as surprised as I thought I should've been.

McNab nodded. "Anyone else to recruit?"

"Not tonight," I said. "We'll meet Jeremiah's mystery man tomorrow."

"I wonder who that is," McNab mused. "I know nearly every soldier in this army and I've never heard of one that was actually from the Black Hills. There just aren't enough Americans out there."

"I guess we'll just have to see."

FOUR

MCNAB and I met with Jeremiah a half hour after breakfast. He told us to follow him and we wound our way through the fort, past the barracks and the mess hall and the rows of warehouses. Jeremiah set a quick pace, which surprised me as I'd expected him to amble and ask questions about the mission, now that he'd had a night to think of them. Him not asking questions was almost unsettling. Like a pause of the wind during a storm.

Still, it was good to stretch my legs. McNab huffed along without complaint and we soon passed the stables and the blacksmith's foundry. Finally, we approached the fort's graveyard.

"You know, Jeremiah, we need a live soldier," I joked.

"We'll get one," he said. He steered us through the entrance and along a path toward the back.

We slowed our steps as we walked. It didn't seem respectful to move fast in so somber a place. Rows of the dead stretched out of sight to both the left and the right as well as ahead. The cost of so many battles in the war with the Jotun.

There were men I knew here. Men I'd fought alongside. Yet they were but a drop in an ocean of headstones.

Despite the sun, I shook off a shiver.

McNab did too. His face looked grim.

"Thinking about the men here?" I asked.

He shook his head, but didn't explain.

Jeremiah led us down a side path and around a small copse of elm trees. At the end sat a small slapped together wooden shack not much bigger than one of our field tents. Shovels and a pick ax leaned against the wall. A pair of worn boots encrusted with dried mud sat in front of the door.

"So who is this man?" I asked.

"Goes by the name Injun Joe," Jeremiah said. "I've told him it's ridiculous, but he just smirks at me."

"He's Sioux?" I asked.

"He's also the gravedigger," a deep bass voice said.

The speaker filled the shack's doorway. A tall Indian with bulging biceps gave us a not-quite glare. He wore loose army pants tied with a rope belt and was barefoot. His uniform shirt hung unbuttoned but his undershirt was tucked in and clean. He had dark piercing eyes, high cheekbones, and a hook nose which made him look like a giant hawk standing on the ground.

I blinked. He looked an awful lot like Otaktay.

"Injun Joe!" Jeremiah said. "This is Sergeant-Major McNab and Lieutenant McCarty. You know him as Billy the Kid."

The Indian cocked an eyebrow. "Huh."

"We're headed to the Black Hills," Jeremiah continued. He nodded at me. "Billy's in charge. He knows a little Arapaho, but we could use you along."

"Huh."

Injun Joe didn't look convinced, so I decided to chime in. "The Sioux asked for our help. There's a new town where there shouldn't be one."

"So? You white men have taken our land many times."

"It isn't us," I said. "But you don't have to take my word for it. Some of the Sioux are here. You can ask them."

At that, he perked up.

"We're leaving at noon," I said. "If you want to meet them before we go, we can do that."

"I'll get dressed," Injun Joe said. "Then we go."

Injun Joe didn't look much like a soldier when he got his full uniform on. It looked slovenly, even if all the buttons were buttoned and none of the fabric obviously stained. Mostly, it looked like it didn't fit. Like his muscles were trying to burst through his sleeves or his pants legs. I half wondered who'd be better in a saber duel, him or Zeke.

We made our way through the camp without much delay. When we arrived at the Sioux barracks, we found Private Brody outside. He sat reading in a rickety wooden chair in the shade by the door. He ran his finger over the page as he did, and his lips moved slightly. His eyes grew wide when he saw us and he stood and snapped to attention. He looked at Injun Joe and his mouth dropped open. When we were close enough, he saluted.

I returned the salute and said, "We're here to see the Sioux."

"Yes, sir!" He went into the barracks, and a moment later, Otaktay came out.

"You!" Injun Joe cried. "What are you doing here?"

I stood and stared at Otaktay, and then at Injun Joe. They really could be brothers. But not friendly ones from the way they glared at each other. Injun Joe balled his hands into fists. Otaktay crossed his arms across his chest and gave a contemptuous snort.

"Umm...," I said. I glanced over at McNab for suggestions on what to do, but he gave me an intentionally bland look in return. Jeremiah seemed to be biting his lip.

"So..., Private," I said to Injun Joe. "You know this man?"

"My cousin," he spat. "Otaktay."

Otaktay said something harsh in Sioux, which I didn't understand.

Injun Joe shouted back in the same tongue. He stepped forward and raised a fist, but then his eyes darted to me and he paused.

"Um, is there going to be a problem?" I asked.

"No," Otaktay said in English. "Anoki knows his place."

Now I was just bewildered. Were we gonna have a fight before we even got going?

"Maybe you should stay here, Private," I said to Injun Joe.

"No," he said with a growl. "I'm going. Sir."

"He comes," Otaktay stated firmly. "He is why we are here."

"Um, what?"

Private Brody, who'd followed the Sioux back out of the barracks, stepped forward.

"Sir," he said. "We offered to bring their message here and save them the trip, but they insisted on coming. They didn't say why, though."

"We need not explain," Otaktay said. He rocked on the balls of his feet and kept his glare on Injun Joe. Or Anoki. Injun Joe was a stupid name.

I sucked in my breath. I was probably the youngest man here, and also the smallest. But I was also the one with the highest rank. Somehow the bars on my shoulders gave them extra weight.

"Actually," I said, "you do need to explain. We're supposed to help you with this new town, and we can't do that without knowing everything."

"Not yours to know," Otaktay said. He barely kept the snarl out of his voice.

"Yes, Lieutenant," Anoki said. "It's between Otaktay and myself."

"And Washta," Otaktay growled.

Anoki grimaced, but nodded.

"Who's Washta?" I asked.

"My wife," Anoki said. "And that is all I will say."

I glanced from one Indian to the other. They continued to glare at each other, as if in a staring match.

"Fine," I finally said out of frustration. I turned to Anoki. "If you're going with us, we're leaving at noon. Be here, or I'll assume you're not."

Everyone stood around, looking expectantly at me. Then I realized why. I hadn't said something I was supposed to. Again.

"Dismissed."

I spent the rest of the morning worrying about whether bringing Anoki was a good idea or not. The thing was, if the Sioux had come specifically for him, I didn't see how I could leave him behind. Apparently, they'd asked Lieutenant Caldwell's help in finding him, but no one had told me. So they were serious.

Even if they weren't, I didn't speak Sioux and Anoki spoke English better than Otaktay. I was sure that'd come in handy. In the end, I decided if Otaktay wanted him along, I wasn't going to get in the way. The General had made it clear I wasn't to create problems with the Indians if I didn't have to.

So I packed up my rucksack and made sure my replacement on the scout patrol knew his job. I'd never become friends with those men, other than Zeke, but they deserved a competent commanding officer. Fortunately, my replacement, a recently promoted lieutenant from Minnesota, seemed to listen closely and have some idea what he was doing.

To my pleasant surprise, everyone was ready to go when I arrived at the Indians' barracks. I did a quick count—four soldiers from Fort Randall, four Sioux, McNab, Zeke, Maria, Jeremiah, Anoki, and myself. McNab had somehow wrangled up four packhorses as well, which were fully laden with food and other supplies. Anoki stood on the far side of the group from Otaktay but didn't seem to be able to stop glancing his way from time to time.

They kept that distance as we rode out. Lieutenant Caldwell took the lead, with the Sioux party right behind. Anoki rode in the back with McNab and the packhorses.

I decided to see if I could learn more about this town. I brought my horse up alongside Otaktay's. He acknowledged me with a nod.

"So," I said, "have you seen this town?"

He nodded.

"Up close?"

He shook his head.

"Did you see any of the people?"

He hesitated, and stiffened. I bit back my urge to ask him another question and waited.

"Rode ponies," he said. "Many—ten, twenty. Shot arrows at us from far away. Too far to hit."

"They were just trying to warn you off," I surmised.

He nodded.

"Anything special about 'em? Like uniforms?"

He shook his head again and then paused. "No uniforms. But small. Small like children. Not big like men."

I blinked. *That* was news. But then, I was small for a man, and that hadn't slowed me down. So I asked, "Small like me?"

He looked me over. "No. Smaller. Children."

Huh. I pulled out of the formation long enough to wave back at Jeremiah and motion him forward. He spurred his horse and soon joined me and Otaktay. I filled him in on what Otaktay had said.

"That doesn't sound like trolls," Jeremiah said. "They're a little shorter, but—"

"No trolls," Otaktay interrupted. "Human."

"Hmmm," Jeremiah said. "The only things we know for sure came through the rift at Andersonville were Jotun, trolls, and dragons. But they could be dwarves. Those are part of Norse mythology, but I don't think they lived in Jotunheim. I'll have to check the Edda."

"The what?"

"The Edda," he explained, "is a bunch of old Viking poems. They're stories about their gods and heroes and monsters. Some of them are about the Jotun, which is why Sam Clemens wonders if Andersonville wasn't the first rift to their realm."

I tensed at that thought. Another rift? At first my heart sped up, but then reason set in. If the Vikings had opened a rift, it'd long since been closed, and it couldn't have been very big. Or at least not as big as Andersonville. If it had been, humanity would've been enslaved long ago.

"Did they have beards?" Jeremiah asked Otaktay.

"Too far," he said.

I nodded. If people'd been shooting arrows at me, I wouldn't have tried to see if they had beards or not.

"I'll see what I can learn before we get there," Jeremiah said. "I brought a copy of the Edda with me. You have to know your enemy and all."

"Can I read it?" I asked.

"If you want, but it's pretty hard to follow."

I nodded. If it was hard for Jeremiah, it'd be doubly hard for me. I might take a look at it, but I'd let him finish with it first.

Besides, there was that other book I might read. My chest tightened as I thought about it. Did I really want to read about myself? I still wasn't sure. But I had plenty of time to figure it out.

That night, we camped along a stream bank on a field that hadn't yet been planted. There were plenty of gleanings for the horses, but McNab still checked with the farmer to see if he minded. The man offered to sell us some eggs, which McNab accepted and we cooked those up for supper.

I was just settling back against an ash tree after supper when Private Brody found me. He stood about ten feet away, clutching his dime novel. He shifted nervously on his feet and repeatedly tapped his fingers on the cover, but the eager look in his eyes belied his jitters. His grin was wide and forced, like someone who knew he should be smiling even if he didn't feel it.

"Yes…," I said.

"Uh… sir, uh… I was wondering, sir…?"

"Spit it out."

"Sir, uh… would you be willing to talk about Colorado?" He looked down at the book. "It's too short, and there's too much missing and I have questions, and… please, sir?"

I stared at him, not quite sure what to say.

FIVE

PRIVATE BRODY'S face warred between fear and eagerness. His eyes darted to mine, and then away, and then back again. I sensed that if I sent him off, he'd go, tail between his legs. I also sensed that if I gestured him forward, he'd fall over his own feet in a dash to be at my side.

And I couldn't see Jeremiah anywhere nearby. So I'd get no rescue from the book's writer.

"Sir?" Private Brody said.

"Sure," I said. "C'mon over." After he'd settled onto the ground next to me, I asked, "What do you want to know?"

"What's it like?" he asked, "Fighting giants?"

I couldn't help laughing. "You're asking me? There are men here who've fought giants a lot more often than me. I'm surprised you haven't yourself."

His face fell. "I, um, well, I've never been to the front."

"It's not as exciting as you might think," I said. "You spend most of your time walking."

"But that's not all the time, right? I mean, you get to fight, right?"

I snorted. Just about every one of my old injuries chose then to remind me of the abuse I'd taken. Everything twinged or throbbed except maybe my left big toe. Of course, as soon as I thought of it, that throbbed too.

"Fighting's not that great," I said soberly. "A lot of men die, and a lot of it's luck."

"But you were good!"

I gestured at the book. "You've read the whole thing, right?"

"Four times!"

I had to suppress a grin. I'd read dime novels over and over until the pages were falling out. With only four reads, Brody had a ways to go.

"Well," I said, "you remember that part where Cassidy got the poisoned scratch?"

"Yeah." He let out a fast breath. "That was… that was what killed him." His eyes widened when he remembered the passage. "Was gonna kill him," he quickly amended.

"Well, it was dumb luck that he got scratched instead of me. He was good. Better than me. A true hero, and he died because of dumb luck."

"Oh." Brody grew quiet. He was still restless, though, and he couldn't quite keep from drumming his fingers on his thigh.

"Listen," I said, "I'll tell you what it was like, what it was really like, but you've gotta do something for me first."

"Anything!"

"Go back through that book, and count all the times we got lucky, all the times we could've died, but didn't. Maybe then you'll understand."

He didn't seem convinced, but he knew when he'd been dismissed. He scrambled to his feet and gave me a salute. "Thank you, sir." Then he strode off toward the fire.

"You were pretty abrupt with him." Jeremiah stepped out of the growing shadows. I couldn't make out his expression, but from his tone he was only mildly chiding me.

"Yeah, well, I should've done it when I read those books about Cassidy. Figured out when he got lucky, I mean."

"Maybe," he said, "but I don't think it would've discouraged you."

I grimaced as I realized he was right. I'd seen Cassidy in person, after all, even before I'd read the books. I'd watched him defeat three giants with ease and the books had paled by comparison. Nothing would've discouraged me at all.

"Well," I said, "we'll just have to try and keep him from getting killed then."

Jeremiah laughed.

"What's so funny?"

"I've heard that line before. From Cassidy."

I glared at him, and, laughing, he walked away.

It took us several uneventful weeks to get to Fort Randall. We didn't encounter any trouble and the weather stayed largely fair. We suffered through a couple of harsh rainstorms, but thankfully no late spring snows. We bought food from farmers when we could, until the farms faded out into nearly endless prairie. The Sioux rode ahead and hunted from time to time, and we spent half a day once preserving the deer meat they'd gotten.

In the evenings, Private Brody would find me with the book and ask about parts of it. Sometimes he did so at the fire, when Lieutenant Caldwell, McNab, and the others could hear. He'd ask for the details of a given scene and I'd do my best to explain what had really happened.

His questions seemed endless, though. He repeated a bunch, too. Was I scared? How did I stop from just freezing up? What did I think when Cassidy did something brave? Wasn't I frightened? Had I really been lucky? What about all my good shooting? Was I scared when I missed?

I did my best to answer politely. I couldn't fault him for his curiosity, after all. When McNab was around, he sometimes chipped in, though Maria remained silent. Lieutenant Caldwell and Zeke and the others would smile but not interrupt. Jeremiah was usually off trying to learn some of the Sioux language from the Indians.

Of course, the trip was more than just humoring a lone private. I tried to get the Sioux to talk with me and tell me what was coming. Otaktay said very little, and nothing new. The new town was big. The riders had threatened them and they'd decided not to force a fight in case it was us Americans.

But now that he knew it wasn't, I sensed he was itching for a battle. He wouldn't come right out and say so, but his body tensed and his eyes narrowed when we talked about it.

Anoki kept to himself. He hung back from the fires at night and rode in the back with the packhorses. He'd volunteered to care for them and it seemed to take all his time during our stops. He occasionally spoke with Jeremiah and one of the Sioux warriors, but kept his distance from Otaktay. I didn't like their apparent feud, but I didn't know what to do about it.

Still, I was thoroughly sick of it when we arrived at Fort Randall. I wasn't sure I could trust Anoki if things got hot. He mouthed all the right words, but his attention was always on Otaktay instead of what I was saying. When I tried asking about what was going on, he brusquely changed the subject.

Thankfully, I didn't have to deal with it at Fort Randall. Otaktay decided his men would camp outside the fort's walls. The rest of us were given beds in the half-empty barracks. The garrison had been stripped to a skeleton crew that was mostly there to keep the fort from being taken over by Indians or squatters, as the fort commander, Captain Logan, told us over dinner.

"Every man we could spare got sent to Chicago," he said. He was a lean man with a very bushy blond mustache that kept catching crumbs of bread and gravy as he ate. "We're the only fort still manned in the area."

"Do you know what we're riding into, sir?" I asked.

"Only what the Sioux have reported." Captain Logan propped his elbows on the table and gave me a grave look. "The squadron I sent never returned. The second squadron I sent to look for the first was turned back by a blizzard. The tracks were lost then."

"We don't even have any old intelligence," Lieutenant Caldwell added. "Our patrols don't go that far west, and there aren't any settlers out there."

"That doesn't stop the occasional fortune seeker from heading out that way," Captain Logan said. "They come through the fort from time to time. Most we never see again."

I nodded. It wouldn't be too hard to just keep going on to Golden City if one wanted.

"Sir, what about the Indians?" McNab asked.

"We don't hear from them," Captain Logan said. "We haven't had contact in months, other than the Sioux you've met, of course."

I frowned. We truly were heading out into the unknown.

The next morning at breakfast, Lieutenant Caldwell gestured for me to join him at his table. He sat alone with the remains of his meal, drinking what smelled like real coffee.

"Where'd you get that?" I asked as I sat down with my own eggs and toast.

"Ask the cook," he said. "He has some special he's set aside."

"How'd he manage that? We barely have any at Fort Chicago." There just wasn't enough shipping from South America these days.

He grinned at me over the rim of his mug. "If I tell you, you'll steal it for yourself."

I snorted. "Like you'd let me."

He just kept grinning. Then he nodded toward the kitchen. "Get your own cup and we'll talk." Of course I hopped up immediately.

I took a deep sip as soon as the cook gave it to me. The rich bitterness nearly scalded my tongue, but I sighed in happiness. The army would've run on coffee if there'd been enough.

When I sat back down, Lieutenant Caldwell had finished his cup and pushed his plate away. He had his elbows on the table and waited with a small smile until I'd taken another long sip.

"I'd like to ask you a favor," he said when I was ready. "I'd like to transfer Private Brody to your command."

My eyebrows went up. "Are you sure?"

"He's going stir crazy stuck in Fort Randall with us. Frankly, it's an easy assignment, but he wants more."

"Yeah, he wants to be a hero." I sipped some more of that glorious coffee.

"True," Lieutenant Caldwell said, "but didn't we all? My first battle cured me of that notion."

I nodded in understanding. It hadn't been my first battle—that had just been too rushed for me to even realize what was going on. But later on…?

"He's good with both a gun and a saber," Lieutenant Caldwell continued. "He works hard and he's never given anyone any trouble. He doesn't drink, either, and he's at church every Sunday."

"He and Zeke will get along then," I said with a chuckle.

"Yeah…" He let out a long breath. "I don't think that'll be a problem…"

"What'll be a problem?"

"He grew up in the South," Lieutenant Caldwell said. "His family owned slaves and his daddy died fighting for the Rebs. He was only nine, and he's never *said* anything about Negroes… but he's never worked with any either."

"And I'm riding with two." I gave a sigh of frustration and crossed my arms across my chest. "If he can't handle working with Zeke and Jeremiah, then I don't want him."

"He didn't have any problems on the way here." Lieutenant Caldwell made to stand. "I'll talk to him. You're headed out mid-morning?"

"As soon as McNab says we're ready. He can meet us at the stables."

By mid-morning, we had the packhorses loaded and fresh supplies for the rest of us. Maria had somehow found time to have a bath and looked almost radiantly pretty. Her black hair glistened in the sun. She smiled at me when she caught me looking but didn't seem perturbed. Instead, she set about checking that her bags of medicines were tied on tight to her horse.

The rest of our team either attended to their own horses or rested in the shade of the stables. Zeke had his Bible out and was reading it. Jeremiah hastily scribbled in one of his notebooks. McNab was directing some soldiers from the fort on where to load the last of the supplies.

I didn't see Anoki.

He'd stayed in the barracks with us instead of outside with the other Sioux, but I hadn't seen him since the night before. He hadn't been in the barracks when I'd awoken.

I didn't see Private Brody either, and I wasn't quite sure how I felt about that. If he couldn't handle Zeke and Jeremiah, he was better off staying in the fort. But I'd grown to like the kid a little.

I snorted. The "kid" was my age. Maybe even a little older. But it felt like we were from different generations.

I'd aged more than I thought.

"Hey, Jeremiah," I said. "Have you seen Anoki?"

He looked up from his notebook. "Injun Joe?"

"Yeah. He's not here." I looked around again just to be sure. "He wasn't in the barracks this morning when I woke up, either."

"That's strange," Jeremiah said. "There's not exactly anywhere to go around here."

"Lieutenant McCarty!" a voice called from behind me.

I turned to see Private Brody staggering toward us, holding up a very drunk Anoki.

SIX

AFTER A LONG LOOK at the drunk Anoki, I quickly glanced around. The Sioux were outside the fort, waiting for us, so they hadn't seen Anoki's state. McNab and Zeke were already hustling over to help Brody. Anoki seemed unable to stay on his feet. He kept lurching from side to side and only the efforts of the others kept him from falling on his face.

Eventually, they steered him to the side of the stables in the shade and eased him down so that his back was against the wall. His eyes barely focused and wandered all around. His breath stank. Stains covered the front of his shirt and his hair hung tangled around his face. Once he was fully seated and not in any danger of tipping on his side, McNab and Zeke stepped back. McNab looked expectantly at me.

I crouched down next to Anoki and waited for him to focus on me. His eyes went wide but remained hollow when he finally did.

"What's the meaning of this, Private?" I asked quietly.

He said something, but it was unintelligible, between his slurring and his mix of English and Sioux.

"Excuse me?" I said.

He babbled some more and then lowered his chin to his chest and closed his eyes. He wasn't asleep, but he started breathing heavily.

I stood and turned to McNab. "Well, what now?"

"Well, sir, he can't ride a horse like that." McNab scowled.

I shook off the "sir," which felt wrong. But we were still inside the fort, and a lot of the fort's men were watching from a distance. Instead, I let out an exasperated sigh.

"We don't know where we're going," I said, "so we can't leave him to catch up later. I'm going to have to talk to Otaktay." Which promised to be an unpleasant conversation. Maybe Jeremiah had developed some rapport with him during their language lessons. I gestured at him. "Come with me, Sergeant."

He nodded and we walked toward the gate.

The Sioux were mounted on their horses and waiting about a hundred yards from the fort. They looked almost regal in the sun—their clothes clean and crisp, their horses fresh. They didn't dismount as we approached on foot. Instead, Otaktay looked down his nose at us as we approached.

"Anoki is too ill to travel," I said. It was close enough to the truth. "We need to wait a day."

Otaktay snorted and shook his head. "He catch up."

"But where?" I said. "We're not on any trail."

Otaktay turned and said something to one of the other Indians. While they talked, Jeremiah moved closer to me.

"Ask him what's going on with Injun Joe," he said quietly.

"You haven't found out?" He'd spent far more time among them than any of the rest of us.

He shook his head. "The others just look at Otaktay when I bring it up."

Otaktay broke off his conversation with the other Indians and looked at me. "There is place. Big rock on river. Three trees. Meet Anoki there."

"River, big rock, three trees," I repeated. "So we're going to follow the river."

"Yes. Leave now," Otaktay said next. He gave me a very firm glare. "You slow. Anoki fast. He catch up."

I sighed. Having a big man on horseback staring down on me should've been intimidating, but it just annoyed me.

"We'll get the others and be back," I said, "but first, what exactly is going on with you and Anoki?"

"Not you to know."

"But I need to know," I shot back. "Look, Anoki's not sick, he's drunk. I should just leave him behind. I don't need a drunk soldier on my team."

Otaktay scowled.

"But you want him along. And if you don't want me to leave him, I gotta know why."

Otaktay continued to glare at me.

"Fine," I said. "He can stay behind." I turned to leave.

"He come!" Otaktay shouted. He sat forward on his horse, his hands made into fists. His face was almost a snarl.

I gave him a steely glare. Intimidation didn't work with me. We stared at each other for a full minute, and then I turned to leave once again.

"Washta dying," Otaktay said to my back. "Want see Anoki. Me promise. Must take him to her."

I froze in my step. Jeremiah at my side let out a low whistle. It took me a few seconds to remember that Anoki had said that Washta was his wife. Then my gut sank. I slowly turned around once again.

"Does Anoki know?" I asked.

"Told yesterday." Otaktay leaned back and crossed his arms over his chest. He was still mad that I'd forced a confrontation, but he knew he'd won.

"I'll make sure he catches up with us at the spot you mentioned. River, big rock. Three trees."

Otaktay didn't say anything and just watched as Jeremiah and I returned to the fort.

We found the others right where we'd left them, sitting in the shade by the side of the stables. Anoki had fallen asleep and now lay on his side, his breathing ragged. Maria crouched next to him, gently wiping his face with a wet cloth.

I told the rest of the team to join me a few feet away. We stood in a small circle in the hot sun while I briefly filled them in on the conversation with Otaktay. McNab looked dour and Brody couldn't hide his shock, but it was Zeke who truly surprised me.

"I will care for Injun Joe," Zeke said solemnly. "We will meet you at the river."

"You sure?" I asked. As the biggest of us, Zeke was probably the only one who could manhandle Anoki if he needed to. I certainly wasn't strong enough to lift the Indian onto a horse. Brody had staggered under his weight even though Anoki had at least been trying to walk.

Zeke nodded. "He's not a bad man. He's just a lost sheep."

"Well, if you can shepherd him to the big rock by the river, we'll all be happy."

He nodded seriously.

"So let's go," I said to the others.

As we mounted our horses, Zeke moved to Anoki's side. He glanced at the sleeping Indian, pulled out his Bible, and started to read. I couldn't help a smile as we rode out.

The big rock turned out to be impossible to miss. It jutted out into the river and was big enough for three horses to stand on comfortably, if they could've climbed up its side. Three huge cottonwoods formed a gate at its base. They shaded the shore and some distance inland from the water.

McNab chortled when he saw it and suggested to Brody that they try some fishing from the edge. As the sun was already sinking toward the horizon, Jeremiah offered to help Maria with supper.

Me, I decided to take care of the horses and take some time to think.

The fact was, taking care of the horses was about the most useful thing I could do. I hadn't done much else for the weeks we'd been on the road. McNab had more years on the trail than I'd been alive. He knew how to pick campsites, set them up, and take them down with an efficiency that was the envy of most of the army. I would've been a fool to tell him what to do.

I didn't have to pick the route, either. The Sioux led the way and knew where all the water and shady stops were. They told me that we'd get more cover in the mountains, which I was looking forward to. The heat on the plains grew the closer we got to summer. I'd started to wish for more rain, if just to cool us down.

So… I was glorified baggage. Which I hated, because I was supposed to be in charge. How could I prove to General Sanborn that I could lead my own team if I didn't really lead?

But they didn't need me, really. And I wasn't stupid enough to give orders to people who already knew how to do their jobs. Too many stupid officers in the army already did that, and I wasn't stupid.

So sometimes I hunted, but the Sioux were far better and more than willing to share their meat. Sometimes I tried to plan for what was ahead, but this time we didn't know enough. All we knew was we would find a mysterious town in the hills with what Jeremiah was now convinced were dwarves.

"I think they have to be," he'd said. "They're the right size and stature, from what I've read. They certainly could use bows and ride horses, even though that doesn't really fit."

"What do you mean?" I'd asked.

"According to the Edda, dwarves are smiths, not warriors. They made magic weapons for the gods and the giants."

"Wait," I said. "Magic weapons? Magic doesn't work in our world."

"Which makes it stranger that they'd be here. But that's not the biggest question. The Edda indicates that dwarves are from Nidavellir or Svartalfheim—it's not clear which—but anyway, it's not Jotunheim. They're different worlds entirely."

"So they didn't come through the Andersonville rift."

He'd shrugged. "They could've. But I don't know why. Jotunheim isn't their home. It makes more sense for there to be a new rift."

I hoped they hadn't come through another rift. I hoped, hoped, hoped they hadn't come through another rift. Because the only way to create a rift was human sacrifice.

Which was also the only way to close one.

And I didn't think I could kill someone to close a rift. I'd done it once, and it still sometimes haunted my dreams. I'd rather die than do it again.

Except I didn't want to die, either. Just thinking about it made me shudder.

And of course I'd thought about a possible rift for days. My mind ran loops as we rode, and sometimes I'd talked to Jeremiah about it. He'd said we'd just have to wait and see before we needed to worry about anything.

The waiting was hard. We still had a couple of weeks on the trail, according to Otaktay. These were the parts that Jeremiah left out of the books, but I had to live them. And I was bored beyond belief.

I'd just finished rubbing down the last pack horse when Otaktay and one of his men hustled toward me. I wiped my hands on a rag as he approached. Twilight had started, which made it hard to read his expression, but his tense body language was clear.

He pulled up a few feet away. "Must leave! Crow war band!" He pointed south.

"There's a Crow war band?" I said in disbelief. "Here?" We were less than a day from the fort and several days' ride from Crow territory.

"Leave! Now!"

"Let's tell the others," I said. Then I yelled. "McNab! Jeremiah!" I jogged toward the main camp and called again. "McNab! Jeremiah!"

Jeremiah stood next to the cooking fire, while Maria still crouched next to one of her pots nestled on the rocks of the fire ring. Both looked at me, a touch alarmed.

"Crow war band," I said. I looked at Otaktay. "How many?"

"Five hands," he replied, flashing one hand with all fingers extended.

"Twenty-five warriors," Jeremiah said. "That's too many for us."

"Leave!" Otaktay urged. "Leave!"

"They may not be looking for a fight," I said.

"Not with us," Jeremiah said, "but them?" He gestured toward Otaktay and his warrior. "The Crow and Sioux have been at war off and on for a long time."

"How soon will they be here?" I asked Otaktay.

"Soon." He bounced on the balls of his feet, clearly eager for action. "Soon!"

"How quickly can we pack?" I asked Jeremiah and Maria. She'd already started gathering her foodstuffs and pans and dishes.

"I'd guess five minutes," Jeremiah said, "unless you want to leave our gear and supplies behind."

I shook my head. "We'll need those supplies." Besides, if we left right away, Zeke and Anoki wouldn't know where to find us.

McNab and Brody came into camp. McNab had two fishing poles over his shoulder and was out of breath. Brody's pants were soaked but he held a small net with a footlong fish inside it.

"We've got a Crow war party approaching," I quickly told him. "I think we should ride out and meet them, before they catch sight of the Sioux."

McNab frowned, but then nodded. "Take Jeremiah. I'll get us ready to run if we have to."

"Sir!" Brody said. "Permission to join you, sir!"

I hesitated. On the one hand, he'd be safer if I left him behind. On the other hand, better three soldiers at any parley than two.

"Granted," I said. "Let's go."

SEVEN

THE CROW WEREN'T hard to find. Other than the three big cottonwoods and some scattered saplings, there just wasn't a lot else besides grass and sky. The Crow stood tall on their horses against the horizon. They were a scary bunch, being twice our number and all clearly hardened warriors. They didn't react at all when the three of us rode toward them in the fading light.

To my left, Jeremiah rode easy. His hands were light on his reins, and he sat like a man riding home from church. Only his eyes betrayed his tenseness, for they darted everywhere. Private Brody, on my right, was his opposite. He looked more jittery than a prairie dog caught away from his hole. If he held his reins any tighter, his hands would start to bleed.

We stopped a few feet from them. The leader, judging from the way the others kept looking at him, urged his horse forward a step. Then he said something.

Which I didn't understand. It wasn't English. I glanced at Jeremiah and Brody, but they were as blank-faced as me.

The Crow leader repeated what he'd said, then said something different. Then he switched to what sounded like a different language.

"Do you speak English?" I asked.

He and his warriors returned our blank faces.

"Do you speak Arapaho?" I asked in that language.

"Yes," the leader replied, also in Arapaho.

I let out a relieved breath and continued, "I am Lieutenant McCarty, Army of the West. We are here in peace."

"Not with the Sioux," he growled back.

So they'd seen them. That made life tougher.

"We are riding to the Black Hills," I said. "To…," I paused because I didn't know the Arapaho word for investigate. "To… look at a town."

His eyes narrowed to unfriendly slits. "Black Hills are Crow land."

That was not an argument I wanted to get into. I looked at Jeremiah but he just shook his head. It didn't appear he was following and I couldn't remember if he spoke Arapaho or not. I decided I had to ignore the Crow's statement.

"The town is not Sioux," I said haltingly. "Not Crow. Not American. We find out who."

His nostrils flared as he regarded me. Then he looked over at Jeremiah and Brody and then stared at the trees that shaded our camp.

"We go with you."

I managed to avoid groaning out loud. Having the Crow and Sioux riding together for a few weeks was setting your gunpowder next to your cooking fire. One spark…

But what choice did I have?

"Camp now," I said. "Leave in morning."

He nodded and then said something in Crow to the men around him. He pointed upriver from our camp, to a scattering of willow bushes along the riverside. Then he turned back to me.

"Together," he said. "In morning. You leave without us, we hunt you."

I paused. I didn't know my Arapaho well enough, but I was pretty confident "hunt" was the right word. That certainly made my gut tighten.

"Morning," I agreed. Then I gestured to Jeremiah and Brody and we turned and rode back to camp.

It promised to be a long night.

Zeke and Anoki hadn't shown up by dawn. We'd kept watch all night, with me taking third watch personally, but hadn't seen a hint of them. Meanwhile none of us could avoid looking upstream to where the Crow camped.

So when the sun rose, I couldn't keep from worrying. The fort was only a day's ride. If they'd set out any time in the afternoon and ridden hard, they should've caught up. I hoped nothing horrible had happened to them. But it didn't make sense to ride back looking for them. The trail had been straight and clear and there was no way they could've gotten lost. They shouldn't have been waylaid either—the only possible enemies this close to the fort were the Crow, and they were with us. Zeke and Anoki were either still at the fort or just late.

But all my worrying didn't change anything, so I started working on breakfast before the others arose. I stirred the coals and added some wood to the fire pit. Maria joined me about the time I put the kettle on for some birchbark coffee. It wasn't really even close to the real thing, but McNab had only managed to snag a little of the real stuff, and I wanted to hold it back for when we really needed it.

I'd heard many a soldier say that coffee was the only thing that got them ready for battle. I planned to keep what coffee we had until battle was imminent. Which, despite our skittishness about the Crow, was not today.

Maria started mixing flour and water for flapjacks and asked me to refill the canteens. I headed over to the river, to a spot where I could watch the Crow camp. They'd started to move about, with the usual commotion of a camp waking up. I returned to the fire just as she dropped the first pancakes into some sizzling bacon grease in a hot pan. It smelled heavenly.

"No Zeke," she said as she cooked. It was as much a statement as a question.

"Yeah, I know," I said. "Do you think we should wait for them?"

She paused and held the spatula up. Then she swiveled to face me full on. Her face was firm, her eyes like my Ma's when I knew I was in trouble.

"You're in command," she said. "You decide."

"Can't I ask for advice?" I said with a hint of exasperation.

"You can, but what can I tell you that you don't already know?"

She had me stumped at that one. But then the question niggled at me. What should I know that I didn't?

The way ahead, I realized. We might be able to leave Zeke and Anoki a note telling them where we were going next, but I didn't know where that was. Not that I thought that was a good idea—it was too easy for them to miss a note or for it to get taken by someone else like the Crow—but it would still help to know where we were going.

So I went looking for Otaktay.

He and the other Sioux had camped a little ways downstream from the rest of us. That put us Americans between them and the Crow, which I suspect they liked just fine. They'd picked a grassy spot close to the river where a light breeze blew. They were just finishing packing their horses when I arrived. Otaktay frowned when he saw me approaching, and he and his men stepped away from the animals. He crossed his arms in front of his chest and waited for me to speak.

"Anoki and Zeke aren't here yet," I said. "We can wait, or we can leave them a sign that tells them where we're going next. But I don't know where that is. Is there a good landmark ahead like this one?"

He furrowed his brow and stared at me. I realized he might not have understood everything.

"Anoki and Zeke," I said slowly. "Not here. We wait or—"

"Wait." Otaktay's tone was firm. I suspected he'd reached the same conclusion I had—if we left them, we might never see them.

"Okay," I said with a shrug. "Will you watch the trail?" I pointed back the way we'd come.

He scowled, obviously not interested in taking an order from me, but also not knowing how to object.

I nodded, and then turned and returned to the camp.

I told the rest of our team as they gathered for breakfast. McNab nodded at once when he heard my decision and Jeremiah followed.

Brody looked a little confused until McNab said something to him as an aside. Maria, of course, was silent. She just continued to fry cakes and pass them about.

Then came the hard part. I had to tell the Crow.

I took Jeremiah with me again, but left Brody with McNab this time. They'd been talking fishing and Brody was clearly eager to show McNab what he could do. It was endearing even to me, in a way.

So Jeremiah and I rode upstream. We could've walked, but I didn't want the Crow to be able to look down on me. As it was, they, too, were mounted and ready to ride as we approached. Their leader rode forward on horseback. I still didn't know his name.

"We need to wait," I said haltingly in Arapaho. "Missing two." I held up two fingers to make sure he understood. "Wait."

His eyes narrowed and he glared at me.

"Must wait," I said. "You can go. We wait."

"No," he snarled. "You go with us."

"Not without my men." I let my hand drift down over my Colt revolver. I was much better with my rifle, but the threat was the same. "We wait."

He huffed, turned his horse, and rode back to the other Indians.

"That went well," Jeremiah said as we rode back to our camp.

"Why do you think that?"

"They didn't shoot us."

I snorted. I wasn't sure how long that would last.

The day grew warmer, but thankfully didn't cross over into hot. The shade under the cottonwoods was quite nice, especially when a small breeze drifted by.

But there wasn't much to do other than wait. By noon, I was starting to feel trapped. I'd seen the Crow out riding, both upstream and to the west, but sometimes to our south. They stayed far enough that I supposed they could be hunting, but it looked more like scouting to me. They didn't have their guns raised, for one.

McNab noticed, too. He'd taken a break from packing up our

camp to get some water. Instead of drinking, he just stood holding his canteen and watched two of them riding by. After a while, he must've felt my eyes on him because he turned and shrugged at me. He didn't need to say anything else.

Finally, finally, about mid-afternoon, there was commotion in the Sioux camp. One of their warriors came running toward us and waved for us to join them. McNab and I were on the move in an instant.

We spotted Zeke and Anoki immediately. Both big men were climbing down from their horses and surrounded by Sioux warriors. But they weren't alone. Lieutenant Caldwell and two of his soldiers were with them.

Lieutenant Caldwell saw us approaching and waved. He'd already dismounted and jogged out to meet us. I slowed to a stop, just outside of easy earshot of the Indians.

"What's happening?" I asked.

"Trouble," he said. "So we were ordered to join you."

I nodded.

"More Sioux arrived last night at Fort Randall." He gestured toward the Indians, and I realized there were several more warriors than before. "They say one of their camps got attacked by the Crow. Women and children were killed. They said by treaty, we're supposed to help them."

"What treaty?" I said.

"Apparently we signed one that said we'd help them if they were attacked, but it was meant for the Jotun, not the Crow." Lieutenant Caldwell wiped some sweat from his brow. "Captain Logan's sent a team to Fort Chicago to ask for orders, but it'll be weeks."

"It's worse than that." The knot in my stomach tightened. "The Crow are here, now. They found us last night." I quickly filled him in on my conversations with their war band.

"There's twenty-five of them?" he asked when I was done.

"Roughly," I said. I glanced at McNab, who nodded agreement. "I didn't get an exact count."

"We brought four more Sioux with us," Lieutenant Caldwell said. "That brings us to eighteen, counting your witch."

"Still not quite a fair fight," McNab murmured.

"But even enough to make them think twice about attacking us," I said. "At least I hope."

"They haven't attacked yet," McNab said, "when they could've easily won."

We were interrupted by Otaktay and Anoki walking over. They both looked grim, but for once they weren't shooting side-eyed angry glances at each other.

"You told them," Otaktay said to Lieutenant Caldwell. When the Lieutenant nodded, Otaktay turned to me and continued.

"Leave now," he said. "Fast. Escape Crow."

"They're not threatening us," I said. At least they weren't directly. Yet.

"They may not know we're at war again yet," Anoki said. "If we can't fight them, we must run."

I wasn't sure we could do either. The Crow were probably better riders than some on our team, and they didn't have baggage horses. I wasn't ready to leave ours behind.

"We can't run right now," McNab said. "They're watching us and we don't even have the cover of night."

I let out a deep breath. That made decisions easier. I still had a lot of doubts about being in charge, but I knew what to do.

"We ride up river," I said. "At least until nightfall. Then we'll see what we can do."

EIGHT

WE RODE until well after dusk. The moon brought plenty of light, and the still air carried the calls of distant birds. We stayed close to the river and let Otaktay and the Sioux lead. The Crow rode to the left of us and behind us. With the river on the right side, there wasn't a way to escape without notice. Otaktay and I both kept looking but never saw a break. So, instead, we camped in the grass.

The next morning, the Crow seemed to have grown in number. I tried counting but the only thing I could be sure of is that there were more than had been there the night before. A lot more. I guessed closer to forty now, which made some of the Sioux visibly nervous. Otaktay, of course, glared at them, but worry now appeared at the edge of his eyes.

We struck camp early and rode a bit harder than usual. It became clear by mid-day that the Crow were indeed surrounding us. They hadn't attacked, but I was beginning to wonder if that was just a matter of time.

I shared my thoughts with McNab as we rode at the back with the packhorses. He was with a bay that had a tendency to wander if you didn't tug his lead line from time to time.

"Their leader—he still hasn't told me his name—says they're hunting," I said, "but they never shoot anything and they always ride in a group."

"A patrol," McNab said. "The number's the same even when the warriors change."

"But why? They don't want to fight us or they'd have done it already."

"Yeah," he said with a morbid chuckle. "They don't want a war with the army, thank goodness."

"Well, the army doesn't want a war with them, either. My orders were pretty clear about that."

"That they were. But the treaty with the Sioux…?"

"Yeah. I wish we had orders about that."

He nodded in agreement. There didn't seem much else to say, so we rode quietly for a while.

Late in the afternoon, Otaktay rode back to find me. To my surprise, he had Anoki with him. Both men looked grim. I pulled on the reins and brought my own horse to a halt.

"Camp soon," Otaktay said. "Where small river joins big river. Tomorrow, leave big river."

I nodded. Following the river had taken us northwest, and we still had a ways to go due west. There must be a small tributary not far ahead.

"When we leave the big river," Anoki said, "the Crow will surround us. We won't be able to defend ourselves like we can now."

I grimaced. I'd come to the same conclusion. With the river at our backs, we had at least some protection. But out in the open…

"Not allow," Otaktay said. "No."

Anoki glanced at Otaktay, and after his cousin nodded, said, "If we camp at the junction where the two rivers meet, Otaktay and his men can sneak across the little river at night. The Crow won't send men across the little river until daylight—it's too treacherous to cross if you don't know where. But we do. So Otaktay can ride ahead and get help from our tribe."

"And then what?" I asked. "A big battle with the Crow?"

"They start, we finish," said Otaktay.

That was not reassuring. Us Americans would be caught in the middle. Worse, I didn't exactly trust Otaktay. I sensed that if he thought he could win, he'd start the fight himself. But if the Sioux were gone, the Crow wouldn't have a reason to fight us Americans, and maybe they'd leave us in peace.

Maybe.

It looked like Anoki thought so. I wasn't as sure, but I didn't feel comfortable telling the Sioux to stay.

"Okay," I finally said. "Let's camp. But let's talk before you and your men leave. After dinner, okay?"

Otaktay nodded and then they rode toward the front of our little column and the other Sioux.

The more I thought about it, the more I didn't like the Sioux abandoning us. For one, I still didn't know where we were headed, and I didn't want to lose my guides. For another, I knew the Crow would be angry, and I couldn't predict what they'd do.

But if the Sioux didn't go, it might be worse. And regardless of whether they went or not, I had to decide what the rest of us did.

Because I was in charge.

My stomach felt tight and my uniform seemed to press down on my shoulders and back. It seemed a little harder to breathe. It wasn't because I was afraid. No, I'd been afraid a bunch of times and that had never slowed me down. This… was doubt.

Before I'd joined the army, I hadn't felt much doubt. Not for long. I'd been confident and headstrong and stubborn as all heck. And in the army, I'd learned how to watch out for myself. After they'd promoted me, well, Captain Mercer had really been in charge. At least until I got assigned to do patrols, and with those, I didn't have to make many decisions.

Certainly not any life or death decisions. Well, maybe not other people's lives. I could live with risking my own. But Maria's or McNab's or Zeke's?

The more I thought, the more my gut tightened. But that didn't change the fact that I needed to do something. I *was* in charge.

Just like Cassidy. I wondered how he'd handled it. He'd seen people die. Some were his friends, even. But he'd kept going.

I wish I'd talked more about it with him then. But… I hadn't known what to ask back then, either. I'd been a lot younger.

I snorted softly. It'd only been a year since I'd ridden with Cassidy. But it might as well have been a lifetime.

I couldn't take his place, but maybe I could keep his team alive. Maybe that mattered more than getting a chance to be independent of the army.

It was a fight to keep the doubts at bay. But I reminded myself that I only needed to figure out what to do today. Tomorrow and its problems would come soon enough.

We continued riding until we found the spot where the little river merged into the Missouri. I decided we'd pitch our own camp a little west, along the smaller one. That'd give the Sioux space to be next to it but behind us.

After we'd set up camp, I called everyone around the fire. Otaktay and his men had taken their usual spot about a hundred yards downstream from us, while the Crow were further upstream, not counting the riders 'hunting' to our west. But that left everyone else, even Anoki, standing or sitting around the fire as the last bits of daylight faded.

"Otaktay wants to sneak away in the night," I said. "He and his warriors will steal across the river and slip away from the Crow. I don't blame them. Tomorrow we leave the river and head west and they'll never get another chance."

Several people nodded, and a few murmured too low for me to catch their words.

"Now the question is, what do we do?" I continued. "I know as the commanding officer, I'm supposed to decide, and I have some ideas, but I want everyone's opinions."

This led to some more murmuring, mostly among Lieutenant Caldwell and his men.

"Don't we need them to guide us?" Jeremiah asked. "We don't know where this mystery town is."

"I do, roughly," Anoki said. "Otaktay told me. We follow the river until it turns south and then cross it and head west. I think I can get us there after that."

"Maybe we should ask for some of them to stay, sir," Lieutenant Caldwell said, with a tone that made it clear that was his choice, if it'd been his decision.

"Mmmm," Jeremiah said. "I think a better question is whether some of us should go with them?"

I blinked. I hadn't thought of that, but I got it immediately.

"Do you think it'll increase our chances of getting to the Black Hills?" I asked.

Jeremiah shrugged. "It can't hurt."

"It could," Anoki said. "But if the Crow chase Otaktay, there will be a battle."

"Do our men have to stay with the Sioux, sir?" Brody asked. He glanced nervously from me to Lieutenant Caldwell and back and I was mildly surprised the private had spoken up.

"It'd be hard to find the town without them," Lieutenant Caldwell said. Then he looked at me. "Mind you, if it's as big as they say, it'd be hard to miss."

"We could do it," I said, "but I'm also worried about whomever we leave behind. What if the Crow attack?"

"That's the big question," McNab said. He rocked on his heels. "What're they gonna do when they discover the Sioux are gone?" He looked over at Anoki, who just shrugged.

"They don't want a fight with us," I said. "They don't want the army coming at them in force."

"But if they could kill us without the army knowing…?" McNab said. "It wouldn't be the first time an expedition disappeared without a trace. We were too close to the fort when they found us. The further west we get, the easier it'd be."

That, unfortunately, made a lot of sense. It also made up my mind.

"We need to split up," I said. "The only way they'll attack is if they think they can get us all. As long as they think someone might get back to the fort, they'll leave us alone."

"I'll go," Lieutenant Caldwell volunteered. "My men and I can ride with the Sioux for a while and then head off on our own if it looks like trouble. Maybe we can lead the Crow away from the Black Hills."

I nodded. Caldwell's orders were to assist the Sioux, not to investigate the mysterious town. The Crow might know where my team was headed, but they wouldn't know where he was.

"Okay," I said. "It's decided." I nodded at Caldwell. "We'll tell Otaktay after dinner."

Of course, we continued to discuss and debate things over the meal. We'd split into smaller groups, each in their own little circle. McNab and Jeremiah were brainstorming on what the Crow might do, with Private Brody listening in. Lieutenant Caldwell and Anoki were in a deep discussion about the local tribes, both Sioux and Crow. Lieutenant Caldwell's other men were in their own group. So after I filled up my bowl of stew, I went and sat with Zeke.

The big man sat quietly on a patch of grass under a skinny cottonwood. In the fading light, his black skin blended into his uniform to make him look more like a relaxing bear than a man. Still, he smiled when I sat down.

"How're you doing?" I asked.

"Fine," he said. "Stew's good." He smiled and plunged a spoonful into his mouth.

"We haven't talked about what you did with Anoki back at the fort," I said. "How you took care of him."

"Injun Joe? Wasn't much." He shrugged. "Just the Christian thing to do."

I snorted. Like many, I'd struggled to keep my faith, any faith, after the rift had opened and the Jotun arrived. Zeke had gone the other way. He was convinced that the Jotun and trolls were a challenge from God to test the faithful, a test that he would not fail.

"Any problems?"

"No. He talked about his wife a lot."

That caused me to pause. I'd been so focused on the Crow and on getting to the mystery town that I'd forgotten we also needed to get Anoki to his wife before she died.

That complicated things.

"What'd he say?" I asked. "Anything you want to share?"

"No," Zeke said. "They was old stories about her. He loved her. I dunno why he left."

"Ah." I didn't know, either. In any case, there wasn't much I could do.

"So what about you?" I asked. "You have any complaints?"

He shrugged again. Then he thought for a minute.

"I miss Bible study," he said. "And pie. Peach or apple. I miss a good pie."

"You and me both," I said with a laugh. "This is good." I pointed at the stew that he'd just devoured. "But pie would hit the spot."

"Maybe there'll be some in that town," he said.

"Yeah," I said. "Maybe they'll sell us pies."

He grinned. "It'd be mighty nice if they did."

We finished our meal quietly, talking and joking about food we missed and how the dwarves might sell it to us. I had no doubt that they wouldn't, but it was still fun to think about.

"You know," I said as the conversation hit a pause, "I'm mighty glad you're on this trip. But I never gave you a chance to say no, like I did with the others."

He shrugged.

"Would you have wanted to stay?" I asked. "I know it's your mission to stop the Jotun and trolls."

"Well…," he curled his lip as he thought. "Well…"

"Go on. I won't hold it against you."

He smiled. That big broad smile.

"I prayed about it," he said. "I prayed good and hard. And I read my verses." He nodded toward his Bible, close at hand.

"And…?"

"We do what the Lord calls us to do. Not what us sinners want."

"And what does the Lord want?"

He fell silent again, and just stared west. After a bit, I fidgeted, and that seemed to break the spell.

"Sergeant-Major McNab said I was to look after you," Zeke finally said. "Like you had me look after him, in Tennessee. And when I prayed, the Lord agreed."

I sat quietly, not knowing quite what to say.

The crickets and other bugs had come out in force, filling the quiet night with their noise. Zeke and I had finished our meal, and he'd excused himself to use the latrine. I dusted myself off as I stood and went in search of others.

I found Anoki. He still sat with Lieutenant Caldwell and they remained deep in conversation, though both looked up as I approached.

"Anoki," I said as I knelt down beside him. "If you come with us, how will you see your wife?"

He grunted. "He told you about her?"

"Otaktay? Yes, he did."

"That was not his to tell," he grunted.

"Maybe," I said, "but you should've told me."

"I did not know she was dying until Otaktay told me at the fort."

I sighed and looked at Lieutenant Caldwell. He gave me a sympathetic look but didn't speak up.

"You're going to see her before she dies, right?" I asked.

He grew gloomy and shrugged.

"That's why Otaktay wanted you along."

"Otaktay," he said with a grimace, "is strict in what is right, and what is wrong. He believes I have a duty to her, even though my leaving was for the best."

My eyebrows rose, but he did not go on.

"So… are you going to see her?" I finally asked.

He shrugged and continued staring off into the distance. After a bit, it became clear he wasn't going to continue, so I stood.

Otaktay and one of his warriors entered our camp. Night had fallen, but his silhouette stood out against the grey sky. He seemed to tower over me, which only made my spine stiffen.

"Leave now," he said.

"Lieutenant Caldwell and his men will go with you," I said.

"We will allow."

I was glad to hear that. I hadn't expected him to object, but one never knew.

So I continued, "Anoki stays with us."

He crossed his arms across his chest. I was sure he was scowling at me, but his face was too shadowed to tell.

"I'll make sure he visits his wife," I said. "On my honor."

His body language didn't change.

"We need him as a guide," I said. "If he wears his army uniform, the Crow should leave him alone." As much as they left us all alone.

"We leave now."

"We'll try to keep 'em distracted."

He turned and strode off without another word.

The problem was, I didn't know how to keep the Crow distracted. I knew they were watching our camp, but from far enough away that we'd have to do something big to get their attention. Worse, it had to be something that wasn't obviously a distraction. They'd probably figure it out the next day when they noticed the Sioux were gone, but better the next day then while it was happening.

Actually, the next day probably wasn't too great either. It was all too easy to imagine them causing trouble because they were mad.

But nothing "normal" in camp would be sufficient as a distraction. And riding out of camp away from the river would be too obvious.

That left only one option, I realized. Some of us were going to have to ride into their camp. If they were busy talking to me, they might not watch the river closely. But if they did and they saw the Sioux...

...I'd have placed myself in their hands.

NINE

THE NIGHT WAS QUIET, far too quiet, as Zeke, McNab, and I rode toward the Crow camp. I'd picked McNab because he was the most experienced fighter on the team. I wanted Zeke along because of his skill with the blade. It was as close to safe as I was gonna feel.

I'd made sure we were all in our uniforms, with every button in place. Each of us had his revolver on one hip and his saber close to the other, with our rifles strapped within easy reach. I was hoping there wouldn't be trouble, but if there was, we'd need our weapons close at hand.

We rode forward, the huff of the horses and the jangle of the tack drowning out the sounds of the river. A light breeze ruffled my hair. My mind kept drifting back to Otaktay and the Sioux. How hard was it going to be to ford the little river here? It looked shallow, though that could be deceiving. He'd said they'd known where to cross, but in the dark, would they be able to manage it?

I'd worried about the river quite a bit. My own team wouldn't be able to cross it, if worse came to worse. Jeremiah, McNab, and I had talked and decided we'd ride south if needed, and then figure out a way west. Jeremiah and Brody had everyone packed and ready to go just in case.

The Crow had pitched their own camp a few hundred yards west of ours along the banks of the small river. A handful of small fires lit up the area, easily five or six, and that was just a guess. I couldn't help wondering if more warriors had joined them since we'd counted last. My gut tightened at the thought, but I forced myself to sit straighter on my horse and ride on.

We rode slowly. I wanted to make sure they saw us. That a lot of them saw us.

They didn't disappoint. By the time we got within fifty yards, there were over a dozen warriors standing at the edge of their camp. They clutched their rifles at their sides, and some kept glancing behind them. From the commotion, I suspected there were more coming.

Then their leader pushed through the crowd.

I pulled up on the reins. Every time we'd met before, we'd both been mounted. Now I was the only one.

He clutched his rifle. He wasn't pointing it at me, but the threat was clear.

"Cover me," I said quietly to Zeke and McNab.

McNab nodded and drew his Colt, but kept it by his side. Zeke put his hand on his own. I took a deep breath, and dismounted from my horse.

I put my hand on my gun as I slowly walked toward the Crow leader. He tensed and waited. I stopped when I was a few feet away.

"We go Black Hills," I said in halting Arapaho. "Find town. You not come."

"We go with you," he said, so firmly his words felt like steel. "Black Hills, Crow land."

"Town not Crow. Not Sioux. Not American. Maybe…" I searched for the word for "dwarf" but didn't know it in Arapaho. I held a hand up, about waist high. "Maybe short men."

None of the Crow looked at all surprised. I wasn't sure if they understood.

"Not human." I held my hand waist high. "Short human like child."

Again, I didn't see a flicker of shock or concern.

"We go," I said. "You not come."

He snorted in derision and glanced at the mass of men around him.

"You with Sioux," he said.

"No," I said. "Crow and Sioux fight. Not us. We not fight Crow. We not fight Sioux. We find town."

Sweat beaded on my brow. Trying to make myself understood in a language I barely knew had my brain in knots. I couldn't tell if the Crow leader didn't understand or just wasn't happy with what he'd heard.

"We go with you," he repeated.

"No," I said with a big shake of my head. "You and Sioux fight. We no fight. We find town."

He stared at me and I stared back. Time slid by as we glared at each other.

A yell came from the river. Then a second. Indian yells.

The Crow reacted immediately. Most ran toward the river. The leader barked something to some of his men and gave me a single glance before rushing toward the river himself. The men he'd left behind shouldered their rifles and pointed them at us.

McNab and Zeke reacted immediately and raised their pistols. I raised my hands.

"No fight!" I said in Arapaho. "No fight!"

That drew their attention. I had several rifles pointed directly at my chest from only a few yards away. Four, I quickly determined. Despite my tight gut, my mind remained calm. In the low light it was hard to see their faces. I couldn't tell how ready they were to shoot.

Still, I kept my hands up and slowly walked backward. McNab and Zeke did the same at my side. I glanced over my shoulder quickly to make sure I knew where my horse was, but mostly I kept my focus on the warriors.

They watched me, but made no other moves. It wasn't until I mounted my horse that one of them called out. I didn't understand what he said.

Gunfire erupted near the river. Several shots, all at once. The Crow facing us turned to look.

"Let's go!" I yelled. I wheeled my horse around and rode hard.

Scattered gunshots came from behind us. I bent down and clutched my horse's neck. I prayed that they'd miss. Or that they weren't really trying to shoot us. I quickly glanced to the side. Zeke and McNab rode hard beside me.

Then McNab grunted and slumped. He kept ahold of the reins and kept galloping. I pulled my Colt and fired backwards toward the Crow without looking. I wouldn't hit anything, but maybe I'd make them duck.

McNab started to slide in his saddle. His grip loosened and his horse began to slow. I steered mine next to his. He looked up at me and gave me a pained grin.

"You gonna make it?" I yelled.

He just gave me a pale look.

But we were close to camp. I could see the others, all mounted, their silhouettes against the sky. More gunshots came from the river.

I glanced back. No Crow. We weren't being chased.

When I got close to my team, I yelled, "South!"

Several of them spurred their horses immediately. The smallest hung back, and as we closed I realized it was Maria. While the shadows cloaked her features, no one else was of her size.

"McNab?" she asked.

"He's been shot."

"How badly?" She turned her horse to meet ours.

We slowed to a halt next to her, and then I motioned for Zeke to follow the others. "Dunno," I said.

"I can ride," McNab panted. He struggled to sit upright. "It's my shoulder. In back."

"Let me see," Maria said as she slid off her horse.

"I can ride!" McNab protested.

I glanced back. We still weren't being followed. "Better let her look at it."

McNab slumped in defeat and then started to dismount. He winced, so I hopped off my own horse and helped him down. Even in the moonlight, I could see the wetness on his upper left back, just above his shoulder blade.

Maria produced bandages from somewhere. She didn't bother

undoing McNab's uniform coat or shirt. Instead, she put a thick wad directly on top of the wound and tied it down by wrapping long strips of cloth around his neck and side. She then bound his left arm to his torso. I figured it was to keep his shoulder blade from moving. He winced again when she cinched them tight.

"That should help until we are safe," she said. "Then I want a better look."

He nodded and turned to his horse. Then he paused.

"Let me help you up," I said.

"Yeah. Give me a boost, Billy."

It took a little bit of shuffling and wrangling, but we got him up. As he settled, I mounted my own horse. We'd been delayed, but I didn't want McNab to bleed out as he rode, either.

We turned our horses south and I glanced back toward the Crow camp, and what I saw made my throat catch.

A dozen horsemen were galloping our way.

"Let's go!" I yelled. It was all I could do to keep the fear at bay.

We dashed off, as hard as we could ride, the distant Crow in pursuit. We rode south, and they followed. We swung east, and they stayed on our tail. With nothing but grass or river in all directions, I didn't think we could shake them. That meant our only chance was to outrun them.

When we got close to the Missouri river we turned south again, following it downstream. We rode hard. I constantly spurred my horse on, and I could feel his muscles strain as it raced as fast as it could. McNab and Maria stayed close by my side.

We kept riding hard. I focused ahead, on going as fast as we could. I spurred my horse, urging even more speed. McNab seemed to be hanging on for dear life, but he hung on.

After a long but too-short time, my horse started to falter and tire. I urged him on again, and he did his best, but I could sense he was nearing his limit. With reluctance, I slowed up enough to look back.

I couldn't see the Crow.

So I turned and slowed my horse to a walk. I scanned the horizon for horsemen silhouetted against the sky and didn't see any. The land wasn't completely flat, but I was sure I'd see them if they were there. Instead, I saw nothing but grass and sky.

Maria and McNab had stopped beside me. His mouth was open and he was panting hard. In the low light, I thought he might be sweating hard, too, but I couldn't be sure. Maria nudged her horse next to his and leaned closer to examine his bandages.

"I think… I think they turned back," I said.

"But…," McNab gasped, "Where's our guys?"

I looked all around and particularly west, where they should've been. I didn't see a single soul.

"We must treat McNab's wound," Maria said.

I nodded. "What do you need?"

"Fire," she said. "Water. Some light."

A fire would've been instantly spotted out here in the grasslands. I looked toward the river. The shore was lined with bushes, but nothing that looked like serious cover. Still, it offered our only hope.

"Let's see if we can find some place with a high bank." I pointed toward the river. "Maybe with a sandbar or something below it. It's the only way we can have a fire." I didn't think we'd be able to hide the horses, but the light from the flames was what would give us away.

We ended up having to ride downstream much further than I thought, but we finally found a spot where bushes grew at the top of a rise, with a long stretch of muddy grass by the water. We tied the horses at the top and clambered down the little drop, McNab was obviously in pain as we went. Our boots squelched in the mud, but there was at least one spot where the grass was thick enough to sit. Maria started examining McNab's wound while I looked for rocks to make a fire pit and then wood dry enough to burn.

I didn't find much, but it was enough. Maria boiled a small pot of water and sponged out McNab's wound. It wasn't as bad as I'd feared, but the bullet was too deep for Maria to remove. Meanwhile, I took care of the horses and kept watch.

As I stood there, all the excitement of the chase drained out of me. I didn't see a thing. Nothing moved in the moonlight.

I thought about what'd happened. The Sioux had been spotted.

We'd thought they'd be hidden enough in the night and that my distraction would work. We'd been wrong, obviously.

That made my gut tighten even more. The doubts arose and I started second-guessing all our choices. Had we really done the right thing by having the Sioux head off on their own? Could I have distracted the Crow better? Had anyone else been hurt? Or even died?

I didn't like those thoughts. I didn't like them at all. But finally my thoughts ran down. Waves of exhaustion took their place. For the first time, I noticed the soreness in my legs from the wild ride. I had to fight the urge to sit on the ground.

We needed to rest for the night, I decided. With McNab hurt, it didn't make sense to do much more riding, even if we knew where we were headed. We've have a better chance of finding Jeremiah and the others in the morning.

That was, if the Crow didn't find us first.

TEN

MCNAB SLEPT SOON after we put out the fire. We'd moved up from the wet river bank to the drier grass. Maria and I split watches for the rest of the short night. I slept hard when it was my turn and awoke just as dawn began.

The sky was cloudless, which promised a warm, if not outright hot, day. A light breeze blew from the west, but it wasn't enough to do more than tease. The insects stirred, but that was it. I couldn't even see a bird in any direction.

McNab looked better, more alert. He sat on his bedroll chewing some jerky and dried berries. His left arm was still strapped to his side, but now with a leather cord instead of a simple bandage. He forced a pained smile when I crouched beside him. That was good. My bad choices back with the Crow hadn't killed him.

"This is getting old, Billy," he said with a nod toward his shoulder. "I'm tired of getting beaten up."

"Sorry," I mumbled. "I'm glad you're alive."

He snorted. "Yeah. But life's supposed to be more than pain, you know?"

"Sorry," I said again.

"You're not the one that shot me."

"Yeah." I grimaced. "But you're out here because of me."

He laughed.

"Billy, my boy," he laughed "do you really think I'd be out here if I didn't want to be?"

"Well, the General did order you to come out."

"And you think I don't know how to get orders changed?" He chuckled. "Oh, Billy, you got a lot to learn."

I tried to keep the red out of my face. He was right, as he'd been so often in the past, so I changed the subject.

"I think we should head due west," I said. "If we follow the river, we'll run into the Crow." I figured we were probably two to five miles south of the little river we'd intended to follow west.

"Well, we might run into them anyway," he said.

"True. But what else can we do? I'm pretty sure Jeremiah and the others will be somewhere to the west."

"Maybe a little north, too," McNab replied. "Jeremiah wouldn't have ridden any further from the little river than he had to."

I nodded in agreement. Besides, Jeremiah was logical like that. I looked over at Maria, but she just gave me one of her inscrutable smiles.

McNab glanced down at his bound arm. "You'll have to help me mount my horse."

"Easy," I said, "this time we've got the light."

And it turned out, it was easy. Once we were packed, I just needed to give McNab a boost, and he was up. We were on our way shortly after dawn.

We didn't see anything until mid-morning. Well, other than grass and sky. But then Maria pointed to the north, where black figures moved in the far distance. We paused and squinted until I was sure they were horsemen. We stopped and watched.

They were hard to see, and it took me a while to get a feel for the number. I guessed there were about a half dozen or so. Certainly more than four or five, and fewer than a dozen, unless there were a bunch hidden behind the others. In any case, it was also more than Jeremiah's group. Jeremiah should've had himself, Brody, Zeke, Anoki, and a couple of pack horses. I looked carefully again. I could count at least six riders and none of the horses were riderless.

So a small Crow band.

"Let's go further south," I said. "Before they see us."

Maria and McNab nodded and we snapped the reins, though we ended up going more southwest than south.

The Crow didn't follow, to my relief.

We rode with the wind in our face and the hot sun on our necks until we came to a small stream flowing north toward the little river. After we'd refreshed ourselves and our horses, we decided to follow it north a ways.

And we spotted the Crow again.

They were ahead of us, downstream, a little closer than they'd been before. There seemed to be fewer of them, maybe four or five. They were all mounted, but appeared to be just standing. They weren't riding anywhere.

Then I realized they were looking our direction.

"Let's go." I quickly cantered due west, and Maria and McNab followed. After several minutes I slowed and looked back.

The Crow were riding west, too.

They weren't headed toward us, though. So we kept going.

After about an hour, we came to another stream. We slowed and then stopped. I'd built up too much sweat in the heat and the horses were breathing hard. We let them drink and I checked on the Crow again. They'd stopped as well—the same distance away, the same direction.

They weren't trying to attack us, but they weren't letting us out of their sight.

"They're tracking us," McNab said with a grimace. "Another of their dratted scout patrols."

"Just a patrol? That doesn't make me happy. Where's the rest of them?"

He shook his head. He knew I could guess as well as he. I looked at Maria in case she had any ideas and she just shook her head too. Their tracking us bothered me. Maybe we could outrun them.

"Your shoulder good enough to ride hard?" I asked McNab.

"Only one way to find out." He grimaced, and I suspected the ride had hurt him, but he didn't want to admit it.

So I decided to go for it.

Several minutes later, the three of us raced across the plains. I didn't think we'd shake the Crow patrol, but I at least wanted to make them work for it. My hat flew off at one point, but the cord caught it, and it swirled around my neck. I ignored it and rode harder.

After a bit, we crested a small rise. My heart skipped—ahead of us, horsemen in blue with a pack train walked slowly north. Jeremiah! They saw us and halted. Jeremiah took off his hat and waved, his dark skin obvious in the bright sun.

I glanced back. The Crow were galloping on our tail.

We raced ahead, and then I saw Jeremiah and Zeke—it had to be Zeke right next to him—point behind us. They spurred their horses toward us, and I could see Jeremiah already reaching for his rifle. When we were all close, I turned my horse and looked back. Around me, rifles snapped to shoulders as the horses paced and pawed the ground.

The Crow had pulled up and stopped. They stood just close enough to make out rifles in their arms. But we were well outside rifle range for both sides.

"Let's go," I said, "at a walk."

Zeke kept his rifle high and waited until we'd all ridden past him. The big man made quite a show as he trained his gun on the distant Indians. It was intimidating, even to me, and I knew he didn't have a chance of actually hitting them.

We walked, turned to look at them, walked some more, and then turned again. After a bit, it became clear they weren't following.

Jeremiah nudged his horse next to mine. He was tense. Worried. "You okay?"

I nodded. "We just got separated. McNab's got a bullet in his back, but Maria's already done what she can."

"Oh boy," Jeremiah said. "I told him he should just retire."

I raised an eyebrow, questioning.

"He wanted one last ride," Jeremiah explained. "Did Maria get the bullet out?"

I shook my head.

Jeremiah set his jaw. It wasn't necessarily fatal, but it wasn't good. Soldiers survived with bullets inside them, unless they got infected. That was the tricky part.

"When did you pick up the patrol?" he said with a jerk of his head toward the Crow.

"An hour or two ago. They're the only ones we've seen."

"They're the first we've seen."

"Think they'll follow?" I asked, though I knew the answer.

"Of course," he said. "Keep going?"

"Yeah." I raised my hand and turned so I had everyone's attention. "Let's go!"

We rode for the rest of the afternoon at a regular pace. About an hour before dusk, Zeke spotted the Crow band again, but they hung back, just at the edge of sight. I decided we'd do double watches that night and arranged them when we were all settled around the fire for dinner.

The plains cooled with the setting of the sun. We'd found another stream to camp by, with a broad low plain beside it. The horses drank greedily, and I took the opportunity to wash my face and hands in the cold water. As dusk continued to fall, the crickets and other bugs came out in force and their songs seemed to flow across the grass. It felt peaceful, but I couldn't shake the sense that the Crow were out there, watching.

Private Brody joined me after we'd eaten. I'd remained seated on a rock near the fire watching Maria and sipping some chicory tea. She was cooking some tincture for McNab, who'd unrolled his bedroll a few feet away and stretched out. It smelled foul, like dung mixed with sulphur. I didn't want to ask what it was.

Private Brody had his book clasped between his hands. He wore his usual expression of eager curiosity, but more tinged by wariness. He hadn't shaved in several days, but his beard was too scruffy to do more than make him look like an overgrown kid. I imagined mine was no different.

"So..., um...," he began, "I wanted to ask about something, uh, before talking about the book."

"Sure," I said.

"The Crow," he said. "Why are we running from them? It's just a patrol. Why don't we go fight them?" His voice had sped up there toward the end. Eager, but a bit scared.

"We're not gonna fight them if we don't have to," I said. "For one, I don't like killing people. Jotun, okay. Trolls, god yes. But I haven't killed another human yet and I don't want to."

"But... they'd kill us."

"True. But isn't there enough evil in the world without us adding to it?"

He swallowed as he digested my words. I decided to let him off easy.

"Besides," I said, "if we attacked and any of them escaped, they'd bring the rest of them down on us. That's not a fight we can win."

"So why not try to lose them? Sneak away so they can't follow us?" The confidence in his voice was back.

"What's the point? They know where we're going."

He fell silent and just stared east for a bit. At the fire, Maria pulled the horribly stinking pot off the flames and added something to the mixture that made it hiss and crackle. But it also dampened the smell, for which I was grateful.

"So…, um…," Brody held up the book. "I had another question."

"Okay." I could indulge him some more.

"In the book, you're angry a lot," he said. "But here, now—"

"I'm not?" I snorted softly. The Billy of the books seemed like a lifetime ago, even if I allowed for Jeremiah's exaggerations in writing. I remembered being more hot tempered then. These days… I was more tired.

The army had done that to me. It was better, out here on the trail with my friends. Much better than marching or training or dealing with orders that made no sense. But complaining in the army just earned problems. Problems I'd had enough of.

Besides, I'd grown less sure of myself. The younger me had known exactly what he wanted and charged ahead, recklessly at times. Now I knew how reckless I'd been. It scared me to think about.

Private Brody shifted restlessly. He was waiting for an answer.

I gave him a rueful smile. "I've learned that anger doesn't help. That doesn't mean I don't feel it, but storming away from the team like a polecat with a splinter in his foot? Like I did in the book? That's just… immature."

He blinked in surprise, and I hoped the answer was good enough for him. I wasn't sure what else to say.

He thought for a moment, and looked about to ask something else, when the sound of running feet grabbed our attention. Zeke, who'd been on watch, skidded to a halt a few feet away.

"Sir, Billy, sir," he said between gasps for air. "Riders coming. A whole bunch. Coming fast. They'll be here in minutes."

ELEVEN

"MOUNT UP!" I yelled. Not that I needed to. Plates got set in the dirt. Brody fumbled and dropped his book. To my surprise, he let it lie. Maria took whatever she was cooking off the fire, but just set it nearby. Everyone scrambled for their horses.

I'd left my rifle close to my bedroll and cursed to myself. I knew not to leave it out of reach. By the time I'd grabbed it and reached the horses, I realized how foolish my order had been. We'd taken the tack off to let the horses rest while we ate, and there was no way we'd get it back on in time. Not that Jeremiah and Brody weren't trying. They were helping McNab mount up before I turned to look east. Zeke had his saber out, already looking the same way.

I strode over and clasped him on the arm. "Let's go. We'll give the others time to escape."

"Lord be with us." He marched forward so fast I had to quick-step to keep up.

It wasn't hard to spot the riders. Between the night glow from the moon and the empty plains, I could see the bunch of dark horsemen coming our way. A big bunch. They were still far enough away that I couldn't make out individuals, but they'd be here soon.

I raised my rifle and fired a shot in the air. The crack of the shot rang out loud, and the horsemen slowed. They didn't stop, though. Instead, they spread out. That made it easier to guess their number.

It looked like thirty. Maybe more. With a sinking pit in my gut, I realized it was more than a scouting patrol.

The main Crow war band had found us.

"Oh, Dear Lord," Zeke said beside me. He'd figured it out, too.

I knew we couldn't outrun them again. Not all of us, even if we abandoned all our supplies in camp. I hoped Jeremiah and some of the others would at least try. But even if they all got away, Zeke and I wouldn't.

So we waited. Zeke moved his saber to a guard position. I set my rifle to my shoulder, but didn't aim. Instead, I waited.

The ends of the horsemen's line broke off and galloped, past us to the sides, moving behind us. The middle came straight at us and continued to slow as they approached closer.

I held my fire but moved enough to make it clear I was holding my rifle up. Eventually, the nearest horses slowed to a walk and then stopped about ten yards away.

In the dark, I could tell they were Crow, but not much else. Shadows hid their features, even if the silhouettes matched what I'd seen before. Eventually, one horseman pushed through the knot. He sat tall on his horse, and I thought I recognized him.

"You no leave!" he said in Arapaho.

I let out a long breath. Their leader.

"We go alone," I replied, as loudly and forcefully as I could.

He said something sharp and loud that I didn't understand. All the warriors surrounding him raised their rifles and pointed them at me and Zeke.

"Kill us and it's war!" I did my best not to move, despite how much I was sweating.

He glared at me, and none of his warriors lowered their guns.

"War!" I slowly lowered my rifle. "The Army of the West hunt Crow to the ends of the Earth." I wasn't sure I'd gotten the Arapaho right, but from the way some of the guns wavered, I'd been understood.

"The Army and the Lord!" Zeke suddenly added in his deep English. "This is Billy the Kid! The hero of Colorado! The hero of Louisville! He does the Lord's work and the Lord's hand is upon him, and if you harm him, the Lord shall smite you heathens down!"

The Crow shifted around more, and a few murmured. I doubted they understood his words, but they understood the tone. A couple of rifles dipped.

"You hear me?" Zeke yelled. "The hero of Louisville! You kill him and General Sanborn himself will hunt you down."

"Sanborn?" The Crow leader's voice actually contained a note of doubt.

"Yes. General Sanborn send me to find town," I said in Arapaho. "Learn about town."

He glared at me for a full eight heartbeats before he barked another command I didn't understand, except that all the Crow lowered their weapons.

"We go town together," the leader said. "You. Us." He gestured back toward our camp. "Yours. Sanborn agree."

That confused me. "No. Me, mine, we go alone."

"No. Crow shoot first, Sanborn come. You shoot first, Sanborn not come. You shoot?"

He held his arms wide, his rifle out, baring his chest and offering me an easy shot. I could kill him as easily as swatting a fly.

And then all his warriors would kill me in a heartbeat.

I didn't believe Sanborn would care who started the shooting, despite what the Crow said. But I'd be just as dead. That didn't seem like a win to me.

"Me, mine, we go alone." I slung my rifle over my shoulder. No point in even threatening something they knew I wasn't going to do.

"Then you walk. Long time."

I blinked. Walk? Sure, we were on foot, but…

"Oh, no." I couldn't help glancing back toward our camp.

"What?" Zeke asked.

"Our horses. They're gone."

The Crow escorted us back to our camp, or what was left of it. It was a noisy procession. Several had already ridden ahead and were coming back. I could hear others yelling in the distance.

At the camp, I was relieved to see that all of our team had escaped, except for Zeke and me. True to the Crow leader's word, all the horses were gone too. I didn't know if Jeremiah had taken Zeke's and mine, or they'd run off, or the Crow had them. With all the Indians milling about, I couldn't look around.

Their horses stomped through the remains of our camp, and I realized they might trample the supplies we'd left. I scooped up the pots and bags that Maria had left by the fire. It had died down to orange coals, and I briefly wondered if the Crow would camp here or push on. But that was a dumb thought. Of course they'd push on.

But when I'd finished gathering up all the loose gear, I spotted something else. Brody's book. I picked it up just as the Crow leader called out something, and all the Indians quieted down.

"You." The leader pointed at me. "Ride with Daxpitchée." He pointed at a burly Crow with bulging muscles and a scar on his forearm. Then he pointed at Zeke. "You with Bishée." Zeke's warrior was as big as he was, with more long black hair on his head and body than I was used to seeing on an Indian.

"Your name?" I asked.

"Cheéte." He pronounced it chay-tah and I didn't think that was an Arapaho word. Not knowing Crow was turning into a problem.

"Ride," Cheéte said. "Now."

I tucked Brody's book into one of Maria's discarded bags and briefly wondered where my haversack had gotten to. Hopefully McNab had it, along with our horses. I looked around to see if there was anything I missed. If there was, I couldn't see it. Then I slowly ambled over to Daxpitchée. If they were going to make me ride with someone else, I wasn't gonna be in a hurry.

But when I got close to the burly Crow's horse, he pointed at my rifle and gestured for me to give it to him.

"No." I unslung it from my back and held it tight.

Cheéte appeared at my side. "Give rifle. Give rifle or walk."

My gut tightened and I felt the anger build. My pulse raced and I started to see red. I looked around. I could probably kill one or two of them before they could react. I'd need to grab a horse or find some cover before the others shot me. That would be mighty tough—

"They giving 'em back when we get to the town?" Zeke asked. His tone was casual, as if his question was just a curiosity.

I blinked. I'd seen Zeke with a head of fury and now he seemed as calm as could be. I didn't believe for a moment we'd get our guns back, but I figured I had better make it clear what I wanted. They'd already decided not to kill us, which meant that sooner or later they'd either have to do so or let us go.

I turned to Cheéte. "You give guns back at town. Give back."

He scowled, but then nodded.

I didn't like it, but I didn't see what choice we had. We were prisoners now. The Crow didn't want to kill us and bring the Army of the West down on them. With the rest of my team, not to mention Lieutenant Caldwell's squad riding with the Sioux, they'd have a hard time doing it quietly.

With a heavy sigh, I handed my rifle over, and then my Colt. I had a knife on my belt but they either didn't see it or ignored it. My saber had been with my horse but Zeke still had his and they let him keep it.

Apparently they weren't worried about him cutting them down with his sword. I stifled a grin. I'd seen Zeke mow through trolls like they were grass.

The Crow were making a mistake.

We rode north along the stream for about an hour and then camped for the night. The Crow made sure Zeke and I were in the very middle, with guards on all sides. But they fed us and let us sleep by the fire, which showed how much they had faith in their numbers. As long as they were watchful, we weren't going anywhere. And they were watchful.

The next day, we continued north until we found the little river and then turned west. The day was fair with blue skies, and I tried to scan the horizon, but never saw anyone but the Crow. We didn't move as fast as I expected, but then I realized they were sending scouting parties out in every direction. We went slow so they could find us easily when they returned.

That gave me a lot of hope. They couldn't've found Jeremiah or the others, or we'd be giving chase. Of course, that begged the question: just where were the others?

I couldn't help wondering whether they'd come for us or not. If McNab was in charge, he'd be looking for me. That was his orders. But with his injury, Jeremiah might be the one in command. Or, being old friends, they'd do it together. Jeremiah might just head to the town.

Captain Mercer, my last commanding officer—heck, my current one by all rights, not that it mattered—had believed that the mission mattered most, to the point where men under him regularly died. He fulfilled his missions but left a trail of blood. I knew he'd sacrifice himself if it was needed.

Just like Cassidy had done.

That tugged at my gut, but it was an old tug. More reflex than anything these days.

So part of me hoped that Jeremiah, McNab, and the team were lurking around somewhere, out of sight, just waiting to ride to my and Zeke's rescue. But another part of me was hoping they'd continued on instead.

As a result, each time the Crow scouts came back alone, my heart quickened. By evening, they still hadn't found a thing, which suited me just fine. Cheéte ordered us to camp along the river. Zeke and I were given some food and two blankets near the fire. Our guards, Daxpitchée and Bishée, stretched out nearby on their own bedrolls. Night fell fast and left me wondering about what I could possibly do the next day.

Somewhere in my wondering, I drifted into a dreamless sleep.

I jerked awake to the sound of gunshots. Several, to the west. The Crow were already shouting and running. Daxpitchée was on his feet, yelling and waving his rifle. I quickly closed my eyes and feigned sleep when he looked my way. Through my eyelashes, I watched him snort and then turn and rush off in the direction of the shooting.

Leaving, tucked into his blankets, my rifle and revolver behind.

TWELVE

IN THE LOW light of the fire, I could see the butt of my rifle not more than a dozen feet away. I scrambled up and looked at Zeke. He was pulling himself to his feet, much more slowly than me. I didn't wait but raced toward my gun.

Someone nearby shouted, harsh and loud. I turned to see Cheéte leveling a rifle at me from five yards away.

So much for escape.

I slowed and raised my hands. He gestured with the barrel of the rifle toward my blankets. With a sigh, I returned to them and sat down.

Cheéte stepped back and lowered his rifle. He yelled something over his shoulder and Daxpitchée and Bishée came running back. They stood a few feet back and glared at us. Cheéte disappeared into the dark.

I huffed in frustration. We hadn't even made it a few feet.

Zeke gave me a sympathetic smile. He shifted around until he was cross-legged with his blanket over his lap. Then he folded his hands in his lap. It struck me as odd, which had the surprising effect of helping me calm down.

"You seem awful relaxed," I said.

He shrugged. "Not much to do."

"You don't wanna escape."

"Sure. But they'd just track us down. They always do."

There was something in his tone that made me think he wasn't talking about the Crow. I'd known Zeke almost a year now and I knew he'd been a slave as a boy, before the War Between the States. I didn't know if he'd ever tried to escape. He was an easygoing man. Well, most of the time.

"But shouldn't we try?" I asked.

"Why? They're taking us where we wanna go."

I blinked at that. He had a point, though I hated it. I wanted to be on my own. I wanted to be with McNab and Maria and Jeremiah. Yeah, the Crow hadn't treated us badly. However, we were still prisoners.

But we weren't abandoned, I realized. If there were gunshots, that meant Jeremiah and McNab or the Sioux were attacking. I guessed Jeremiah and McNab, since the Sioux should've been long gone. So the gunshots meant that Jeremiah and McNab knew where we were. They might not have been able to rescue us this time, but I was sure they'd keep trying. So maybe the best thing to do was sit tight and wait.

I hated sitting tight. My stomach did acrobatics that threatened to make me sick.

But still, I didn't have much choice. I decided to follow Zeke's lead and sat cross-legged with a blanket over my lap. Except my mind kept racing, so all that did was make me as twitchy as a squirrel.

Zeke noticed and grinned. I glared at him, but it didn't wipe the smile off his face. Instead, we sat in the flickering firelight and waited for the commotion to end.

We waited what seemed like forever and was as least long enough to make my legs and arms all stiff. I itched to get up and try to see what was going on, but I held back. The Crow had added some sticks to the fire, which popped and crackled, but not enough to drown out the sounds of distant shouting. Finally Cheéte stormed up. His rifle was slung over his shoulder and he stomped right up in front of me. Unsteadily, I climbed to my feet.

"You no leave!" he snarled. "No leave!"

I just stared at him.

"No leave!" he repeated. He spat on the ground at my feet and then strode off.

"What was that?" Zeke asked.

"I think… our guys got away."

"Thank the Lord."

Our team didn't try again the next day. The Crow sent out more scouting patrols, but in fewer directions. Mostly west and south. Once, Cheéte dispatched a large group—maybe half the warriors in camp. They rode hard, but came back several hours later alone.

We camped again by the small river. Some of the Crow had been hunting and brought deer meat for us to eat. Zeke sat on a small rock while the Crow started a fire in a small ring of rocks nearby. It was still light enough to see, so he got out his Bible.

I plopped onto the grass next to him. I was tired from the ride, and it was good to just sit. I watched as he thumbed through the pages until he settled on a section and tapped the page twice.

"What're you reading?" I asked.

"Daniel." He didn't look up. "He trusted God in the lion's den."

I snorted. This wasn't a lion's den, and I still wasn't sure if I believed in God or not. I'd seen too much evil to believe He was there, taking care of us. On the other hand, if He *wasn't* watching out for me, I'd been amazingly lucky the past few years.

I toyed with asking Zeke to read out loud to me, but then decided I didn't want the sermon that'd come with it. I'd seen him explain the Bible to other soldiers before, most of whom just humored him. I wasn't in the mood for that.

But, I realized, I could still read. I had Brody's copy of the book about me.

My gut clenched. I'd been honest when I'd told Jeremiah I didn't want to read it. I knew it'd bring up some memories I wanted to forget. Worse, I knew he'd exaggerated things to make me more heroic than I was.

But maybe not as bad as I'd feared. Brody's questions had been good. That wouldn't've been true if Jeremiah had lied too much.

I decided I could read it slowly. After all, I already knew how it ended. There was no reason to get caught up in it like I'd done with all the dime novels of my youth.

<hr>

We spent several days moving west, following the same general pattern. We followed the little river while Crow scouts rode both ahead and south looking for our team. They never found them. We started seeing rock mesas in the distance to the north of us but the scouts never headed that direction. They must've figured they weren't good hiding places for one reason or another.

Eventually, the river turned south. There was a wide ford there, and we crossed it and started heading northwest. We'd apparently skirted the southern edge of the mesas we'd seen. Another two days' riding brought us close enough to see tree-covered hills in the distance ahead of us.

One evening we stopped early, to my surprise. Cheéte found us and looked us over. Then he pointed at the lieutenant's insignia on my uniform's outer frock coat.

"Give," he said.

"What?" I gasped in surprise.

"Give," he repeated. "I return."

I blinked, but decided I had nothing to lose. It was easier to take the entire uniform frock coat off than to remove the insignia, so I did, leaving me in just my shirt.

He took it and walked off. Two hours later he returned with it, but ignored my question about why he needed it. Zeke just shrugged as well, and I made a note to find out later.

The next day we continued our ride northwest. The distant hills were speckled green with all the spring growth. I myself was mighty relieved to see them. After all the flat, flat, flat, the hills reminded me of the mountains of home. Just enough to make me a tad homesick. Maybe if I earned my own troubleshooter squad, I could visit Colorado more often. I was certainly ready to see some of those faces again.

We moved slower once we reached the hills themselves. We'd long since abandoned any trails and more than once stopped while the scouts worked out the best way ahead. The hills were actually more like small mountains and steep in spots, but not so bad that we couldn't ride through if we picked our path.

Meanwhile, I kept an eye out for Jeremiah or McNab. If there was ever a place for a rescue raid, these hills were it.

So we wound our way through the scattered trees and up the slopes. We eventually camped in a small valley that wasn't much more than a crease between two hills. That night, our regular guards were joined by four more. They all watched us warily and wouldn't speak to us. I stayed awake for a while in case of another raid, but heard nothing.

Eventually, I slept.

Cheéte shook me awake just as the sky was beginning to turn from black to grey. I rubbed my eyes while he continued to shake my shoulder. I was cold and stiff, but he didn't seem to care. Once my eyes opened, he stood up and put his fists on his hips.

"Go," he said. "Go now."

"What hurry?" I said in Arapaho. "You still no tell me why you take us to town."

"Go now!" He gestured for me to stand.

I clambered to my feet and saw Zeke stirring as well. Our guards were already up and had their rifles in their hands.

Then I heard the shooting. Several shots from the northwest. Followed by several more. Then loud yells. Then more shots.

Cheéte said something to Daxpitchée and Bishée. They glared at me and Zeke and lifted their rifles, though didn't point them at us. Then Cheéte waved at the other two guards and all three ran in the direction of the shooting.

The sleep drained from my body and I felt my muscles coil. I was tense, tight. Ready to spring. Zeke shifted his stance. He stood shoulders wide and on the balls of his feet.

The Crow regarded us and then both took a few steps back, to a distance where it'd be hard to rush them before they leveled their guns.

Hard, but not impossible.

Still, we waited. The yells and the gunfire continued, getting louder and closer. We could see Indians running through the sparse trees, but in the low morning light it was all blur and shadow and movement.

Then a bullet crashed into a nearby pine, shaking the branch it hit. Daxpitchée's head turned.

I took two running steps and launched myself at him. He turned, but I hit him waist high. We tumbled to the ground.

Once there, we started to roll. He punched me in the side and pain shot through my ribs. I jumped back before he could grapple with me. Given how much bigger he was, if he got on top of me, I'd be through. But as I retreated, he kicked out and caught my leg. I fell to my back.

I could hear Zeke wrestling with Bishée nearby, but couldn't spare them a glance. Daxpitchée bounced to his feet while I was still scrambling away on the ground. I grabbed some dirt and threw it at his eyes. He turned his head just before it hit, but that gave me a chance to climb to my feet.

Daxpitchée stalked forward.

But then there was a loud crack, followed by a thud. Both Daxpitchée and I looked to the side. Bishée was down with Zeke standing over him. The big Negro held Bishée's rifle by the barrel like a club.

Daxpitchée hesitated just a step, which gave me time to dive for his bedroll, where he'd stashed my own guns. He smashed into my side just before I reached them and was on top of me, punching and grabbing. He cocked his fist back to drive it into my face—

A gunshot! Right beside us!

"Stop!" Zeke yelled.

Daxpitchée looked his way and froze. Zeke had the rifle leveled at him.

"Off!" Zeke yelled again. He gestured with the rifle to show what he meant.

Daxpitchée rose off of me. I scrambled to the side fast. There were still shouts and gunshots all around us. I grabbed my revolver and shoved it in my waistband and then pulled my rifle from Daxpitchée's blankets. Still on his knees, he just glared at me, when he wasn't glaring at Zeke.

"Let's go!" I gestured for Zeke to follow and took off through the woods, sideways to the sounds of the battle.

Zeke was fast behind me. We just ran and ran and didn't look back, weaving as we did. I didn't know how long it would take Daxpitchée to give chase, and I feared he'd try to shoot us, but no bullets came. We just fled until Zeke started to falter. He was panting and sweating and finally slowed. We stopped so we could catch our breath. Only then did I look back.

I couldn't see any pursuers.

But that meant I couldn't see any friends, either.

It didn't take long before the way ahead of us turned into a steep slope. Judging from the morning shadows, I figured we were headed west, which meant the attack had come from the north. From the continued gunfire, the fight was more than a raid, which got me wondering. Was it just our team, or had the Sioux joined in? Or the dwarves?

I wanted the high ground. So Zeke and I strode forward, up the mountain, listening and watching. The cries and gunfire were more distant and scattered, but all off to our right. The hill ahead of us grew steeper, but we kept a steady pace. We still didn't see anything and the sounds of battle continued to fade. I kept having to wet my dry mouth, and sweat dripped from Zeke's brow, but we kept on.

Finally, we reached the ridge, where the trees were thinner. Zeke was almost staggering and my legs burned. We'd climbed harder and faster than I'd done before, and the sounds of battle faded. We found a clear spot where we could look around, and my eyes went wide.

To the north, where our ridge met another, the land had been cleared of trees and brush. Toward the top of the other ridge, stone walls rose. A tower with actual battlements broke the sky above them.

We'd found the town.

THIRTEEN

"OH, DEAR LORD," Zeke said beside me. "What have we here?"

It was a good question. At this distance, the grey stone walls looked like they'd been carved from the hillside. I couldn't quite tell their height, but they appeared more human-sized than giant-sized. I looked at their shadows, which were about as long as those of the few remaining trees. So the walls weren't too tall. I let out a breath of relief.

The tower's sides were dotted with what looked like arrow slits instead of windows. On top, I thought I saw sentries behind the battlements but couldn't be sure. The morning sun was still cresting the ridge, leaving most of the town in shadow.

I looked at Zeke. "Let's go along the ridge."

"Think we'll find the others?" He slung his rifle over his shoulder and put his hand on his saber, though his revolver was gone.

"I hope so." I was actually pretty confident we would. I was more concerned that they were all right. That fight had lasted longer than I'd thought possible. They'd come to help us, but now they might need our help.

We worked our way along the top of the ridge, keeping an eye on both sides for trouble. Nothing changed near the town, and we didn't see anyone down among the trees on the other side. The gunfire had died out and we couldn't hear any shouting either.

We walked for maybe twenty minutes as the sun slowly rose higher. I felt thirsty, but could only lick my lips. All of our stuff, including Brody's book, was still back in the Crow camp. For a moment I regretted leaving it, but I missed my canteen more. I settled for wiping my brow with the handkerchief I still had in my pocket.

We paused when we reached a spot that had a good view of the town to the left. By now we were close enough to clearly see figures on the top of the tower and the top of the wall. We could also see a gate. Wooden doors with bands of metal sat closed in front of what looked like a road. I couldn't make out much of that road given the slope of the land, but nothing moved on it.

Gunshots rang out from our right, followed by yells. The slope was gentler here and the trees sparser. After a few more gunshots, we spotted horsemen riding our way hard through the woods.

In blue uniforms!

My heart raced. I unshouldered my rifle and Zeke quickly did the same. Then, pulses pounding, we waited.

The first riders burst out of the trees—Brody, McNab, and then Maria in her blue dress. Brody spotted us and cried out. They turned their horses toward us. Bent low, they rode hard.

A moment later, Jeremiah and Anoki emerged from the trees. They wheeled as they did and fired revolvers back into the woods. Gunshots answered, but Jeremiah and Anoki just turned and spurred their horses toward us.

"Cover 'em," I told Zeke. We both raised our rifles.

Two Indians thundered out of the trees. They rode hard, their horses at full gallop. I held my fire—I couldn't tell if they were Sioux or Crow.

Then one of them rose up and fired his rifle at Jeremiah. The Indian had to be Crow.

I dropped my sights to his chest. But I couldn't do it. Not to another human. I switched my target to the horse and shot it instead. It tumbled, throwing the Indian.

More gunshots, from our side. The other Crow turned to ride back toward his comrade.

But gunfire also came from the the tree line. Anoki's horse suddenly screamed and collapsed, but Anoki was able to jump free.

As he scrambled toward us, I watched the trees. The gunfire slowed, probably because they didn't want to hit their own man, who was now up and running for cover. No one else emerged. I decided to encourage that with a couple of shots into the most likely shooting blinds. No one screamed, but no one shot back.

Jeremiah slowed and pulled Anoki up on the horse beside him. Meanwhile, the others had reached Zeke and me. Brody immediately started firing his Colt back at the trees. From horseback, his shots went wild, but maybe enough gunfire would discourage pursuit. I continued my own shooting until my magazine ran dry.

McNab noticed and rode next to me. I realized his arm was still in a sling.

"Climb on!" he called. I scrambled up and Zeke climbed up behind Brody. When Jeremiah and Anoki joined us, we galloped down the ridge to the west, away from the Crow.

And toward the town.

We rode hard. I clung tight to McNab's waist as the horse dashed down slopes so steep I thought we'd fall. When the slope leveled out, he slowed and turned. No one was following us over the ridge.

"Think we got away?" I panted. I glanced around. The rest of the team had stopped as well.

"Maybe." McNab huffed, catching his breath. "If they're chasing the Sioux instead."

"The Sioux?"

"Yeah. We found 'em and they said we should attack."

I snorted. "I'll bet."

"It worked," he said. "The Sioux drew the Crow out of their camp." He gestured at the others, "We rode in easy. But you were gone."

"So you tracked us."

"Nah. Just guessed where you were going." He pointed at the town. "Is that it?"

"Has to be."

Brody and Jeremiah were openly staring at the town. Anoki kept looking back at the top of the ridge.

"So now what?" McNab asked.

"They have to have seen us," I said. "So I think we just go up to the gate. We run if they attack us." I waved the others over, and when they were close, I told them the same thing.

"I don't like it," Jeremiah said. "Do remember, Otaktay said the dwarves shot at them."

"But we're not the Sioux." I grimaced as I thought. "What about a flag of truce?"

"You think they'll know what that means?" McNab looked at Jeremiah, who just shrugged.

"We could use my shirt," Brody volunteered. "Well, my spare one. It's white."

"That might work," Jeremiah said. "We could hang it on a rifle like we did in Harrisburg."

I vaguely remembered the passage from *The Road to Harrisburg* that Jeremiah referred to. I snorted softly. I'd read that book until it'd been falling apart. I'd been able to recall not only scenes, but exact lines. But that'd been over a year ago. How…

"Fine," McNab said. "We can run if they shoot." He gave me an expectant look.

Yeah. I needed to give an order. "Let's do it."

It didn't take long to create the makeshift flag. While Brody was digging through his saddlebags, I dismounted from McNab's horse and stretched my legs and borrowed his canteen. My thirst satisfied, I looked at our group.

We had seven people and four horses. I didn't like doubling up, but I didn't like the idea of walking, either. If we needed to run, we'd need to run fast. In addition to the dwarves, assuming that's who lived in the town, the Crow could come over the ridge at any time. I didn't want to leave anyone behind, especially not me. I'd spent plenty enough time with the Crow as it was.

I sensed McNab and Jeremiah felt the same. McNab kept looking nervously at the ridge. We didn't know why the Crow had abandoned pursuit. Maybe the Sioux had been close.

So we mounted back up—me with McNab, Anoki with Jeremiah, and Zeke with Brody, while Maria got a horse to herself. That was probably for the best. Her saddlebags bulged and I could see a small bottle peeking out of the top of one. We'd be in trouble if a second rider broke any of those.

Then we rode slowly toward the town gate.

The sun had risen high enough to make it easier to see details. The walls weren't a single sheet of stone like I'd first thought, but several large blocks, some the size of a horse, cunningly fitted together. The cracks between them ran like lines of a spider's web and I was sure they were too small to use as footholds. The wooden door, too, looked smooth, though it was more than one board.

There were definitely soldiers on the wall and tower as well. They wore metal helmets that glinted in the sun, and a couple soldiers were clearly bearded. More ominously, every single one had a bow in their hands. They weren't raised or pointed at us, but that just meant it'd take another second or two to shoot us.

Zeke and Brody rode in front, with Brody holding our makeshift flag high. There wasn't enough breeze for it to do more than flop against the rifle. I couldn't help wondering if the dwarves would know what it meant.

We paused about a hundred yards from the gate—far enough to make their bow shots difficult, if they decided to fire on us. Then we waited.

And we waited.

Sweat started to bead on my brow. Seated behind McNab, I had to lean to the side to get a good look at the town. It got awkward fast. Even so, the sentries seemed to be doing nothing.

"Crow!" Jeremiah yelled.

I whipped my head around to look over my shoulder as McNab also turned the horse.

About a dozen Crow warriors rode fast down the ridge behind us. No war cries or shouts—they were bent low and riding hard. Their horses' hooves pounded the ground.

Then yells came from up the road to the east. The Sioux, with Otaktay in the lead, charged down. Otaktay waved his rifle.

I quickly glanced around. The dwarves had done a thorough job of clearing away all the brush. We were in an open grassy plain with a dirt road and absolutely no cover. With the gate closed, we were surrounded on three sides. The only way we could flee was—

I swore. Another dozen Indians rode hard at us from the west, up the road toward us. They looked like Crow, but it was hard to tell. What wasn't hard to tell is that we were surrounded.

Shots echoed off the hills. The Crow coming down the ridge and the Sioux had gotten close enough that some of their warriors had stopped riding and started shooting. McNab's horse skittered with the blasts. We started circling, trying to look in all directions at once. The others in our little group did the same.

With a loud creak, the town gate opened.

A half dozen short men on ponies stood in the center. As soon as the doors were wide enough, they trotted forward. All six raised bows with arrows nocked.

I started swearing. We were surrounded.

The only thing that made sense was to join up with the Sioux. Fast. As fast as we could. But the Crow from the ridge had already veered off toward them. Gunfire was almost constant now, and I saw a Sioux warrior get hit and fall off his horse.

If we ran toward that fight, we'd be lucky if none of us shared that fate.

"What do we do?" McNab yelled. He didn't look back but kept his eyes on the dwarves, who were now the closest.

"Let's meet them," I said quickly. Then louder, to the rest of the team. "Follow us!"

We hurriedly closed the distance with the dwarves. I intentionally didn't draw a gun, and to my relief, none of my team did either. Two of the dwarves pointed their arrows at us, but none let fly.

But I felt silly, behind McNab, leaning out to see. Finally it got the best of me and I tapped McNab on his non-injured shoulder.

"Stop." I slid to the ground before he could reply. I stepped away from the horse and found myself only a dozen feet from the lead dwarf. If you could call being a half length ahead "lead."

On the pony, he was taller than me. I looked up to see a deep frown glaring back at me. He wore armor made of interlocking metal rings over a leather shirt and an iron helmet. His black beard hung halfway down to his waist. A green ribbon wound around one upper arm, but otherwise his clothes were plain.

I hoped he spoke English.

"We come in peace," I said. "We seek parley."

He blinked, but otherwise his expression didn't change.

"No fight," I said. I pointed at him and then swept my arm to encompass my team. I wanted to make it clear our weapons weren't pointed at the dwarves. "No fight." I spoke loud to overcome the distant yells and gunfire.

His brow furrowed, and I silently cursed the language barrier.

Another gunshot rang out—this one close and sharp.

The dwarf's eyes went wide, and he tumbled from his pony.

FOURTEEN

I WHIRLED to find the shooter just as chaos erupted around me. Horses spun and bucked. Rifles and bows went off. The lead dwarf's pony ran. I scrambled to the side to avoid McNab's bucking horse and then raced toward the downed dwarf. One of his companions had also dismounted.

A pony went down screaming. Its rider rolled free just in time but lay stunned. I heard Jeremiah over the screams of injured horses. The gunfire was now closer and louder.

I kept my eyes on the dwarf. He sprawled face down in the grass. Blood already stained his back above his hip where the bullet had exited. Maybe if I helped him the dwarves would be grateful! I reached him just at the same time the other dwarf, a burly one with a short beard, did. He began by rolling the leader dwarf over.

Leader Dwarf shuddered and gasped. Blood soaked his stomach and he coughed hard. Mostly phlegm, thank God. I knelt next to him and yanked a handkerchief out of my pocket. I pressed down on the wound in his gut and ignored the stickiness of the blood on my hand. It didn't look good, but he wasn't dead yet. He put his hand over mine, and then pressed the cloth down himself.

I leaned back and looked around. The gunfire was louder now, and horses raced this way and that. I barely got a glimpse of Jeremiah—still mounted and firing his rifle as fast as he could back in the direction of the Crow. But then Short Beard said something and I turned back to him.

Short Beard reached under Leader Dwarf's shoulders and tugged him up. He gestured toward Leader Dwarf's feet. Between us, we managed to lift the wounded dwarf. Then Short Beard nodded his head toward the town. We started running as best we could. I stumbled twice, but we didn't drop Leader Dwarf. He was surprisingly heavy. It took all I had to keep ahold of him.

A horse raced by us before we got to the gate, but only close enough to make me flinch.

We ran. We stumbled and we tripped but didn't fall. We kept running.

Suddenly, I was surrounded by dwarves. They pulled Leader Dwarf out of my hands. One dwarf shoved me toward the town gate, and I realized we were only a few yards from it. I ran through it, but I ran so hard, I tripped just inside. I tumbled to the ground and rolled. I sat up and looked back at the battle.

Horses charged back and forth across the plain. Several were down, some dead, some screaming from wounds. I saw Brody and Zeke on their feet backpedaling toward me. Brody had his rifle on his shoulder and fired occasionally. Zeke stood by Brody, saber drawn, protecting him.

I couldn't see the others. The Crow seemed to be retreating, but the dwarves were firing arrows in the direction the Sioux had come. Or at least the dwarves that were still mounted. I spotted one face down in the dirt.

"Are you hurt?"

I startled at the voice in my ear and sighed with relief when I realized it was Maria. "The others?"

She pointed to where McNab sat on the ground holding his left arm. His face was pale with pain.

"His wound opened up when he fell off his horse," Maria explained, "but he should survive."

"Jeremiah? Anoki? Any of the Sioux?"

She shrugged.

"Go see if the dwarves need help."

She nodded and hurried over to the cluster of nearby dwarves surrounding a prone body. I slowly clambered to my feet and realized I'd lost my rifle somewhere along the way. Fortunately, my revolver was still at my waist. I drew it and looked out at the battle. The fighting had moved away from the town. Brody and Zeke were halfway back to the gate while two dwarves had rushed forward to one of the bodies that lay on the road. Brody appeared to be covering them.

There didn't appear to be anybody I needed to shoot. I wanted to rush out to help Zeke and Brody. Then I realized it was silly. There were plenty of sentries covering their retreat. They didn't need one more doing that. Zeke and Brody would be fine.

McNab, on the other hand…

He sat cross-legged off to one side, inside the town about ten feet from the open gate. As I approached, I realized he was pressing a large, dirty white cloth to his shoulder. It'd been loosely and hastily tied, but there didn't seem to be much blood. Mostly, he looked like he was about to faint.

I knelt next to him. "Lie down." When he looked confused, I added. "You don't want battle shock."

"Ah. Yeah."

I helped ease him to the ground. I checked the back of his shoulder first. There was barely any blood seeping through his jacket. Hopefully, the wound hadn't opened that much.

"What happened?" I asked.

"Horse got shot. Glad you were already off."

"Glad they didn't shoot you."

"They already did." His smile drove some of the pale out of his face. But that could've just been him lying down.

"You think it was the Crow that shot you?" I hadn't seen who'd been aiming at us in all the chaos.

"Don't know. They were shooting at us."

"The Sioux, too, I think." I looked out the gate. Brody and Zeke had just backed in, along with the last of the dwarves. With a loud creak, the gates started to close. "Or at least they were shooting at the dwarves."

"You think so?" McNab asked.

"Dunno for sure," I said. "I guess I better find out."

I walked over to Brody and Zeke to check on them. Both were tired but unhurt. Brody looked very uncomfortable and almost ill, but promised he was fine. I told them to go sit with McNab and make sure he didn't go into battle shock.

Then I turned to face the dwarves.

I thought they'd been ignoring us, but two holding bows stood at the ready watching us while the others bustled about. I took a moment to size them up. Both were stocky and about a foot shorter than me. They had beards down their chests and dark skin. The one on the left kept shifting his weight from side to side.

I realized I was still holding my Colt. I holstered it and held my hands out to show they were empty. Then I took a few steps closer until I had the two dwarves' attention.

"English?" I asked. "Do you speak English?"

They glared at me but didn't respond.

"English?" My gut started to knot in frustration. I couldn't help raising my voice. "English?"

One of them turned and yelled something to the dwarves tending one of their wounded. He looked over, and then trotted off deeper into the town.

I put my hands on my hips and surveyed the area. We were in what looked like a courtyard behind the gate. Two narrow dirt streets ran off between low stone-walled buildings. Another ran along the wall itself. The buildings themselves were the same fitted stone as the wall, though with rougher surfaces and wider cracks. They, at least, had windows, with what looked like real glass.

The two dwarven soldiers continued to stare at me. They appeared more bored than tense. Their bows pointed at the ground, though I suspected they could raise them faster than I could draw my Colt. Not that I would. With the gate closed, we were basically trapped inside and at their mercy. Which I hoped was good.

I couldn't hear gunfire anymore. I checked the sentries on the wall.

They'd lowered their bows, though they continued to watch the field. The busyness in the courtyard had calmed, too. The last wounded dwarf was carried off just as three new dwarves came marching in. The new lead dwarf, helmetless and with his black hair in long braids, took a quick look around before marching directly over to me. The other two trailed a half step behind.

"English?" I asked.

"You are in charge?" His accent was harsh and unfamiliar, but understandable.

"I am." I straightened up a bit, but didn't salute. "Lieutenant McCarty, Army of the West."

"Your men?" He nodded toward McNab and the others.

"And Maria." I looked around and didn't see her. I hoped she was okay.

"You with Sioux or Crow?"

I blinked. "Neither. The Sioux told us about you, but we're here for ourselves."

"What do you want?"

"To learn about you. To find out if you help the Jotun."

"Jotun!" He spat. Then he glared at me. "You come." He gestured with his hand toward the street he'd arrived down.

"All of us?" I nodded toward my team.

"All. Now."

"Do you have a name?" I didn't want to have to make one up for him if I could avoid it.

He paused for a moment and looked at me. "Vestri."

"Okay, Vestri," I said, "let me get my men." I headed over to them, but he and his two fellows were only a step behind. I still didn't see Maria anywhere, but I couldn't afford much time to look. It only took a dozen strides before I was next to McNab.

He looked better, a lot better. The pale had faded from his face though he was still clearly in pain. Brody knelt next to him, with a comforting hand on McNab's good shoulder. Brody looked up at me, his eyes full of worry, but the cause wasn't exactly clear.

"Can you stand?" I asked McNab.

"Yeah." He sat up and extended a hand to Zeke, who pulled him the rest of the way up. He trembled a little, though. It didn't look like battle shock, but it didn't look good. Either he'd lost more blood than I thought or something else was wrong.

I turned to Vestri. "Let's go."

The dwarves turned and marched us down the street that was headed toward the center of town. They set a quick pace, which forced me to quick-step to keep up. McNab managed it, too, but he was clearly in pain. I was breathing too hard to talk, but I could look around.

Not that there was much to see. Stone and dirt. Stone walls, much like I'd seen in the courtyard, with pinewood doors and the occasional glass window. Few buildings had a second story and none had trees or plants growing around them. Most of the stone was plain grey or some splotched variation, but I did spot intricate carvings on some of the buildings. Most looked like some form of writing but a few were clearly small reliefs of animals, mostly badgers and raccoons.

We passed a few side streets before the main street opened up into a square of some sort. This one had wooden roofed stalls lining the edges, but all were deserted at the moment. We marched right past them to a two-story building with steps leading up to a double door. That door stood open with dwarves on either side in the same armor of linked metal rings, but with axes instead of a bow.

Vestri marched us right inside.

My eyes didn't immediately adjust to the darkness within the building. We walked through some sort of outer hall and then into a larger room which had a high ceiling and plenty of torches.

I'd half expected a throne room, with some sort of dwarf king. Instead, a large wooden table covered with both papers and small clay figures stretched from nearly one side to the other. Several dwarves milled around it. We stopped a dozen feet away just as the room fell silent.

One of the dwarves stepped out of a small cluster of them near the table's end. His grey hair was in long braids, including his beard. A deep scar creased his forehead and his eyes were narrowed. He walked forward with a casual, deliberate air. One I'd seen only from Hickok or Cassidy.

This was clearly the dwarf in charge.

Vestri bowed and said something in what I presumed was Dwarvish. The leader dwarf replied in the same tongue.

Vestri turned to me. "Alviss welcomes you to New Svartalfheim. We have much to discuss."

FIFTEEN

THE ROOM GREW STILL. I stared at Alviss and tried to read his emotions. It wasn't easy. His skin was almost as dark as Zeke's, though much more rugged and worn. His eyes, though, pierced me as if he was seeing more of me than I was of him.

"What do we need to discuss?" I finally managed to say.

"This land," Vestri answered. "We claim it as ours. Not the Sioux's. Not the Crow's."

I had to admit, I wasn't surprised by his words. They wouldn't have built a town, out of stone no less, if they weren't planning on staying. The town walls and bowmen also made their intentions clear.

I figured I needed to know more. "How much are you claiming? All the Black Hills?"

Vestri repeated my question to Alviss, who replied in words I couldn't understand. Then Vestri turned back to me.

"All the land within a day's ride from here and all the gold under the ground."

That was why they were here, I realized. Jeremiah had told me about how the dwarves in the Edda loved gold. Except we Americans had promised this area to the Sioux and I didn't know if Vestri and

Alviss knew that. I also doubted General Sanborn would be willing to send enough of the army to get rid of the dwarves.

"We claim this land as ours," Vestri continued. "You agree. You get Sioux, Crow to agree."

"That may not be easy." In fact, I had no idea how to do it.

"They fear Army of the West. You get them to agree." Vestri crossed his arms and gave me an expectant look.

I didn't know what to say. I didn't know if the Sioux and Crow really feared us or not, but I was happy to play along with that. But Vestri was clearly waiting for me to speak. He gestured for me to go on.

I paused. His gesture was exactly like that the merchant Boggs used back in Golden City. In fact, he looked a lot like Boggs, though Boggs was clean-shaven. Both were short, mostly muscles, and humorless. I'd done a lot of business with Boggs, including buying my first Winchester rifle from him. He was always dead serious when it came time to negotiate.

Which got me thinking—what had I learned about negotiating from Boggs?

Never agree to anything immediately. Make sure you understand what they're offering. Think of all the ways it can go wrong or you can get cheated. Not that Boggs himself ever cheated, but he was almost impossible to cheat. The last man who had thought he could had ended up with a broken arm and been run out of town.

I didn't think I could do much if the dwarves decided to cheat us, but I could do the rest.

"What're you offering?" I asked. "Why should the United States of the West acknowledge your claim?"

Vestri actually smirked. "Trade."

He said something in Dwarvish to a cluster of younger dwarves at the table. One hurried off toward a hallway on the far side of the table. Then Vestri relaxed.

Other dwarves produced a handful of pinewood chairs that they placed in a small semi-circle facing the open area of the room. They gestured for us to sit. McNab's paleness had returned. He looked at me questioningly, and when I nodded, sank into the nearest chair. Brody joined him, though Zeke circled around behind them and remained standing.

I decided to stand. Alviss and Vestri were, so I would, too.

Several minutes later, a dwarf hustled back into the room. He carried what looked like an Army of the West saber, except straighter and far smoother and shinier than I thought possible. Its blade gleamed in the low light.

Vestri took it and the other dwarf nodded and backed away. Then Vestri turned to me. His eyes darted to my waist, but my own saber had been strapped to my horse and I had no idea where it was. Then he looked me in the face.

"This blade strong." He raised the saber up. "Stronger than yours. Show you." He paused and curled his lips as he thought. "Practice… practice fight."

"You want to spar?" I said.

"Yes. Spar. Spar is the word. We spar."

I shook my head. "Not me. Zeke, you willing?"

"Sure," he said with a nod. He stepped around the chairs and drew his own saber.

Vestri stepped back and the other dwarves spread out until they'd formed a loose circle around Vestri and Zeke. The two combatants stood several feet apart with their blades in guard position. Zeke towered over the dwarf, a mountain facing a boy.

"You attack," Vestri told Zeke. He gestured with the tip of his blade.

"You sure?" Zeke said. "These are sharp. Don't wanna hurt you."

"You attack," Vestri repeated.

Zeke nodded and stepped forward. He swung hard and fast, but clearly short. His blade wouldn't even whisk past Vestri's head.

But Vestri countered. His own sword shot up, blocking Zeke's—

—and cut right through it. The top half of Zeke's saber went flying and clanged to the floor several feet away.

I stared at Vestri. We all did. Even Zeke lowered what was left of his saber with a look of disbelief.

Vestri smirked. "We offer trade. For gold, you get these. They kill Jotun."

I nodded. It seemed we had much to talk about indeed. "Give me and my men some privacy to confer."

The dwarves showed us to a small room with two wooden benches and a small table with a red cloth covering it. I blinked in surprise—it was the first bright color I'd seen in the town. A small window let in air and light, and the walls were ornately carved. I didn't inspect the carvings closely, but they seemed to be figures of dwarves fighting dragons and other monsters.

McNab and Zeke sagged onto one of the benches while Brody spoke briefly with Vestri. Then Brody told me that he'd be back after a quick visit to an "indoor outhouse." I briefly wondered what that meant, but he and Vestri departed before I could come up with the words.

A few minutes later Vestri returned with a ceramic pitcher of water and several brown ceramic mugs. The dwarf also handed McNab a small glass flask and told him to drink it. McNab took a sniff of it, then did so.

I motioned to Vestri as he turned to leave again. "Our nurse, Maria. She was helping some of your men. Could you bring her? And leave the saber? We'd like to look at it more closely."

He scowled, but then nodded. He drew the saber from his belt and passed it to me. Then he was gone.

I joined the others at the table. It felt good to sink onto the bench. My legs were more sore than I'd thought. McNab looked better. Still in pain, but less likely to pass out. Zeke just stared at the saber.

I passed it to him. "See how this feels while we wait for Brody and Maria."

"You want me to take some swings?"

"Yeah."

The big man took the saber and adjusted his grip. The handle was plain and straight without ornamentation or a sculpted grip. It was shorter than the ones we used, and seemed lighter. He waved it around a bit before standing. Then he moved into position and starting doing the practice swings we'd all been taught. We watched as he thrust and stabbed and parried. He worked through all the basics and then ended in a guard position. It all looked flawless.

I couldn't help but smile in amazement. He couldn't shoot worth anything, but with a blade in his hand?

Zeke gave us a satisfied smile. "It's light. Balanced good. I could swing it all day."

That didn't actually tell us much about the sword. Zeke could swing anything all day.

He reached out and lightly touched the edge with his thumb, before pulling his hand back fast. He stuck his thumb in his mouth and sucked on it.

"Sharp," McNab chuckled. For the first time since we'd come inside, he actually smiled.

Zeke nodded without taking his thumb out of his mouth.

"Those would slice through Jotun armor," I said. We'd heard they had started wearing thick high boots to protect their ankles and vulnerable knees.

"We need to find out how many they've got," McNab said.

"Yeah," I agreed.

"And why don't they have guns?" he asked.

Now that was a *good* question. I arched an eyebrow to see if he'd continue with a suggestion, but he just shook his head.

As I thought, Brody returned accompanied by a dwarf. As soon as Brody was in the room, the dwarf departed. I scowled. Apparently, they didn't trust us enough to go to the privy by ourselves. He frowned when he saw Zeke sucking his thumb.

"What'd I miss?" Brody asked.

"The sword's sharp," I said with a gesture at Zeke. "But we're wondering why the dwarves don't have rifles."

"Maybe they can't make gunpowder," Brody said.

I nodded, but my gut tightened. That made sense. The Jotun and the trolls didn't know how, and a lot of men had died to make sure it stayed that way.

A lot of men I'd known. Too many faces flashed through my mind. I almost had to close my eyes.

Instead, I looked to McNab. His eyes were filled with the same haunted look as mine. We knew too many of the same men. Heck, he himself had almost died on that raid.

"Yeah." I put my elbows on the table and took a deep breath.

"Huh? What?" Brody asked as he looked from one of us to the other.

"You had to be there," McNab said.

Brody scowled. I thought about saying something, but I didn't know what. As it was, my mind was already drifting.

At the beginning of the battle, I'd almost shot a Crow warrior. I suppressed a shudder. My gut turned to knots. Maybe I should've, but… I never wanted to do that. Was that a line I'd be forced to cross?

I'd only killed one human in my life. Cassidy. I'd had nightmares for a year. But I wasn't sure I wanted it to get easy.

"What is it?" Brody asked.

I shook my head. I didn't know what to say. I was saved by Vestri returning with Maria.

She looked tired and had bloodstains on her sleeves and the hem of her dress. She looked us all over and immediately went to McNab. I only got a brief nod on the way.

"How are you?" She bent close to his shoulder wound.

"Tired. They gave me this." He held up the flask.

She examined it closely and gave it a sniff. Then she set it on the table. "Take off your shirt. Let me see your wound."

He let out a resigned sigh but started undoing his buttons.

"Did you learn anything we could use, Maria?" I asked as she waited for McNab.

She shook her head. "They let me help with the wounded, but only one spoke a little English. They have a nice hospital, though. Very clean."

That didn't surprise me. The whole town was clean. Almost—sterile. At least what we'd seen so far.

"How many of those swords do you think they have?" Brody asked.

"Good question," I said. "We'll need a lot."

"He said 'trade,' not 'give,'" McNab said. "They didn't name their price. We gotta make sure we we get some up front. Our guys won't sign a treaty without seeing the goods. Even Congress ain't that dumb."

I grimaced. Congress was so far away in San Francisco that I barely thought of them, but General Sanborn had mentioned them when he gave me my orders, back all those weeks ago.

"Can I keep this one?" Zeke asked. He still stood, holding the blade, but had wrapped his thumb in a handkerchief.

Maria noticed and gestured him over. "Let me see that when I'm done with McNab."

McNab had gotten his shirt completely off. He faced us, so we couldn't see the scars on his back, and the ones on his chest were small and thin. The bullet wound in his shoulder oozed when Maria pulled back the bandage, but it didn't look any different than I'd expected. She pulled some clean bandages out of a little pouch and dabbed at it. He winced at first, but then let her clean it up.

"Does this hurt?" she asked.

"No," he said in surprise. "I can barely feel it."

Maria paused and stared at him. Then she picked up the medicine flask and looked into it again. She dipped a finger in and gathered up a little bit to taste. Her eyebrows went up.

"This is like poppy juice," she said, "but stronger." To McNab, "How is your head?"

"Fine," he said. He looked as surprised as the rest of us.

"Not foggy, or thick, like with poppy juice?" Maria asked.

He shook his head.

She turned to me. "We must get more of this. It could save lives."

My heart beat faster. We now had another good reason to make a deal with the dwarves. But could I pull it off?

The room felt stifling hot all of a sudden. I tugged at my collar to maybe stop some of the sweat from pooling there. My gut churned as well. I could almost feel McNab and the others looking at me. Waiting.

McNab interrupted the silence. "So… what's it gonna be, Billy?"

I took a deep breath. "My orders were to find out if this town was a threat. We don't know that yet. Yeah, they're being nice to us, but that could be a ruse."

Zeke and Brody shifted uncomfortably, but McNab nodded.

"But I don't think they're gonna just let us poke around," I continued. "So we gotta be sneaky, and I'm not sure how to do that."

"I can keep working in their hospital," Maria said. "Maybe I can find where the medicine comes from."

I nodded. "And we need to find Jeremiah and Anoki anyway. We can tell the dwarves we're going to negotiate with the Sioux."

"Do, uh, we all need to go, sir?" Brody asked. "I could, uh, tell them I want to help with the swords or something…"

There was something in his eyes that was off, but I didn't know how to ask. But then I shook my head.

"Not you. Zeke. They already know he's the swordsman. He can tell them he wants to train with the new blade. The last thing we need is someone hurting themselves with it."

"New blade?" Maria looked at Zeke, and I remembered she hadn't been in the hall during the demonstration.

"It cut through my sword like it was pig fat," Zeke said as he placed the blade in front of her.

She looked at it and then tilted her head. Her eyes narrowed, and then she carefully picked it up and held the blade close to her eyes.

"This has the grey fog of a rift," she said quietly. "This sword is not from our world."

SIXTEEN

AFTER MARIA'S WORDS, the room was so silent I could almost hear my heart beat. I certainly felt it hammering away. I had to force myself to breathe, and judging from the faces on some of the others, they did, too. But Maria looked as calm as always as she examined the blade.

"Yes," she said as she set the sword down. "It has come through a rift. It was probably magical in their world."

"And it's not here?" I couldn't believe that. It'd cut through an army saber like nothing! How could it not be magic?

"It might as well be," Brody grumbled. "We can't make anything like that."

I couldn't help but nod in agreement, but Maria shrugged, obviously not wanting to argue.

McNab grimaced and reached for the sword. He gingerly held it up. "So why'd they offer to trade it?"

"What are you getting at?" I asked.

"You don't trade something like this if it's the only one you've got," he said. "Which means they can get more."

As the implications sunk in, I started swearing. Not quietly either. Brody looked at me in surprise but McNab grinned.

"Uh… I don't understand," Zeke said.

"The dwarves could've come through the original rift, at Andersonville," I explained. "Jeremiah thinks they did, though he's still got some questions. But they can't get more from a rift down in Andersonville."

"Doesn't matter. It's closed." McNab said.

I blinked. I'd heard that, but no one had said it as firmly as he'd just done.

"Anyway," I continued, "if they brought this with them, they'd only have a few, and they'd keep them for themselves. Not trade them."

"Do you think this blade could have been forged here?" Brody asked Maria.

She started to shake her head, but then paused. "Perhaps," she said, "but I do not see how it would have acquired the rift fog that surrounds it."

I stared at the sword. "Rift fog?" What was a "rift fog?" I couldn't see any "rift fog." But then, I couldn't see ghosts either, and Maria could.

"Does the medicine have the rift fog?" I asked.

She raised an eyebrow at the question and reclaimed the bottle from McNab. She pulled the stopper and peered inside. Then she stuck her finger in. When she withdrew it, she examined the milky white fluid on her fingertip.

"Yes," she said. "The bottle does not, and it is faint on the medicine, but it is there." She stoppered the bottle and instead of returning it to Jeremiah, passed it to me. "There is a little left. Keep it safe so we can examine it more later."

I nodded at her words, but still fought to hold my frustration back. Both the things we wanted weren't from our world?

"This doesn't change anything," McNab said quietly. "We still have to learn about this town."

"Yeah," I agreed. I let out a deep breath. "But now we know what we're looking for. We wanna find out if they've got their own rift."

I couldn't help feeling grim. I was sure they did, but proving it wasn't going to be easy.

We talked a little more, but mostly we just went over what we'd already decided. Zeke wanted to come with us to look for Jeremiah and Anoki, but I wanted to leave as many people in the town as we could. We wouldn't find out if the dwarves had a rift by talking to the Indians. Zeke might not either, but he'd still be in a better position to try.

I kept mulling over the exact words to use when we next spoke to Vestri. McNab had some ideas, which I liked. I thought that maybe he could do all the talking since he had more experience with these things. But he laughed when I suggested it.

"You're the boss, Billy! I'm just the quartermaster. They won't listen to me."

I snorted softly. I didn't agree, but I didn't see how I could argue.

We talked and waited for maybe an hour. Eventually, a dwarf arrived with some bread and thick sliced ham. He took our water pitcher, but Vestri was the one that returned with it. I briefly considered standing, but he walked around the table to my side before I could. Since I was sitting and he was standing, I was actually shorter than him by a bit. I tried not to smile as I looked up at a dwarf.

Vestri got right to business. "You agree? Our land?"

"How many swords?" I held up the bottle. "How much medicine?"

Vestri scowled. "Trade. Not gift. Only that one yours." He pointed at the blade that Maria had returned to the table. "Replace one we broke. But no more except trade."

"Fine. Trade. How much? How many?"

"One pound gold. Each."

"Both medicine and swords?" I asked. "How many of each?"

"Both. Many of each. One hundred swords, start."

I crossed my arms as my gut tightened. They had a rift! They had to, if a hundred swords was a "start!" But I couldn't let my worries show on my face.

Vestri didn't notice. He put his hands on his hips. "But only when our land."

"I'll need to talk to the Sioux and the Crow. I'll go talk to them with these two." I pointed at Brody and McNab. "Maria stays and helps in hospital. Zeke stays and you teach him how to use new sword."

He snorted and shook his head.

"We must talk to the Sioux and Crow," I insisted. "The Army cannot promise you the land if it means war."

To that, he nodded.

"Maria's a good nurse," I continued. "The best. She can help your healers."

He pursed his lips, but then nodded.

"And Zeke—"

Vestri shook his head vehemently before I'd even finished.

I plowed on anyway. "Your sword isn't like the ones we carry. He needs to learn."

"We not teach. Soldiers not stay here. Only her." He pointed at Maria, as if there was any doubt about who he meant.

I grimaced. I didn't see a way to win this argument, at least not right now. So I changed to the next subject.

"Some of us dropped our rifles during the fight. Did you find them?"

Vestri shook his head. For some reason, I didn't quite believe him.

"What about horses? Do you have any of our horses?"

"One," he said. "Hers. We sell you ponies."

"Give," I said. "Or loan. We don't pay if we bring them back. We need the ponies to find the Sioux and the Crow."

He scowled, but eventually nodded. "You bring back."

"We will." I considered extending my hand for a shake to seal the deal, but, did dwarves do that?

"Get ponies." Vestri gestured toward the door. "Take to courtyard. You finish food and you go find Sioux. Find Crow. Get them to agree —our land."

I nodded, even though inside my gut was fluttering. How the heck was I going to manage that?Otaktay and the Sioux hadn't travelled all the way to Chicago to give up the Black Hills. I was also pretty sure Cheéte and the Crow would happily kill me and everyone on my team if it got them what they wanted. The only reason I wasn't dead was that they feared the Army of the West.

Which I wasn't sure was warranted. Would General Sanborn actually send a force if we somehow didn't come back?

I certainly hoped so. But I also knew fighting the Jotun came first. If he was forced to choose…

Vestri stood. He impatiently huffed and crossed his arms.

"We'll eat," I said, "and then go."

He nodded and left the room.

After we'd finished the food, Vestri and two dwarvish soldiers arrived to escort us back to the main room. To my surprise, it was nearly empty. Alviss sat at a chair at one end of the long table with a single soldier by his side. The rest of the milling crowd from earlier had left.

Vestri led us over to Alviss. Vestri bowed, and then said a few words in Dwarvish. Alviss replied and Vestri straightened up with a blink. He spoke again, more urgently, but without raising his voice.

Alviss responded with a single curt word and a shake of his head.

Vestri grimaced and grew tense. Then he turned to us.

"I am commanded to go with you," Vestri said. "Stay with you while your nurse stays with us. Alviss says this is the way of equals. Dwarves, army are equals."

I furrowed my brow and looked to McNab.

"Yeah," he said. "We're trading *guests*." His eyes darted to Vestri, who didn't seem to catch the emphasis. But I did. He meant hostages.

Oh, God. I hadn't meant for Maria to become a hostage, but that's what she'd become. Alviss had just made that abundantly clear. I began to wonder if I'd made a mistake by suggesting she stay behind… but we desperately needed to find out about that rift…

In the end, I couldn't change anything. I looked at Vestri. "Welcome to the team."

It was already noon by the time we gathered in the courtyard behind the town gate. I'd started to sweat, standing there, having lost my hat as well somewhere along the way. Zeke rode Maria's horse while the rest of us sat on ponies. These looked a lot like the horses the Crow rode. That made me wonder. Had they brought the ponies through a rift too, or traded with the Crow to get them? Or something else?

I thought about asking Vestri, but I thought that'd be too obvious. Besides, he rode with such a scowl that I was kind of nervous about approaching him.

In contrast, McNab sat easy on his own pony—a piebald with a long mane. Maria had bound his right arm to his side to reduce the chance of him opening it up again. She'd even given him a couple of stitches. He said that it didn't hurt very much at all, thanks to the dwarvish medicine. Mostly he was just tired.

Me, I was jealous. Too many of my old scars ached in envy.

Brody was perhaps the most changed. The eagerness in his eyes had been replaced by wariness. He slouched as he sat and his hand kept sliding back to his Colt. When we finally headed out, he fell to the rear beside Zeke.

We rode east along the dirt road. It ran uphill to a spot where it crossed the ridge Zeke and I'd walked earlier. Then it petered out among a large grove of stumps. I couldn't help grimacing. Knowing where the dwarves had gotten their timber didn't tell me where to find the Indians.

"Any suggestions on where the Sioux would be?" I asked McNab and Brody.

McNab pointed east, down the far side of the ridge. "We camped down there, about a mile, but I doubt they're around. We only stopped there because it was dark."

I shrugged. "We've got nowhere better to go."

We found the old campsite, but if McNab and Brody hadn't known where it'd been, I never would've realized what it was. Grass was trampled and most of it near a small creek had been grazed down to stubs, but the Sioux had broken up their fire rings and scattered the ashes. We found a couple of good hoof prints but no hint as to which way they'd gone, or even if they'd come back this way after the battle.

Vestri had ridden in silence the entire time. His snarl had faded from "I'll kill you if you talk to me" to "you annoy me but you'll live." He now reminded me of some soldiers back in the fort on mornings before they got their coffee.

I took a breath and rode up to him. "Do you have any idea where the Sioux are?"

He shrugged. "Only see Sioux two times."

"Two times?" I distinctly remember Otaktay saying the dwarves had fired arrows at them when they'd approached the town.

"Two times. First time, they meet wood cutters. Say this their land. Get angry when we say no. Second time, they attack town. We win, they leave."

I tried to keep my jaw from dropping. Had the Sioux lied to us? They must have! Or… was Vestri lying now? My blood started to boil. I didn't like being lied to.

But I didn't want that to show. I kept my jaw set. My eyes flicked to McNab, who was within hearing distance. He kept his face stiff, too.

"And what about the Crow?" I asked as casually as I could. "Did they attack you, too?"

He frowned, as if he were trying to find the right words. "Crow first friendly. Now, not."

I thought of the ponies. "You traded with them."

"Yes. At first. Then they make demands. We refuse. No more trade."

"Ah." I didn't know what else to say. At least the Crow hadn't fought with the dwarves. Well, not at first. I had no idea who'd been shooting at whom during the recent battle before the town gate.

Vestri just scowled.

"So," I said, "if we can't find the the Sioux, we should find the Crow."

"Well, that might not be a problem," McNab said. He pointed off to the south. "'Cause here they are."

SEVENTEEN

THE CROW RODE SLOWLY out of the scattered pines on the far side of the creek. Their rifles remained slung across their backs, but their faces were grim. Those that I could see. With the sun behind them, some of them were too shadowed to read.

There weren't as many of them as before. Maybe a dozen. Still, that was twice our number, so part of me was relieved that they didn't appear to be looking for a fight. If they were, we could run, but their horses had to be faster than our ponies. Still, my hand drifted up to grab my rifle, before I remembered I didn't have it.

Then I spotted Cheéte. He rode slowly and splashed across the creek, followed by two Indians I didn't recognize. When he saw Vestri and me, he turned his horse and headed straight toward us. He paused a few feet away. Then he glared at me, which got my spine up. I glared back.

"Bad you run," he said to me in Arapaho. "Many die because you run."

"If you had let us go," I retorted, "we not run."

He huffed, turned to Vestri, and said something in a language I didn't understand. Vestri responded in the same tongue. I sat uneasy, listening to them. From their expressions, Cheéte was as mad at Vestri as he was at me. Vestri wasn't taking it, though. His words sounded equally harsh. When they were finished, both looked on the edge of grabbing their weapons.

Cheéte glared back at me. "Our land. You no trade with them. Trade with us. You give guns, horses. We give knives. Our land. They not pay. You not trade with them. Our land. *Our* land."

I blinked. I was in over my head on this. I could handle shooting things. Figuring this out… that was gonna be much harder. My nerves started to kick in. I wasn't sure I could do this.

But then I mentally played back what Cheéte had said. Knives. I glanced at his belt. Sure enough, he had a knife there with a long plain handle like the dwarven sword's. But he didn't carry a saber.

This was getting complicated. I honestly didn't know what to do. In the dime novels, Cassidy had always been quick with what to say. But these days, I suspected that was because the writer edited out all his indecision. I'd have to remember to ask Jeremiah about it when we found him. My gut tightened as I wondered where he and Anoki were.

Well, in any case, I wanted to talk to McNab. And not where Vestri or Cheéte could overhear. Not that Cheéte would understand if we spoke English. I gave Vestri a sideways glance. Just how good was his English?

I couldn't think of any way to find out, but it was something to think about. Except right now, both the Indian and the dwarf were staring at me. Waiting for me.

"What about the Sioux?" I said to Cheéte. "You're at war with them now. That can't be good."

"We drive them from land," he practically spat. "We kill their warriors. Take their women. The Sioux be no more."

But then his eyes darted to Vestri, who didn't look like he'd understood a thing.

Something was up between them. I needed to find out what.

"Billy, you remember Harrisburg?" McNab murmured. Vestri's eyes darted to him, but he frowned in confusion.

But my eyes widened as I realized what he'd meant. In the book *The Road to Harrisburg,* Cassidy had gotten two feuding families to work together by reminding them of their common enemy, the Jotun. Which I might be able to do.

I cleared my throat to get Cheéte and Vestri's attention. Then I spoke in Arapaho to Cheéte. "America and the Army of the West not claim this land. Like you," I looked at Cheéte, "we wish to drive enemy from land, but our enemy is Jotun."

To my surprise, Vestri seemed to be following the conversation. Did he speak Arapaho, too? I turned to him in English.

"Our enemy is Jotun. You help fight?"

He grunted.

I looked at Cheéte again. "Enemy is Jotun. You help fight?"

He snorted and glared at me. "Jotun not here. Sioux here. We fight Sioux."

"Sioux not here either," I shot back.

"We find Sioux." His eyes darted to the side, toward… the northeast?

But the Sioux were still a problem. Even if I could somehow convince the Crow not to attack them, I doubted I could get the Sioux to do the same. They'd lost women and children. They were out for blood. And Jeremiah and Anoki were probably with them, so I couldn't just leave them alone.

But how to find the Sioux without leading the Crow right to them?

I shook my head. That wasn't the immediate problem. The immediate problem was the Crow. I didn't think they'd attack us, but they weren't going away either. I'd already spent enough time in their company. That made my blood boil enough.

But as the anger simmered in my gut, I mentally played back through what Cheéte had said. He wanted us to trade with the Crow instead of directly with the dwarves. He hadn't said what, though.

"What do you want from us?" I asked in Arapaho. "If we trade? What do we give you for knives and…" I fumbled for the word for medicine. "… healing water?"

"Healing water?" His eyes went wide and he looked at Vestri, who gave me a dirty look. Which answered the question about whether Vestri understood Arapaho.

I nodded. "Medicines. We trade for them. What you want?"

"Army fight Sioux."

I shook my head. He knew as well as me that wasn't going to happen.

"Rifles." Cheéte continued to stare at Vestri, but the dwarf's surprised look had turned to a glare.

That was enough. I was tired of Cheéte trying to intimidate me. Yeah, I was smaller than him and without my rifle, but I'd killed giants! He wasn't as scary as them.

"No rifles," I snapped. "We not have rifles." I pointed at my back where mine should've been. Gone. Taken by enemies. You? You take?"

Cheéte's eyes narrowed. I figured he got the implied threat, but I didn't care. If he reached for his rifle, I could draw my revolver faster. It was my turn to glare at him.

"We not have rifle," he spat. His eyes didn't leave mine as we slipped into a staring contest. The big Indian and little me.

"Maybe not," I snarled. "But you have other stuff. Like my book."

He blinked in surprise and pulled back. I gave him my best feral grin. He snorted and said something to one of the other Crow. A minute later, two books thunked to the ground in front of my pony— Brody's book that I'd been carrying, and Zeke's Bible.

"Dawn. Tomorrow. At town." Cheéte spat. "You agree our land or it bad." With that, he turned his horse and rode off, the rest of the Crow trailing behind.

I decided we should take a break to water and feed the horses, not to mention ourselves. The day was downright pleasant, with enough scattered puffy clouds to give some shade at times, but also some warm sun. I figured there was no point in running off until we knew where we wanted to go. Besides, I wanted to talk to McNab without Vestri listening in. The dwarf kind of got the hint and went to water his pony a little ways downstream.

Zeke was thrilled to get his Bible back. He immediately sank onto a nearly fallen log and started paging through it. He went fast, not like he was looking for a specific verse or anything. When he'd reached the end, he looked up with a big grin.

"All the pages are there." He lowered his head and started flipping through it more slowly.

I chuckled. Even McNab looked amused.

Brody accepted his book back with a perfunctory thanks. He turned it over in his hands and then walked to his horse and tucked in in a saddlebag. He still looked glum when he wandered back to where McNab and I stood.

"You're not happy to have it back?" I asked.

He shrugged. "It's all lies."

I blinked in surprise. "Not all of it."

"Nah, not even most of it," McNab added. "Jeremiah just cut the boring parts."

Brody scrunched up his face like he was going to say something, but then shook his head and walked over to the creek. He knelt down, and I thought he was going to take a drink, but then he stood up and skipped a rock across the water.

"I'll talk to the kid," McNab said and made to walk over to him, but I stuck out my arm and blocked his path.

"No," I said with a sigh. "I think I have to do this."

He grimaced, but went to sit with Zeke.

I tried to make my walk as casual as possible, but Brody still stiffened at my approach. He'd actually sat down on a lump of grass with his feet dangling over the creek. Rocks still splooshed and kerplunked when he couldn't get them to skip.

"Hey." I sat beside him and looked out at the water. It bubbled along nice and peaceful, its tinkling almost musical.

Brody threw another rock.

I picked up one and threw it myself. Then he threw one, and I followed up. Mine made a satisfying plop. He skipped his next one twice before it smacked a rock on the far bank of the creek.

"I finally read the book myself," I said. "It's not bad."

"It's still lies. It's all lies." He chucked a rock so hard it completely cleared the creek and thudded into the dirt on the far shore.

"No… not all. Most of the facts are true, actually."

He paused, mid-throw, and stared at me. "Even Cassidy's big fight with the giants at the end?"

"Even that." I shrugged. "Jeremiah took out the boring parts and a lot of the parts where we wasted time not knowing what to do. But what he left in is pretty true."

"You said it was lies."

I let out a long breath. "I did. Before I read it. I…" I sagged where I sat. What could I say?

But to my surprise, Brody just waited. He lowered his arm instead of throwing the rock. We didn't move, but just listed to the water burble.

"The books…," I finally said. "The books also leave out all the doubt. All the confusion. All the times we were scared and had no idea what to do. That's how they lie." I snorted. "In the book I'm not an idiot."

"I don't think you're an idiot." His sincerity made me laugh, which caused him to look at me with alarm. "I don't!"

"I feel like one." I gestured toward where Vestri stood next to his pony, dozens of yards away. "I have no idea what to do."

"In the book you do. You and Cassidy both."

I turned to face him. "Now you're defending the book?" I couldn't cover my amusement.

He ducked his head in embarrassment. "Yeah, well…"

"You said it was full of lies."

"It is! Well…" He picked up one of the last of the small rocks in the area and threw it into the creek. "It lies about the fighting."

I nodded. And then I thought a bit. Most of Brody's questions about the book had been about the battles. What'd it been like? What'd I been thinking? It was like he…

"That was your first battle," I said. "Wasn't it? In front of the gate."

"Yeah." If he could've hung his head any lower, it would've been in his chest.

"But you did well. You kept your head and you helped rescue that dwarf. You were steadfast!"

He turned his head and looked at me, his eyes wide with surprise. "Really?"

"Really. I mean, I couldn't've done it better myself."

A genuine smile creased his lips, but then his cheeks reddened and he looked down at his lap again.

"You were great!"

"I soiled myself," he said quietly.

I couldn't help laughing, but I fought it back as his face turned redder and redder.

"It's not funny." He reached for a rock, but there weren't any more.

"No," I agreed, "it's not. But it's *exactly* the thing that gets left out of the books."

"Did you ever…?"

"No. But let's go talk to McNab. I'll bet he knows someone who has. Maybe even Cassidy."

Brody snorted at the thought, but then he nodded. "Sure."

"Besides," I continued. "You won't do it again. You've been in your first battle now. You're a veteran."

He blinked at that and didn't say a thing.

"We should get going." I stood and he joined me.

McNab sat a respectful distance away and he nodded at us. But before I could walk over, Vestri gestured for me to come to him. He had already walked half the way over. I decided I might as well meet him.

"Enough time waste," he said when we were close. "We go talk to Sioux."

I blinked. "I thought you didn't know where they were."

"Don't know. But have good guess."

EIGHTEEN

I STARED AT THE DWARF. I hadn't realized how wrinkled his skin was, and I began to wonder at his age. But I dismissed the thought—it wasn't important. What he'd said was. He knew where the Sioux were! Where I hoped to find Jeremiah and Anoki. The Crow hadn't said anything about them, and if they'd captured Jeremiah and Anoki, I was sure they would've.

"Where?" I asked.

He pointed northeast. "Over two hills. Then big rocks. Good camp place. Safe."

I nodded. It was as good a lead as any. It also would give me time to talk to Vestri some more. But first, I had to take care of something.

"Brody!" I called.

He stood in front of McNab, and I suspected I'd interrupted the beginning of their conversation. Still, both of them looked at me as I strode over.

"Yes, sir?" Brody asked when I was close.

"Vestri thinks he knows where the Sioux are," I explained, "but if he's right, we can't lead the Crow to 'em. So I need you to hang back and hide and see if they're following us."

"Yes, sir." He paused. "How do I do that, sir?"

"We're going northeast. Once we get into the trees, you get off your pony and hide. Zeke can lead your pony. We'll go, oh, a mile or so and then wait. If you haven't seen the Crow in an hour, come find us. Sooner if you do see them. Do you understand?"

He nodded and swallowed hard. "Why me, sir?"

"You're the best man for the job." I nodded at McNab. "He's hurt. Zeke's too big to hide well, and I gotta go with Vestri. Can you do it?"

He swallowed hard, his eyes wide.

"It's what needs to be done," I said. "You've a veteran now and I think you can do it. Don't let them see you, and make sure you count how many of them there are. If they're following, of course."

"Yes, sir!"

His tone was more enthusiastic than his eyes, which made me wonder, but I figured he'd do the job fine. Yeah, my reasons for *him* doing it were a bit thin, but this way he'd know I had confidence in him. Besides, I didn't think he'd fail.

McNab grinned at me when Brody wasn't looking. He'd knew what I'd done. I just gave him a small nod. Then I called to Zeke and we were on our way.

We rode into the trees. I had Vestri explain where we were going to the others. I then added that if we got separated or if Brody couldn't find us, we'd all go the the "good camp place." Brody nodded and let out a relieved breath before dismounting and passing his reins to Zeke. He looked around and headed for a small cluster of short, bushy pine trees.

He'd be fine.

I waited until we were headed up the first hill before I rode next to Vestri. I figured now was the time to ask.

"You traded with the Crow," I began. "Knives, but not swords. And no medicines."

He shrugged. "They only ask for knives."

"So should we ask for more?"

He didn't reply, and we rode for a few minutes before I decided on my next question.

"What did the Crow trade you?" I asked. "They don't have gold."

"Yes." He set his jaw. "No gold. We want gold."

I wasn't sure what it was with gold anyway for the dwarves, but I knew the United States of the West could get it. It just wasn't as valuable to us as iron and steel these days. And if we could get more of those giant-killing swords…

"So what did they give you?"

We rode a bit longer before he answered. "Ponies. Food."

"No gold," I said.

He shook his head, but I got to thinking… food? Why'd the dwarves need to trade for food? Maybe when they first arrived in the Black Hills, but both the Crow and Sioux had hunted successfully our entire trip. I couldn't imagine the dwarves would've had any problems. I eventually decided it was something to talk to Jeremiah about. But only when Vestri was nowhere around.

I realized I had another question he might answer. "Do you want anything from us besides gold?"

"No. Just gold."

That just begged the question: Why? Humans used gold to trade. It was only worth what you could get for it, unless you really liked it in jewelry. And none of the dwarves I'd seen had worn any jewelry, gold or otherwise.

But if they had a rift, it made more sense. Gold might have a different value on the other side. Like, maybe it was what they used to make their magic.

That said, one thing was clear. If the dwarves wanted gold, it didn't make sense for the Crow to be middlemen, for either us or the dwarves. In fact, it didn't make sense for the Crow either. I was still missing something.

But the Crow were definitely turning into a bigger problem.

I suspected the Army could beat them in a fight, if it came to that, but my gut tightened at the thought of it. A lot of people would die, and we had enough needless deaths in the world as it was. The Crow weren't the enemy. The Jotun and the trolls were.

While I was lost in my thoughts, we reached the top of the first hill. The trees were more scattered here, which gave good views both the way we came and across the small valley to the next hill. I figured this was a good place to stop and wait for Brody.

We waited longer than I'd expected. Vestri remained by my side, though we didn't speak. McNab got off his horse for a bit and stretched out on the ground, like he was gonna take a nap. He gingerly held his shoulder as he lay down, which meant the medicine must've worn off.

I climbed off my own horse and sat on the grass next to McNab. He gave me a pained smile.

"How bad is it?"

"Eh. No worse than some."

"You've been hurt a lot."

He chuckled, deep and dark and unsavory.

"But you keep going on missions," I said. "Why don't you retire?"

"Thought about it," he said. "Almost did."

"Why didn't you?" I knew the army'd give him a good pension when he did call it quits.

"Well…," he gave me a tired grin. "Because of you, Billy. Somebody's gotta help you take over for Cassidy."

The blood rushed in my ears.

"I…," I shook my head. "I can't take Cassidy's place." The man was a legend. Me…?

"Somebody's gotta," he said. "Ain't you been listening to Jeremiah?"

I snorted. The idea was too ridiculous to consider. I'd been a hero in Louisville. It wasn't worth it. All I wanted to do now was get away from the army rigamarole. Besides, no one could really replace Cassidy. That'd be like trying to replace a legend.

He chuckled at my expression.

"Yeah, you're not ready yet."

I stared at him, but he just grinned, leaned back, and closed his eyes.

I figured it was almost an hour before we spotted Brody scrambling up the slope toward us. He emerged from the last of the trees with a big grin on his face.

"They're following!" he called out. "Or at least they were!"

"Did they see you?" I asked when he was close enough that I didn't have to yell.

His grin turned sour. "Yeah. But then they turned around and rode off."

So the Crow were still out there, and still following us. They had to know we were looking for the Sioux. Which meant we had to lose them. That wasn't going to be easy. I was sure they knew these hills well, and they were bound to be excellent trackers. We might not lose them with the usual tricks.

So the more I thought about it, the more I became convinced that the only way to give them the slip was to give them something else to chase.

Still, it made sense to get McNab's opinion, and maybe Zeke's and Brody's too. I called them to gather around. Vestri drifted nearby—close enough to listen but not part of our circle. Then I explained my thinking.

"Yeah, that might work," McNab agreed. His face was drawn. His pain was back. "If one of us hid their tracks and the others left a clear trail…"

"They didn't notice me until they were right on top of me," Brody added.

"More the reason," I said. "So all but one of us start going a different direction. We circle around and make our way back to the dwarf town. The last man goes to the Sioux Camp and tells them to meet us at the town."

"The Crow might be watching the town, too," Brody said.

"True," I replied, "but if the Sioux get inside the walls, there won't be any battle."

"The Sioux won't go inside," Zeke stated rather flatly. "They won't be walled in."

He had a point. They hadn't liked being surrounded by the Crow on the trail. They certainly wouldn't like being surrounded by the dwarves. I glanced at Vestri again. I really hated that he understood English better than he let on. If only Zeke or McNab spoke Arapaho…

…but I thought of McNab's trick with the book. And that made me think of a code Cassidy had used in a different chapter of *The Road to Harrisburg.*

"Uh, McNab," I said. "Do you remember Pig Latin?"

He blinked. "IgPay atinLay? EahYa."

"Good." I checked with Zeke and Brody and they both nodded. Vestri continued to pretend he wasn't eavesdropping.

"I think we should split up." I spoke loud enough for Vestri to easily hear, but not so loud as to make it obvious what I was doing. "If the four of you lead the Crow in a wide circle back to the dwarf town, then I can go talk to the Sioux and persuade them to agree to the dwarves' claim. Of course, it might take a while. You'd have to wait inside the town. Are you good with that?"

Vestri took in a deep breath and held it. He was definitely listening. So I switched to Pig Latin.

"Ouyay ancay ooklay orfay ethay iftray ilewhay ouyay aitway." *You can look for the rift while you wait.*

"Yeah…" McNab fought to keep the smirk off his face. He too raised his voice a couple of notches. "That'll work. No way the Sioux would agree to the dwarves' claim if we led the Crow to them. You think you can talk them into it?"

"I know I can," I lied. "They listen to me. But it still might take some time. Several days at least."

"I don't see much choice," McNab replied. He looked over at the dwarf. "Hey, Vestri! We think we can lead the Crow in a big circle back to your town while Billy slips off to talk to the Sioux. That good with you?"

Vestri turned to face us. "If Sioux agree our land, that good."

"So we'll do it?" I said. "The four of you lead the Crow away while I go talk to the Sioux?"

He grimaced as he thought about it, but in the end he nodded.

"Good," I said. "Let's get going."

We mounted our ponies and continued north, down from the ridge into the next valley. At the bottom, we found a small stream, if the trickle even counted as that. I could've stepped across it without getting my feet wet, but it was good enough. We found a stretch with a long dirt bank that would leave plenty of horse tracks. The others crossed and moved around enough really mark up the bank. Then Zeke led them northwest. Where he could, the big man brushed against tree branches and the occasional bush, bending and breaking off small branches as he went.

I watched them go with a pang of regret. I kinda wished we could stick together. I felt calmer with McNab around. I knew he was looking out for me, even if he had crazy ideas about me replacing Cassidy.

A small breeze picked up and waved the pine trees. Their scent filled the air as I turned my own pony northeast. I went slowly through a rocky area along the creek and then moved across a small gap between the trees where my pony would leave fewer marks. I kept looking back, but I didn't see anything but woods. After about twenty minutes, I figured I'd been cautious enough and urged my pony into a trot.

At the top of the next hill, I spotted the large rock outcropping that Vestri had described earlier. The top was bare and jagged, and a scout could easily lie between the folds of the rock without being seen. If they were camped at its bottom, the sheer face also provided an impassible rear wall. I couldn't see the bottom due to the forest of pine trees in the way. Worse, I couldn't see any Indians.

I checked back the way I'd come. I couldn't see any Indians behind me either. I moved behind one of the few trees at the top of the hill just in case a Crow scout was watching me. Then I waited. Nothing moved but the trees in the wind and the occasional bird. I waited a bit more, and then I rode down toward the base of the rock.

I didn't go quietly. I figured if the Sioux were there, the worst thing I could do was sneak up on them. No point getting shot because I'd surprised a guard.

Which turned out to be a good idea. I'd just about reached the valley floor when a Sioux stepped out from behind a tree and pointed a rifle at me. His long black hair was in braids and he wore warpaint on his face. He barked something I didn't understand.

Instead, I raised my hands above my head.

He said something again and then lowered his gun enough to look at me. I kept my hands up. Apparently he recognized me, or at least my now dirty and worn uniform, because he lowered his rifle the rest of the way and gestured for me to follow him.

I did so, fervently hoping that Jeremiah and Anoki were here.

NINETEEN

THE SIOUX LOOKOUT led me on a winding path through the pines and scattered bushes. After a bit, he made a call like a bird, and then we turned and went toward the rock. It loomed overhead and I thought I saw a falcon nesting halfway up. I was surprised at how quiet it was, other than the sounds of our own movement.

So I was surprised when two more Sioux strode through the trees. One of them was Otaktay.

The big Sioux's eyes went wide when he saw me, but then narrowed into a glare. He crossed his arms and waited until I was close enough to speak in normal tones. I decided to do him the courtesy of dismounting instead of looking down at him.

"You found us," he said.

"The dwarves know of this place." I gestured back the way I'd come. "The Crow found your last campsite. They may be coming."

His scowl turned to a look of alarm. He said something to the Indian with him, who turned and ran back into the trees.

"They followed you?" Otaktay asked.

"I don't think so. But I can't be sure. We split up and the others left an obvious trail while I hid mine."

"We move." He gestured for me and the lookout to follow him, and then set off at a run. I remounted my pony and followed.

The camp was larger than I'd expected, with many more Sioux warriors present than I'd imagined were around. They were already in motion—packing horses, putting out fires, and other things. I spotted Jeremiah about the time he spotted me. I let out a huge sigh of relief.

"Billy!" he called as he ran over. "You're alive!"

"We all are." I looked around again. "Where's Anoki?"

"Now that's a long story."

I nodded. "Same here. And we need to move fast in case the Crow are coming."

"We'll talk on the way."

Jeremiah ran for his horse. Within a few minutes, he and all the Sioux were mounted and ready to go.

Otaktay led us northeast at a fast pace, up out of the valley and across another hill. Then he turned us even further east and kept us going until we'd crossed another ridge and ridden down into a small valley. By then, the horses were winded, and even I was sweating. Otaktay called a break.

I dismounted so I could stretch my legs. Jeremiah did the same, and we wandered a bit away from the main cluster of Sioux.

"So what happened?" I asked. "You didn't come into the town with us."

"We charged the Crow, Anoki and me," he said grimly. "Anoki killed one too, before they shot our horse. Then the Sioux joined the fight and Otaktay showed up. He had a spare horse, and…" He shrugged.

"Yeah," I said, "it was a little crazy."

"Battles always are."

I snorted in agreement. "So… where's Anoki?"

"Remember his sick wife?" After I nodded, he continued, "It seems there's a large Sioux camp about a day's ride from here. Otaktay sent him there to be with her."

"And he went?" I had visions of him deserting first.

"He didn't want to, but I made it an order. I'm still a sergeant." He smirked.

"Yeah," I said. "But that doesn't matter out here. You're just Jeremiah. We don't have to put up with all that army crud."

"If you say so, Lieutenant." He barely kept a straight face.

I swatted him on the shoulder and he laughed.

"So what else?" I asked.

"Not much." He grew somber. "The Sioux lost a couple of warriors in the battle, but Otaktay thinks they got the better of the Crow."

"I do, too." I filled him in on meeting the Crow at the old Sioux camp, which then caused me to back up and fill him in on the dwarves and the town. He whistled when I told him about the dwarvish saber and nodded in agreement when I said there had to be a new rift.

"It'd explain why there's so many dwarves" he said, "and how they built the town so fast."

"Yeah," I agreed. "Even if they quarried all that stone here, that takes a lot of workers. If they'd come through the original rift down at Andersonville with as many as they have now, we'd have known about it."

"Maybe. Many things came through that rift before we even knew what happened."

I conceded with a nod, but I was still sure we would've heard if there'd been more than a few dwarves. But it didn't matter. What mattered was the rift they had *now*.

Jeremiah's gaze drifted to Otaktay, who stood many yards away in conference with several of his warriors. He wasn't trying to listen in, which made me feel relieved, somehow. The Crow and the dwarves clearly didn't trust us, but apparently the Sioux didn't mind me and Jeremiah talking privately.

"You think the Sioux were the attackers, like that dwarf Vestri said?" Jeremiah asked.

"Dunno." I blinked at his sudden change of subject. "*Someone* shot that dwarf at the gate, and the Sioux were closer."

"Yeah." He frowned. "But it could've been the Crow too. They were within range."

"Did Otaktay say anything?"

He shook his head.

"Okay, let's talk to Otaktay."

Jeremiah followed me as I walked over to the cluster of Sioux. Otaktay saw me, but finished his conversation with his warriors before turning to us.

"I have been inside the town," I said. "There are many, many dwarves. They will be hard to remove by force."

"It's *our* land." His eyes narrowed. "You promised. You gave it to us. You must help us remove them."

I grimaced. "They don't want the whole Black Hills. Just everything within a day's ride of their town."

"They claim what is not theirs. If you not help, you not friend of Sioux. Treaty with army over. Sioux at war with army."

That was *not* what we wanted. I was sure the army could defeat the Sioux. But the Sioux and the Jotun at the same time…?

"Fine," I said. "I want to see Anoki." Otaktay tilted his head in confusion. "My men are scouting the town. They're looking for its weaknesses. We need to give them a few days, so I want to see Anoki."

He paused and seemed to be thinking it over. Then he nodded. "We go."

We rode east, out of the Black Hills and onto the plains once again. Few clouds blocked the sun's warmth, and for once it felt like a truly glorious spring day. I wanted to gallop and apparently the Sioux felt the same. Otaktay raised his arm and cried out, and a moment later we were all thundering across the land.

On my pony instead of a full-sized horse, I started to fall behind. They slowed for me, thankfully. We rode hard until the horses began to tire, and then we dropped to a walk. Still, it had been exhilarating, and I shared a happy grin with some of the Sioux. Even Otaktay seemed more relaxed.

After a few hours, a large, lone butte rose up in front of us. The slopes were mostly reddish-grey rock that looked more like a pile of sand than a craggy hill. Only a few trees spotted the steep sides, though the bottom of the butte was green as could be. What made it remarkable was that it was the only hill or mountain anywhere around.

We rode straight toward it. From time to time, we stopped and peered behind us, but saw no sign of anyone following across the grass. Apparently, we had indeed managed to give the Crow the slip.

I spent a lot of time thinking as we rode. My mind kept drifting to McNab's words about me taking over for Cassidy. It was absurd. Ridiculous. But he believed it. Worse, I suspected he wasn't the only one. Wasn't that why Jeremiah had said he was coming along? To write another book about me?

I just wanted to figure out what to do about this town so Sanborn could let me have Cassidy's freedom. I didn't want to *be* Cassidy.

So why did everybody want me to?

I tried to keep my thoughts on the mission and on the dwarves. I didn't have the single-mindedness of my superior, Captain Mercer. He wouldn't have wanted me to be Cassidy. He just would've wanted me to solve the problem with the dwarves.

My mind tired, so I decided to focus on the ride. That, at least, I could enjoy. It felt good to just go toward the distant butte, with the wind in my hair and the sun on my neck.

When we got close to the butte in mid-afternoon, Otaktay steered us toward a small lake, not far from the mountain itself. On the far shore of the lake stood dozens of tipis. We'd reached the Sioux camp.

Several young boys in buckskin shirts and pants ran out to greet us as we cantered into the camp. They yelled and called and some of the warriors returned their cries. One warrior slid from his horse and scooped up a boy of about eight into a massive hug. The others laughed and waved, and soon we were in the middle of the camp itself, surrounded by the merry chaos of greetings.

Somewhere in the middle of that, Jeremiah and I both dismounted, and teenaged boys grabbed the reins. When I yanked back on them, one youth pointed to the lake and then the horse, and then mimed drinking. I let him take my pony.

When I turned back, Otaktay stood by my side. He pointed toward a tipi by the water and gestured for Jeremiah and me to follow him. We fell in a few steps behind him and broke free of the crowd, which was beginning to disperse.

There we found Anoki.

He sat cross-legged on the ground in front of the tipi next to a small fire with a pot on it. He wore ill-fitting Sioux buckskins instead of his army uniform, and his shoulders slumped. He poked at the fire until we were close. Then he looked up at us. His eyes were worn and haunted. They went wide when he saw me.

"You're here," he said. He started to scramble to his feet.

"How's your wife?" I gestured for him to stay seated.

He looked down into the fire. "Not well." He gestured at the tipi. "She's sleeping now."

"Anything we can do?" I crouched down next to him.

He shook his head. "She's in pain. The medicines don't work. It's slow."

"What if we had new medicines?" I suggested. My hand drifted to the pouch at my waist where I held the bottle from the dwarves that Maria had told me to keep safe. It didn't have much but, it had a little.

"Maria's won't work," Anoki said. "I asked her."

"No… but the dwarves' might. It took away all of McNab's pain almost at once."

Anoki looked up from the fire at me. Then at Otaktay, who'd been silently standing by with his arms crossed.

"Dwarf medicine?" Anoki said.

"Mmm hmmm. It's magic medicine." Well, more or less. Now was not the time for nuance.

"Will it work?" Otaktay asked. The note of concern in his voice surprised me.

"I don't know," I admitted.

"Need it work. Save Washta. Please."

I stared at him. Every time I'd talked to Otaktay, every time I'd seen him, he'd been gruff and unbending. Like he had a spear for a spine. And he'd just said "please?"

I glanced at Jeremiah, who raised his eyebrows in a match to my own curiosity, but he kept silence.

"I… I have some dwarf medicine." I fished the little bottle out of the pouch and held it out to him. Maria wanted to examine it later, but this was a better use.

Otaktay snatched the bottle from my hand and stared at it. He said something in Sioux to Anoki, who just shrugged in response.

A weak voice came from inside the tipi. Anoki's head snapped around and Otaktay clenched the bottle.

"Excuse me," Anoki said. Then he turned and scrambled into the tipi.

Otaktay was right behind him.

I stared at the tipi entrance. Then I shifted around so I could sit on the ground. The noise of the Sioux camp still surrounded me, but no one seemed to mind. I glanced around to be sure, and saw one of Otaktay's men watching me from a distance, as well as a couple of the boys.

Jeremiah and I settled in to wait.

The two Indians emerged quite a while later. Both looked shaken. Otaktay glanced toward the butte, whose long shadow now stretched across the plain. I figured we had maybe another hour of daylight. The smell of cooked meat already wafted from some nearby fires.

"We stay night," Otaktay said to me. "Hold tribal council."

"The medicine took away her pain," Anoki said to me. "We know she's not better, but it helped. Thank you."

"You're welcome."

"We have many sick, besides Washta," he continued. "Here, and in other camps. The Black Hills are still Sioux land, but we want to know more about these dwarf medicines. You'll need to convince the council to make a deal."

I swallowed hard, but nodded. I had no idea what I'd say.

TWENTY

THE SIOUX DECIDED to wait until after dinner to hold the tribal council. Not that I minded. I ate more delicious buffalo meat than I'd ever had in my life. It was a bit more lean than I was used to, but after being cooked on the open flame, it was juicy and oh so tender.

After all the craziness of the past few days, it felt good to just sit by the fire and eat. The Sioux made me feel welcome, though it seemed that the entire camp found a reason to come by and see me. At least I was a normal curiosity. To them, I wasn't the Hero of Louisville or a character in some book. I was just a small American man that had come to visit. They basically treated me the same way Jeremiah did, without the hero worship. I kind of liked that.

Jeremiah himself seemed happy to have me around. As we sat and ate, he even said so, after I told him all about the dwarf town and what we'd learned.

"I've been wondering what's been going on," he said. "Otaktay doesn't say much."

"Any problems?"

"No. I don't think Otaktay likes me, but…" He shrugged.

"Any of them speak English besides Anoki and Otaktay?"

"A few words, here and there. Otaktay and Anoki learned from a missionary when they were boys, but most of these warriors are younger."

"Did you ever figure out why they don't like each other?"

"Oldest reason in the book." Jeremiah's eyes twinkled. "They both fell in love with the same woman."

"Washta." I couldn't help looking toward the tipi where the sick woman still lay.

"Correct. Apparently, she was quite a woman. She still is, as far as I can tell."

"Any idea what's wrong with her?"

"No," he said with a shake of his head. "I don't know why Anoki left, either. None of the others know, and he's not saying. But I do know he doesn't want her to die."

"Huh. It's not consumption is it?" Ma had died of consumption. It'd been real miserable at the end.

"No. It's something like it, though. Whatever it is, it's slow."

I nodded. So was consumption. It could take years, but it always killed in the end.

The bigger question was whether the dwarf medicine could cure it. And if it would help the Sioux agree to a deal with the dwarves. I tried to come up with what they might do, but in the end my mind just ran circles. In doing so, it hit upon another question.

"Say," I said to Jeremiah, "what happened to Lieutenant Caldwell and his men? When we split up back at the river, they went with Otaktay, but I haven't seen them."

"I asked Otaktay about that. It seems that when the Crow attacked during the river crossing, the Sioux scattered. He never saw Caldwell after that."

I frowned. Caldwell had to be around somewhere. I supposed he could've gone back to Fort Randall, but that didn't sound like him. If he'd gotten separated from the Sioux, he should've either searched for them, or us, or made his way to the Black Hills on his own. Given the size of the town, I'd be surprised if he hadn't found it. So what'd happened to him?

It was almost a relief when Otaktay showed up and beckoned for us to follow.

He led us to a larger fire not far from the lakeshore itself. Most of the camp sat in a circle around it, far enough back to give a little room to walk around the flames without getting burned.

On one side, three grey-haired old men and one even older woman sat. They all had beading on their brown shirts. The woman wore jewelry with gold and silver and some colorful stones I didn't recognize. The men all had headbands, but none that were ornate enough to clearly mark one of them as the chief. I spotted Anoki sitting next to the old woman.

Otaktay led Jeremiah and me to a spot a few feet in front of them. He said a few words in Sioux to them and then turned to me.

"Tell them about the medicine."

"There's not much to tell," I muttered, and then louder for the crowd, "The dwarves have magic medicine. Better than ours. One of my men was wounded. The medicine took the pain away. The rest we gave to Washta, but the dwarves have more."

I paused while Otaktay translated. When he was finished, the old woman leaned over to Anoki, who murmured something. She nodded and straightened up. Then the man in the middle gestured for me to go on.

"The dwarves want all the land within a day's ride of their town," I said. "The Army of the West has not agreed to this and will not agree to this without the permission of the Sioux. They offer us medicine and swords that can kill Jotun."

After Otaktay translated, the four elders frowned and then conferred. Then the man in the middle said something to Otaktay.

He translated for me. "Too much land. No."

I blinked. That answer implied they might be willing to give up *some* land.

The old woman conferred with Anoki again and then she said something to Otaktay, who translated.

"Need more proof medicines work," he said. "She says once not enough."

I grimaced, but nodded. It was a fair request. None of us knew exactly how well the medicine worked or what it could cure.

"Then we need to go to the dwarves," I said. "We will tell them they have to prove their medicine works first before there's a deal."

Otaktay translated, and the elders nodded. Then the woman said something to Anoki. His eyebrows went up and he asked her something in reply. As she answered again, his face seemed to war between wariness and excitement. Finally, their conversation ended and Anoki cleared his throat.

"We will take Washta," he said loudly enough for the entire assembly to hear, though since he spoke English, I suppose me and Jeremiah were all that mattered. "We will take Washta, and if they do not cure her, no deal."

I let out a deep breath. I hoped to heck the dwarves could do that.

Given the deepening night, the fires were soon banked, and the families and elders all retreated to their tipis for the night. The Sioux led Jeremiah and me to a tipi, which we gratefully used. It felt strange to be sleeping without the stars overhead, but I was so tired, I dropped off immediately.

Just after dawn, the camp bustled to life. Jeremiah had actually gotten up earlier and was gone. I emerged from our tipi to find Anoki sitting on the ground, waiting.

"Washta wants to see you." He stood and waited for me to follow.

We returned to Washta's tipi, but this time a thin woman sat next to the fire in front of it, wrapped in a blanket. She looked frail and worn, and her skin hung loosely on her. She tried to smile, but her face was tight with pain. Her breath was shallow and labored, but a fire burned in her eyes.

"Welcome, Lieutenant McCarty." She gestured for me to sit next to her.

"You speak English." I sat cross-legged, more across from her than beside her so she wouldn't have to turn to look at me. Anoki settled on her other side.

"Anoki, Otaktay, me learn together." She let out a pained breath. "Better days."

"I imagine," I murmured. "Hopefully, the dwarves can cure you."

She snorted softly and gave me a wry smile. "When I found lump, I know I die soon. I accept. Otaktay does not."

"He loves you," I said. I thought about Ma and how I hadn't wanted her to die of consumption. I'd tried to get her to do everything she could, but there wasn't much. I'd cried both when she passed and often in the weeks that followed. But as a new orphan at fifteen, I'd been too busy trying to stay alive to mourn for long.

"Yes. Too much."

I wondered how that was possible, but didn't know how to ask. Instead, I looked at Anoki, whose eyes were haunted.

"We want medicine for others," she continued. "Too many Sioux die that should not. We want them all to live."

"Even if it means giving up claims to the land?" I knew Otaktay didn't want to do that.

She shrugged dismissively. "Dwarves build in place with no trees. It's all dead wood."

"I like the ring to that," Jeremiah said. I hadn't seen him walk up to the fire, but he'd obviously been standing there for a little while. "'The Deadwood Dwarves.'"

"Yeah," I said with a laugh. "I can see it in one of your books already."

Washta gave Jeremiah a look I'd seen from my mother many a time, the "be quiet now" look. Apparently, it worked on him too, because his grin was replaced with a more serious expression.

"Dwarves build where land not good. Town can stay, for medicine."

I nodded, but then realized she'd referred just to the town and not the surrounding land the dwarves had claimed. I'd seen enough of that to know that once you got away from the town itself, the area away from the deadwood was good for hunting and logging.

"Well," Jeremiah said, "we'll have to see everything the medicine does. We'd best find out soon."

"Was there anything else you wanted?" I asked Washta.

"Yes," she said with a firm nod. "I do not care about medicine, like others. I care for Anoki." She gave him a warm smile, and he sheepishly hung his head. Then she faced me again, and the iron was back in her eyes. "When this done, you let Anoki leave army. He come home. Be where he belongs."

I nodded solemnly. "I will do my best."

"More than your best. You succeed." She flicked one hand in the direction of our tipi "Go. We leave very soon."

Somehow, it felt right to bow when I stood, so I did. Then Jeremiah and I headed off to pack.

———

The Sioux war band surrounded me, Jeremiah, and Washta as we rode across the plain. They brought extra horses, and we switched often. We only stopped briefly for water and the occasional bite to eat. The cold morning gave way to a warm noon and an even warmer afternoon. But we made good time and were back to the original Sioux campsite, the one we'd met the Crow in, about an hour before dusk.

We paused there to let the horses drink and to have some food ourselves. Washta had to be helped off her horse. She looked on the edge of collapse, and I was shocked when I realized she'd tied herself to her mount. When Anoki and Otaktay did help her to the ground, she staggered and nearly fell. Otaktay helped her to a small fallen log while Anoki brought her water and pemmican.

Jeremiah came to my side as we watched the two hulking warriors care for the woman as if she were a delicate flower. Jeremiah looked at them and shook his head with a small sigh.

"Did you ever find out why he left her and joined the army?" I asked him.

"Anoki? No. I actually asked, and he said it wasn't a story he wanted to tell."

"Huh." Given how much he clearly loved Washta, I couldn't imagine him leaving her on purpose. But then I also couldn't imagine being in love like that. I'd found some girls back in Golden City pretty, but I didn't know how to talk to them. I was too poor and too intent on learning to shoot and do whatever else I needed to be able to ride with Cassidy, anyway.

And where had that obsession gotten me?

Cassidy was dead. I was stuck in the army. I wasn't a boy anymore, even if they still called me "Kid." I could shoot well, I supposed. And after that…? After that, I'd have to think about it.

But it didn't look like I'd get much thinking. A Sioux brave raced into our little group and ran to Otaktay. They spoke animatedly, and then Otaktay gave orders to the rest. Soon everyone else was remounting their horses while he and Anoki helped Washta back to her horse.

"Let's help," I told Jeremiah. We hustled over. Jeremiah took the horse's reins and held them steady while the two men lifted Washta up. I took Anoki's place steadying her while he raced around to the other side and helped her get settled.

Then I turned to Otaktay. "What's happening?"

"Crow scout," he spat. "Saw us, ran. We go now before they all come back."

I swallowed hard. With this big of a group, there was no way we'd be able to give them the slip.

TWENTY-ONE

I THOUGHT FAST. As Otaktay and Anoki finished getting Washta settled, she tied herself to her horse once again. I got Otaktay's attention as soon as they were done.

"Let's run for the town," I said. "The Crow can't follow us inside, and we'll be safe."

He nodded and called to his men. Meanwhile, I ran for my pony. It wasn't as fast as the Sioux's horses, so I hoped it could keep up.

We raced through the woods to the grove of stumps and then down the road toward the town. Once again, Washta rode in the middle. I lagged behind, but Anoki and two warriors dropped back with me. If the Crow showed, I wouldn't be alone.

We didn't see the Crow. The town's stark walls came into sight, but we didn't slow. Instead, it seemed the horses quickened their gait.

Then maybe a thousand yards from the gate we heard yells. I turned my head to see Crow horsemen thundering up the road from the west toward us.

Again? We were gonna have a fight at the gate *again*?

But, I realized, they were a lot further off. We'd arrive at the gate just as they got to the edge of decent rifle range. If the dwarves let us in, there'd be no fight.

My pulse raced. Would they let us in? Or would we be trapped outside? They'd let *me* in, but I was in the back of the pack. Oh, God! The dwarves wouldn't see me!

I started yelling, "Let me through! Let me through!"

At first, the Sioux ahead didn't hear or understand. I kept yelling and spurring my pony harder, and finally some of them looked around. Their horses parted, and I dashed between them.

Distant gunshots sounded, but I barely blinked. If the Crow were closer than I thought, there was nothing I could do.

I rode through the mass of Sioux, but the leaders were still far ahead of me. I soon caught up with Washta, who had bent over so she was all but hugging her horse's neck. Jeremiah had drifted off to the side.

Of course! I didn't need to be out front—just far enough from the others that the dwarves on the town walls could recognize me. I yanked the reins to the right and spurred my pony harder until I'd left the Sioux and the road and was almost riding straight at the near corner of the wall itself. I started yelling and waving at the wall instead of the Indians.

Soon, I was close to the foot of the wall. They'd built a little ditch that ran along the length which didn't cross, but instead rode alongside, down toward the gate. The Sioux stretched out ahead and behind.

I prayed the dwarves would open the gate. I hoped for it hard. Then I let out a sigh of relief when I saw the doors slowly swinging open.

The Crow were still a ways off, but getting closer every moment. As the lead Sioux neared the gate, the Crow slowed their own charge and continued shooting. The Sioux, fortunately, kept riding. The first two reached the gates and dashed through

But then one of the horses screamed and went down. Its Sioux warrior jumped free just in time and rolled in the dirt. Those behind were too close, moving too fast. They dodged him and the downed horse and kept on their way. More Sioux made the shelter of the gates.

I raced toward the thrown warrior. More gunshots rang out, and I did my best to ignore them. The screams of the downed horse were harder to block. Instead, I tucked myself low, against my pony. It strained and huffed, but didn't slow.

The thrown Sioux was on his feet, but limping. His horse kept trying to struggle to its feet with no success, but it shielded him from the Crow. One of the other Sioux still on horseback pulled up on his reins and raised his rifle. He started returning fire. I didn't look to see if it was doing any good.

Instead, I closed the distance to the downed man and slowed up enough to extend him a hand. He nearly pulled my arm out of my socket as he scrambled up behind me on the pony, but as soon as he did, I raced for the gate. Other horses blurred by and I caught a glimpse of Jeremiah's blue uniform up ahead. Then we were through the gate and I was bringing the pony to a halt and I—

I paused. The little courtyard on the inside of the gate was ringed with dwarven archers, each with nocked arrows pointed at me and the Sioux.

The gates screeched as they closed behind us. The Sioux on the horse with me tried not to lean against my back, but his balance was off. I looked around and didn't see a single familiar face among the dwarves.

Slowly, I raised my arms.

Dwarves holding torches appeared behind the archers. Dusk was further along than I'd realized, and I was surprised at how much brighter the torchlight made the courtyard. The Sioux's horses shuffled and shifted, but the warriors kept them under control. I looked for Washta—but only caught a glimpse of her in a crowd of others. Everyone seemed to be waiting for something.

With a deep breath, I realized it was me.

A jolt of fear ran up my spine. *Me.* They were waiting for *me.* I almost wanted to throw up. I even felt lightheaded. I felt more scared than I'd been in battles.

But I needed to do what had to be done.

I dismounted. Then I strode to what I sensed was the front of the crowd. My knees wavered, but held.

The crowd quieted and all eyes turned to me.

"Where is Vestri?" I asked loudly. "Vestri?"

The dwarves murmured and one ahead of me frowned and shook his head.

"Alviss, then. Take us to Alviss." I pointed at the cluster around Washta. "Them. Me. Take us to Alviss."

The murmurs increased.

"Alviss! Take us." I pointed at myself and the Sioux again. "To Alviss."

A dwarf pushed between the archers. I let out a relieved sigh when I recognized him. He'd been the officer when we'd first arrived and had summoned Vestri.

"Me, them. To Alviss." I pointed again, and realized that Otaktay had broken away from the crowd and was now approaching on foot. I gestured directly at him. "At least take him and me."

The dwarf said something I didn't understand and motioned for us to follow. When some of the other Sioux started forward, the archers aimed their bows at them. I frowned, as did Otaktay. He said something to his men, and then he and I followed the officer. A troop of dwarves fell in behind.

We were led down to the large building where we'd met with Alviss before. The guards at the door stood alert and regarded Otaktay with some curiosity. He didn't give them more than a glance. Our guide didn't slow either. In a fast minute, we were inside the large room with the big table.

This time, chaos filled the room. Dwarves dashed in and out. Most ran to one of two clusters at each end of the table. The room echoed with the din of all the conversations and it stank of sweat and smoke.

The group at one end parted, and Alviss emerged. He looked worried, very worried, as he made his way over to us. Two heavily-armed bodyguards trailed in his wake.

"We're here," I said in English, "to make a deal. This is Otaktay of the Sioux."

The dwarf next to Alviss murmured something in his ear, and the dwarf leader turned to gaze at Otaktay. He carefully looked him over from toe to head, as if memorizing every detail about him. Alviss frowned and called something back to the table. One of the dwarves in a leather jerkin perked up and replied. A moment later, two dwarves ran off and two others carried chairs toward Otaktay and me. I sat, and after a deep frown, Otaktay did the same. Another dwarf brought a chair for Alviss and placed it a few feet in front of us. Once Alviss sat, his bodyguards took up posts behind him.

Then we waited.

The bustle around the table continued. I glanced at it from time to time, but my gaze kept getting drawn back to Alviss. There was something magnetic about his eyes. Something about the way he held himself. This was not someone to be messed with, I realized.

After about fifteen minutes of uncomfortable waiting, three people bustled in. I let out a relieved breath at the sight of the tallest—Maria. Her blue dress was splattered in dark stains, but she looked okay. If it was blood, it wasn't her own. The dwarf closest to her wore brown robes with similar stains. The third wore no beard, and I had to look twice to realize that dwarf was a heavyset woman.

Once they'd made their way over to us, the two dwarves stood beside Alviss while Maria made her way to me.

"Are you okay?" I gestured at the stains on her dress, which I confirmed were blood now that she was close.

"I'm fine. So are the others. Tell you later." She nodded her head toward the female dwarf. "Eira speaks English well."

The female dwarf waited until she had my attention and then looked to Alviss. He said a few words and then she turned to us.

"Welcome, McCarty of the army and Sioux honored guest," she began.

"Otaktay," I said. "His name is Otaktay."

She bowed her head. "Welcome Otaktay. You have come to discuss our request?"

I blinked. Her English was much better than Vestri's. Why hadn't we met her before? And where was Vestri, for that matter?

Otaktay's familiar scowl returned and he glanced at me.

Okay, so it was up to me. "The Sioux are considering your desire for the land. They wish medicine in return, if it is truly powerful enough. They wish to see a demonstration."

Eira conveyed my comments to Alviss, and they conferred for a bit before she turned back to us.

"You may visit our hospital and see the effects."

"We want to see if it works on one of the Sioux," I said. "A sick woman. She has… a lump that's made her sick."

"Oh, no," Maria murmured.

While Eira and Alviss conferred, I raised an eyebrow in a silent question to Maria, asking if she knew anything, but she just shook her head.

"We do not know if we can cure her," Eira said at last. "If we can, do the Sioux agree that this is our land now?"

"No!" Otaktay's scowl had deepened, and the muscles in his shoulders and arms tightened, but he didn't spring out of his chair.

I held up a calming hand. "What he means is, they do not give up the claim to all land within a day's ride. It must be smaller than that."

Alviss frowned after Eira conveyed my words. He stared at Otaktay and then at me. I set my jaw and stared back.

"Let's see if the medicine works before we figure out the land," I said. "Besides, we also need to deal with the Crow." I jerked my thumb in the direction I thought the gate was. I couldn't help wondering if they were still out there or if they'd gone somewhere else.

For that matter, where were McNab, Brody, Zeke, and Vestri? Maria's words were a bit reassuring, but shouldn't they be here?

"Will the Crow accept our claim?" Eira asked.

I thought back to my conversation with Cheéte, remembering how he wanted to control the trade. That meant he didn't mind them being here, right?

"They agree to your town being here," I said. "They have other conditions."

Otaktay gave me a sharp look.

"Which are?" Eira asked.

"We will have to discuss that with them." I sat up straight and put my hands on my thighs. Then I stared straight at Alviss. He was intimidating, but no more so than my commander, Captain Mercer. So, I refused to show any fear.

"But first," I said emphatically, "we need to cure the Sioux woman."

Our staring contest continued for a long minute before I couldn't help but blink and look away.

Alviss snorted. Then he said something to Eira, whose eyes went wide with surprise. She asked a quick question, and his answer came in emphatic tones.

"We will give your woman medicine," Eira said. "Your men will stay in the quarters we show them. Then we talk more."

I looked at Otaktay, who nodded. Then to Alviss and Eira, "Agreed."

The dwarf in brown robes, who'd been standing silently next to Maria this whole time, stepped forward and said something to Alviss in Dwarvish. After a quick exchange, he glanced back at Maria, but then hurried off.

Maria let out a long breath and visibly relaxed.

"What's that about?" I asked, "and where's McNab and the others?"

"They're fine," she said quietly, so that Eira couldn't hear. "Well, mostly fine. Our team is confined to their quarters. But Vestri is dead."

My gut clenched. Dead? I couldn't imagine that tough dwarf getting killed.

"How?"

"Ask McNab when you see him. They've kept me apart from them." She gestured toward the dwarf in brown robes. "He's been my... keeper. He goes everywhere with me and we treat all the patients together. I think his job is to keep me from learning anything they don't want me to learn."

"Well," I asked, equally quietly, "have you?"

She pursed her lips and glanced at Eira, who'd started into a long quiet conversation with Alviss.

"They have too many wounded," she said, "and too many freshly wounded."

"What?" That didn't make sense.

She nodded. "I treated a dwarf today for a cut that could only have come from an axe or heavy blade. And only within the last day."

I swallowed. The Sioux and Crow didn't use swords or axes, and I knew none of my men would have done it.

So what else were the dwarves hiding?

TWENTY-TWO

I SAT THERE and tried not to let my emotions show on my face. Alviss now spoke with two younger dwarves, while Eira stood nearby and watched us. I was sure the hubbub of the room had kept her from hearing our conversation, but Otaktay's eyes kept darting to Maria and me. I guessed he'd overheard us, but didn't know what to say. Either that, or he didn't want Eira to see us talking.

When Alviss finished, the two younger dwarves came over, along with Eira. Both the new dwarves struck me as boys—thin, with softer features and only wispy beards. The one with the thicker beard had a fresh bandage on his forearm. They all stopped a few feet away, so I stood. Otaktay was on his feet as well.

"We'll get your men and show them to their stables and quarters," Eira said. "They will stay there. Then you," she indicated all three of us, "and the sick woman will come to the hospital."

"Better make it four," I said. "Her husband is with her now."

Otaktay glared at me out of the side of his eyes, but I ignored him.

The younger dwarf gestured for us to follow him. As we left the building, guards fell in around us. We all marched at a steady pace back to the gate.

There we found that all the Sioux had dismounted, and some were even sitting on the ground. Anoki sat cross-legged next to a very tired Washta who held a canteen in her hand. Hope flickered in Anoki's eyes when he saw us. I strode over and filled him and Washta in on our discussion with Alviss. Meanwhile, Otaktay gathered his warriors around and spoke to them.

Jeremiah had been huddled with the warriors, so once I was done with Anoki and Washta, I caught him up on what had happened. He frowned and scratched his head.

"Fresh wounded?" he said. "That doesn't make any sense."

"I know. Who are they fighting? Not us, or it'd be bullet wounds and not blade wounds."

He shrugged agreement. "Besides, there's none of us out here. Except maybe that lost patrol."

I blinked. I'd completely forgotten about them. It'd been weeks since Captain Logan had told us that back at Camp Randall. No one had brought them up—not the Sioux, not the Crow, not the dwarves. So either they'd run into some other trouble or someone was hiding something from us. Either could be true, frankly.

But now we had two lost groups. That lost patrol and Lieutenant Caldwell's group. And I hadn't seen my own team, come to think of it, though Maria said they were fine. Except for Vestri.

I really needed to talk to McNab.

"The dwarves have agreed to let two of the Sioux stay with the horses," Jeremiah continued. "It looks like the rest of us will be confined to one of their barracks, but they said there are others there. I presume McNab and the rest of the team?"

I nodded, but before we could talk further, one of the messenger dwarves came over and motioned for us to join the others. Jeremiah and most of the Sioux were led off by a host of dwarf soldiers. Then our own guide motioned me, Anoki, Washta, and Otaktay to follow him.

The sun finished setting as we made our way quickly through the streets on foot. The dwarves didn't slow, though in the darker shadows it became harder to see where I was stepping. While the dirt street was smooth, the occasional embedded rock or small slope made me wary. After a bit, the dwarves noticed and dropped to a walk.

I thought we'd go to the plaza, but we turned onto a smaller street before we got there. This one had only a couple of doors off of it before it ended in a small courtyard with the first garden I'd seen inside the town. Rows of raised beds of soil were separated by small footpaths. In the dark, I couldn't see what was growing in the dirt, other than it was very small.

We strode through the garden and paused before a set of closed double doors. The lead dwarf knocked, and I looked around while we waited. With all the shadows, I could barely make out anything. Otaktay and Anoki both stood stiffly on either side of Washta, supporting her weight. All three looked ahead at the doors.

When they opened, I was relieved to see light beyond. It was distant, but at least I could see! The dwarves up front had a short conversation, and then we were all ushered in.

We headed down a short, dark corridor that opened up into a larger candlelit room. The air was surprisingly fresh, due to what looked like small windows up near the ceiling, though the ceiling wasn't that high above my own head. Tapestries on the walls dulled the click and clack of our feet on the stone. Except for the left wall, I realized. Polished wooden shelves and drawers lined it from floor to ceiling along its entire extent.

The center of the room itself was surprisingly crowded. Eight short wooden beds formed a small square with only space enough between them for a single person to pass. All the beds held mussed blankets and pillows, but were otherwise empty. A few small wooden tables ringed the beds. Maria, Eira, and a dwarf doctor stood by the nearest. The doctor's head only reached Maria's shoulder, despite her being a small woman.

They gestured at Washta to approach. The dwarf doctor then held up a hand to Anoki and Otaktay when they tried to follow. Clearly, they wanted us to stay back.

Washta sat on the edge of the bed and talked quietly with Maria. After a few words, both women smiled. Then Maria took a half step back, and the dwarf doctor stepped in. He looked into Washta's eyes and ears and then put his fingers on her neck. He asked a few questions, which Eira relayed to Washta. Then he gestured for her to lie down. He poked and pressed her stomach through her clothes and then had her remove her outer layer before continuing it. When he came close to her breasts, he stepped aside and let Maria probe the underside.

Maria frowned. Then she said something quietly to Eira and the doctor. After a quick but seemingly urgent conversation, Maria and Eira came over to us.

"The medicines they have now will not heal Washta," Maria said. "They can remove her pain, but not cure her."

Anoki let out a long ragged sigh.

"We have ideas," Eira said, "but they will take time. They may not work."

"Do what you must," Otaktay said. He turned to me. "We not give land for 'not work.'"

I nodded. I hadn't expected anything else.

"We will try tomorrow," Eira said. "She can stay here tonight. We will take away her pain so she can sleep."

"Can some of us stay?" I asked, with a quick glance at both Indians.

Eira glanced at the guards and then the doctor. They spoke briefly in Dwarvish. Then she looked at the guards again. She frowned before turning back to us.

"One," she said. "As long as he does not leave this room."

I had a suspicion at least one of the guards would be staying, too. But even one was a small victory. And the fact that Eira had said "he" meant she hadn't considered Maria. I hoped that meant Maria had the freedom to poke around.

"Anoki stays," Otaktay said. He didn't look at the other Sioux as he did so. He just stared straight ahead.

I furrowed my brow. "You sure?"

"I take care of warriors. Stay with them. Visit tomorrow."

Anoki bent his head. Then he rubbed his temples. "Thank you."

"Do you need anything?" I asked him. He hadn't brought his haversack or any gear.

He just shook his head and looked longingly at Washta. She seemed to sense it, because she turned and gave him a smile.

The walk from the hospital to the barracks was as quick and as dark as our earlier trip. I stumbled once on an uneven patch of road and cursed softly under my breath. The dwarves barely paused, though one did look back and down. His face was shadowed and I couldn't see his expression, but his body language cried out, "That was stupid!"

I felt the fury in my blood rise. I'd tripped on something I couldn't see! How was that my fault?

But then I quickly took some deep breaths and forced myself to calm down. It'd been a long day. Fatigue was starting to fuzz my brain. I was sure the dwarves thought all sorts of nasty things about us they didn't say. I'd begun to have some nasty thoughts of my own about them.

Besides, I really couldn't see where I was walking. The dwarves acted like I could see just fine…

…because they *could*, I realized. Dwarves could see in the dark!

That gave me a chill. I hadn't seen them fight yet, not really. That battle in front of the gate had been too crazy. But if they could see in the dark, I knew I didn't want to fight them at night.

Not that I wanted to fight them at all, actually. They didn't have guns, for which I was grateful, but if they made their arrowheads out of the same metal they made the swords and knives…

I suppressed a shudder. They would pierce anything.

I couldn't help thinking about that all the way to the barracks.

The dwarves had picked a small building with a dozen small wooden slat beds crammed into the first room. I saw hallways leading out on the far side, but I didn't have much time to look, for as soon as I entered, Zeke stood and gestured for me to come over and join him. I let out a relieved breath as I spotted Jeremiah, Brody, and McNab all sitting on the edges of two beds shoved close together. They stood as well, and I almost ran up to them and hugged them all, except I figured that Otaktay was watching.

I stepped back and gave them all a look over. They were worn, and Zeke had a bruise on his cheek, but otherwise no one had any new injuries. McNab was tired and smug, while Brody buzzed with energy I'd not seen in weeks.

"Boy, is it good to see you," I said. "What happened?"

"We got attacked!" Brody said. "But not by the Crow. They were shooting arrows."

"What?"

"Well, we don't quite know," McNab said. "We were riding through the woods north of here when Vestri toppled off his horse with an arrow in his neck."

"They got my horse," Zeke said, "but we drove them back."

"Them?" I asked. "Who's 'them?'"

"No clue," McNab replied. "They fired a bunch of arrows at us out of the trees, hit Vestri, and then ran away. When Zeke tried to chase them, they shot his horse."

"Better my horse than me," Zeke said. He bowed his head. "If I hadn't turned…"

"The Lord decided it wasn't your time." I smiled, and when he raised his head, he had a small smile as well.

"So we put Vestri's body on his pony and came back here," McNab continued. "The dwarves let us in and then brought all of us here. There's a privy down the hall." He pointed toward the passageway. "There's also another room with a water barrel and some food, but no other doors."

"So this is a prison." My gut tightened at the thought. I couldn't help looking around for windows, but of course there were none. The door we'd come in was now closed. I presumed there were dwarf guards on the other side.

"Yeah," McNab said. "They left us our weapons, but they won't let us leave."

My hand drifted to the Colt at my waist. The others had their own, or their rifles were lying around within reach. Zeke kept one hand on the hilt of his "magic" sword.

I still missed my rifle.

But more than that, I hated being confined. The dwarves were forcing us to do what they wanted, just like the Crow had done to me and Zeke before. I was tired of it. I was a lieutenant in the most powerful army on the continent! And the dwarves were treating us like unruly kids.

Enough of that. I looked around at the men. They were all waiting for me. Brody, with a mix of eagerness and fear on his face. Zeke, with his steady calm. McNab was mostly tired, but he still gave me an encouraging smile. Jeremiah's expression was curious, as if he'd already figured out what we were going to do, and was just waiting for me to say it.

"So…," I said, "If this is a prison, how do we bust out?"

TWENTY-THREE

THE ROOM SEEMED SUDDENLY QUIET, though the Sioux continued to talk and move around on the other side. My team was fully focused on me. From their smiles, they liked what I'd said. They were ready to bust out, too.

Jeremiah was the first to respond. "Even if we get out of this room, where do we go? They'll recapture us quickly if we're just wandering the town."

"True." I really hadn't thought about it, because all I really wanted was to stop being told what to do by the dwarves. But we'd stick out like a giant in a field.

"Yeah, we'd need inside help," McNab said. "Judging from that dwarf shadowing Maria."

"Inside help?" Brody asked. "Oh, you mean one of the dwarves. But why would any of them help us?"

"A bribe," I said. "Maybe if we had some gold…"

Jeremiah frowned. "But we don't."

"But isn't that why they're here?" Brody asked. "Here, as in the Black Hills. Didn't Vestri say they wanted 'all the gold under the ground'?"

I blinked, and then I chuckled. "Of course. Good thinking, Brody." I turned to the others. "Let's go find their mine."

"That could be inside the town," Jeremiah said.

"Maybe," I said with a nod, "but you remember the mines up Clear Creek, right? Even the ones that just were holes in the ground?"

"Not particularly. I haven't spent as much time in Golden City as you."

I grinned. "Well, mines have tailings. So even if the main shaft is inside the town, they have to put the rock they dig out somewhere. And I doubt those tailings are in town."

"Mmm," Jeremiah said. "I like it."

"But they'll stick us with someone like Vestri, if we're not careful," McNab said.

"Which is another reason we need to get out," I added. "We need to find who killed him. If it wasn't us, or the Sioux, or the Crow, who was it?"

"That," Jeremiah said, "is a good question."

We talked a bit more before Brody yawned. Mostly, we realized how little we knew. McNab said Vestri had been shot north and a little east of town, and they'd immediately ridden due south. As a result, they'd never made it further west than we were now.

But we weren't the only ones who'd explored part of the area, I realized. We had a room full of Sioux that claimed these hills as theirs. It'd be stupid not to talk to them. I gestured for Jeremiah to join me, and we walked over to Otaktay.

Most of the Sioux had already settled down for the night. The dwarf beds were too short, so most of them had spread out blankets on the floor. Otaktay had picked a spot against the wall close to the little back hall. He sat with his back against the stone. There was just enough light from a candle at the corner for me to see his face. For once, he looked worn and tired instead of stern. He gave me a curious look as I approached.

I crouched down at his side. "My men were attacked north of town. One of the dwarves was killed."

He looked surprised, and motioned for me to go on. I briefly described what had happened.

"So there's an enemy out there," I finished. "We're going to go look for them. We don't know the area, though. We thought maybe you could come with us."

He nodded, but then frowned. "Washta here."

"Yes," I said, "but she's safe. They're looking after her, and Anoki is with her."

He just snorted.

I realized I'd had enough walking softly around him and Anoki.

"Okay," I said, "I know you haven't wanted to talk about it. But it's time. What exactly is going on between you, Anoki, and Washta?"

He glared at me, but when I refused to blink, he gave a tired shrug.

"Her father was chief," he said. "Chose Anoki for her."

"Yeah… but why'd he leave? And why'd she want him back? And why did *you* want him back?"

"I not want him back. Washta want him back."

I let out an exasperated sigh. "So why did *she* want him back?"

"Husband should be with wife before she die."

I let out another huff of frustration. This was getting me nowhere. I had to try a different approach.

"So," I asked, "why didn't the chief choose you?"

To that, Otaktay tensed. He pursed his lips and stared out into space for a moment.

"Chief not like how I fight Crow. Not then. Now…?" He shrugged.

"Wait a minute," Jeremiah said from over my shoulder. "You were fighting the Crow? I don't remember any reports of this. It was back before Anoki joined the army?"

"Yes." Otaktay looked confused. "You not know? Crow want war with you, when giants first arrive. Want us help. We refuse. They attack us. Then giants cross great river. Follow your army west. But trolls cross river too. Trolls attack Crow. Crow ask Sioux for peace. Sioux agree." He snorted. "Bad. Should not have agreed to peace."

"But the Crow beat the trolls," I said. They must have! I didn't know how many trolls had crossed the Mississippi all those years ago, but there weren't any west of the river now, so they must've been driven back…

"Maybe." He shrugged. "Sioux not help."

"And now your war with the Crow has started again." Jeremiah shook his head. "It's amazing what hate will do."

Otaktay glared at him and then stood. Without another word to us, he walked over to one of his warriors and started talking to him in Sioux.

Jeremiah and I watched him for a bit. Then Jeremiah muttered under his breath, "I didn't mean just him."

I nodded. I was sure the Crow hated Otaktay just as much in return.

I decided the best way to leave was simply to tell the dwarves that's what we were doing. They might try to assign us another "escort" like Vestri, but we could refuse. If they insisted… well, I was sure we could manage something. There were a dozen and a half of us, counting the Sioux. One dwarf wouldn't be a problem.

Besides, there was no point in trying to leave until daybreak. Not when we could sleep on actual beds. Well, some of us. Big Zeke spread his blankets out on the floor and was fast asleep in minutes.

But I also decided we shouldn't all go. Jeremiah, McNab, and I huddled on McNab's bed when I explained my thinking.

"If we leave one of us behind," I said, "then they might get sloppy and reveal some clues about where the rift is. Maybe let him look around. Especially if they think he's not in good shape."

"Well, my back does hurt," McNab said. "When that medicine of theirs wore off, I thought I was gonna fall down in pain."

"Mmm hmm. So they should either give you more or let you stay here."

"I could use the rest," he said with a sigh.

"You didn't used to say that," Jeremiah teased.

"Yeah, well," McNab said, "I'm tired of getting hurt, and I want to get out before I lose a leg or an arm."

"Amputees can still lead good lives." It was a line I'd repeated dozens of times in the hospital, but my gut clenched as I said it.

"I'd rather die," McNab said somberly, "than be a cripple."

Jeremiah just gave him a sour look.

"Well," I said, "tomorrow you get to see what you can learn here in town, while we try to find the mine tailings.

"Good enough for me."

The next morning, I managed to convince one of the sentries to send for someone who spoke English. About thirty minutes later he returned with Eira. She walked slowly in the morning sunlight, her shoulders slumped.

"While you take care of Washta," I told her, "we and the Sioux are going to look for the Crow."

That wasn't quite true, and in fact I was hoping to *not* find the Crow, not with us riding with the Sioux. But if I said we were going to look for Vestri's killers, I knew the dwarves would force some of their own men on us.

Eira tilted her head and looked at me. "And where are you going to look?"

"They came from the west when we rode in. We'll go that way."

She stiffened. "We will get you guides."

"We don't need guides." I hooked a thumb toward Otaktay. "We have the Sioux."

"We will get you guides." She turned without another word and marched off.

Jeremiah came and stood by me. "They really don't want us poking around."

"No. So that's exactly what we're gonna do." I was even more determined now to not have the dwarves shadowing us.

"How?"

"Split up after we're far enough away from the town. We'll break into at least one more group than they have guides."

"Oh, that's clever," he said. "So even if they divide their guides, they can't go with everyone."

"Not unless they send a dwarf for every man here. Which I'm doubting they will."

"Agreed. Let's get everybody ready."

About an hour later, we rode out through the gate with four dwarvish soldiers on ponies. The day was overcast, and Otaktay said it was likely to rain, though not until later in the day. We rode west down the road at a casual pace. Like the road leading east to the grove of stumps, this one was rough-cleared dirt with only a small handful of wagon tracks. The road wound mostly downhill, though the slope wasn't too steep. It twisted and turned to follow the edge of the hill.

As we rode, I tried to talk to the dwarves. None of the four spoke English, though. Not only did they not respond to my questions, but when I made rude comments to provoke them, they didn't even blink. They just either looked at me or the road ahead and ignored me. They could've been faking, but I suspected they just honestly didn't understand me.

We rode until the town was out of sight and then about thirty minutes more. Then Jeremiah, Otaktay, and a bunch of the Sioux warriors peeled off and galloped south. The dwarves started in surprise, and then two spurred their horses to follow.

I grinned. That'd worked a little better than I'd expected.

The rest of us stopped and watched them go until they were out of sight. I moved next to Brody and Zeke. The remaining two dwarves glared at us, but I doubted they could hear us. Still, I pitched my voice low and included some Pig Latin.

"Brody," I said quietly. "Indfay erewhay isthay oadray oesgay." *Find where this road goes.* "Zeke, go orthnay to erewhay Estrivay asway illed-kay." *Go north to where Vestri was killed.* "Look around and see if you can find any clues. Otaktay told his best trackers to go with you."

I nodded toward two of the Sioux, who gave Zeke a casual nod.

"Where are you going?" Brody whispered.

"I'm going to stay right here. There's two of them and three groups of us. They can't follow us all."

"Ha!" Brody actually grinned like a mischievous boy. "We'll outfox 'em for sure." His eyes darted through the remaining Sioux until he spotted the two Otaktay had assigned to him. Brody gestured for them to follow and then spurred his horse. Like a shot, they were off, with another dwarf trailing and furiously trying to keep up.

I smirked at the last dwarf and he just scowled in return. Then Zeke and two Sioux left the road and headed north. Given the hills, they didn't ride hard, but the dwarf's consternation plastered itself on his face. The last two Sioux and I just stood there, on our horses. I tried not to be too gleeful as I watched him look from Zeke to me to Zeke to me to Zeke again.

Finally the dwarf growled something at me. He turned his pony toward me and started ignoring Zeke's party.

Well, that was a bit disappointing. I'd hoped to be in the group without a "guide."

So we sat there, listening to the forest birds and the breeze through the trees, until Zeke's group was good and gone. Then the remaining Sioux and I turned west and headed down the road at a pace just little faster than a walk, the dwarf right on our heels. While I was curious how Brody was doing, I didn't want to be in his back pocket right away.

So it surprised me when we spotted them ahead of us about an hour later. They remained mounted, but were mostly milling around. There appeared to be others with them, though on foot.

Had they run into more dwarves?

It looked like they had, because if it'd been the Crow, there'd have been shooting. But it wasn't clear why the dwarves would've been out here.

Until we got to within a hundred yards or so of them. Then we could see past them, to the right, where a gap in the hills opened into a valley.

And what had to be the largest open pit mine in the world.

TWENTY-FOUR

BEYOND THE CLUSTER OF HORSES, men, and dwarves, the ground dropped away and was nothing but dirt and rock all the way to the far side of the valley. The pit stretched larger than the gap between the Table Mesas near Golden City, maybe a mile or two across, and the sun glinted off its huge stair-stepped walls. I couldn't see any people in it, but the sheer size boggled my mind.

We continued slowly, but it didn't take long for the group ahead to notice us. Brody emerged from the cluster on his pony and waved me forward. Now I could see dwarves on foot as well. I figured they must've been here first.

Well, we'd found at least one thing they'd been trying to hide. Though how they thought they could, I hadn't a clue. The pit was too dang *big*.

"We found what's at the end of the road, sir," Brody said when we were close. His grin was as wide as could be.

"They're mining gold, I presume." I looked over at the pit again. They'd basically ripped out the side of a whole mountain.

He shrugged. "I didn't ask, sir. They, uh, they won't let us by."

"I'm not surprised." I could see now that the dwarves on the ground either had drawn swords or nocked arrows. They weren't pointing them directly at us, but the threat was clear. I glanced around at the Sioux. While clearly tense in their bearing, they didn't do more than stare back at the dwarves. Rifles remained slung over their backs or strapped to their horses.

"So what do we do, sir?"

"Go back." I gestured at the mine. "We're not gonna learn anything else here."

"That's it, sir?"

I turned my horse around. "I'll explain later." I gestured for the Sioux to follow.

We rode slowly and the dwarves on foot didn't follow. The "guides" that had chased Brody and me stayed with us, but both were more visibly upset. They talked rapidly and in angry tones between themselves, but I couldn't understand a word.

That just raised a question in my mind. If they had guards at the mine, why did they need to give us "guides"?

The mine was just too big. Too obvious. I mean, we'd followed the only road in the area straight to it. There's no way the guides could've kept us from discovering it.

And come to think of it, there was no way they could keep us from discovering anything. Maybe if they started a fight, but I was pretty sure they didn't want that. I had to grant that there might be a point where they'd do so, but four dwarves weren't going to stand much of a chance against the dozen and a half of us that had ridden out. Even with their special swords.

Heck, when we'd rode out with Vestri, he hadn't tried to "guide" us or steer us away from anywhere. He'd even helped us find the Sioux. The only time he'd done anything, really, was when the Crow showed up.

I blinked. That was it. That had to be it!

Eira had assigned us guides when I'd said we were going west to look for the Crow. *West* wasn't the important part! The *Crow* were!

The dwarves didn't want us talking to the Crow without them there. Just like the Crow didn't want us talking to the dwarves without them there.

I didn't know why, but I could find that out.

But the immediate question was which way we wanted to ride. I suspected Otaktay and Jeremiah were doing just fine to the south and could handle any Crow as well as their "guides," so we'd go north. We headed back up the road to the spot where Zeke and his two Sioux had left the trail and then did the same.

The hills here were steeper and rougher going. We worked our way up the slope and through the pines, and from time to time one of the Sioux would point to a track or a bent branch. They were regular enough that I figured Zeke's group was leaving us a path.

We didn't catch up to them right away, though. We rode for an hour and a half or so without a single sighting. All we heard were birds and the occasional skitter of a squirrel on a branch. Finally, we reached a small open meadow and the tracks stopped.

The meadow was on a gentle slope, with lots of scruffy grass and a few spiny bushes. At first I'd thought they'd gone straight across, but we couldn't find any indication they had. Not upslope to the east or downslope to the west. I used gestures to suggest the Sioux circle the meadow again and look for signs we might've missed. The two dwarves sat on their ponies a few feet away and talked quietly between themselves.

Brody sidled his pony up next to mine. "So what now, sir?"

"Drop the 'sir,' please. I'm just Billy." After he smiled, I continued, "I don't know what to do," I admitted. I gestured at the Sioux. "I wish some of them spoke English. They probably know the best places around here to look if we can't pick up the trail again."

"This is one of those parts that isn't in the book, right?"

"Yeah," I joked. "The heroes get lost. It's not exciting reading, is it?"

"So we're heroes?"

I snorted. "They say we are." When his eyebrows shot up, I amended things, "Well, they say *I* am. Gave me a medal and everything. But honestly, I was just doing what had to be done."

"But... isn't that what a hero does?"

"I suppose so," I laughed. "Right now, what has to be done is finding out who killed Vestri."

"That... that was scary," he said. "One minute we're all riding along. The next, he's falling off his horse. We never saw it coming." He shuddered. "Dead. Just like that."

"That's right! You were there. Think you can find that spot again?"

His brow furrowed. "I thought we were looking for Zeke."

"We are. But he's supposed to be headed to where Vestri was killed. We can meet 'em there." My stomach clenched at the thought that he might not be there, but I didn't see any other options.

"Well, I think it's that way." Brody pointed northeast. "But I'm not entirely sure."

"Why don't you take point?" I suggested. "Then if you see something familiar, we can change direction."

He nodded. A few minutes later the Sioux came over, shaking their heads. I didn't think Zeke and his two Sioux had just vanished, but they'd stopped making their trail obvious, which disturbed me just as much.

The pine forest of the Black Hills reminded me a lot of the mountains I'd tromped through back in Colorado. The undergrowth wasn't as bad as Kentucky and Tennessee and the air was dry, which I liked. The hills were actually steeper than I expected in spots, but thankfully not impassable for our ponies.

We wound through the trees following Brody's hesitant lead. He stopped a lot to look in all directions, particularly when we reached a small ridge. The dwarves had started riding closer to me, almost flanking me, while the Sioux spread out and continued to look every which way. Once again, I felt a bit alone. Brody was the only one I could talk to, and I didn't want to distract him from figuring out the way forward.

Instead, we trudged along. At midday, we found a small stream where we stopped to water the horses and have a few bites of jerky and dried fruit. Brody decided we'd gone a little too far east and said we needed to head northwest. I didn't see any point in arguing, as I figured we could still easily get back to the town by dark.

We started working ourselves down a slope when Brody suddenly spurred his horse and trotted ahead. He headed for a small rock outcropping, pulled up short, and then turned around.

"I know where we are!" he called. "We stopped here so McNab could rest."

"Great!" I said as we caught up with him. "So how much further do we have to go?"

"About a mile that way." He pointed west, down a little crease in the hills.

"Okay. Let's spread out." I dismounted and waved the Sioux over. Then I started drawing in the dirt. I put two small pebbles in the middle of a circle and then pointed at me and Brody. The Indians crouched next to me and watched. Then I added four small rocks on the circle and pointed to each of the Sioux. I did it again a couple times until they nodded. We'd go west in what I hoped was a silent ring of outriders around the two noisy men. That should give us any warning if someone tried to attack.

The dwarves I largely ignored.

The Sioux seemed to figure out what I wanted. They stood and quickly remounted. Then they spread out, encircling Brody and me. The dwarves remained close to me as we rode west.

And we saw nothing.

We went slowly, with Brody regularly nodding and muttering under his breath as he recognized things. I was mostly worried about an ambush, though I had no real reason to suspect one. Whoever had attacked before probably wasn't still in the area.

At most, I hoped to find Zeke. Just where was he? And why'd he stop leaving the trail? I began to wonder if we'd made a mistake by not searching that area more thoroughly before pushing on. Zeke wasn't the smartest man under my command, but he was dogged. If he'd started leaving a trail, it didn't make sense for him to have stopped.

After what seemed like ages, Brody eventually pulled up. He looked all around and then rode over to a large pine with half-dead branches.

"Here," he said emphatically. "Here's where Vestri was shot." He slid off his horse to examine the ground a few feet from the trees.

"Blood?" I dismounted myself, looped my pony's reins over the branch of a nearby small pine, and walked over.

"I don't see any, but there should be some. Oh, there." He scuttled sideways.

I knelt beside him. The dirt and scattered grass had dark spots on them that could've been dried blood. A lot had already faded or been messed up by animals.

A Sioux war cry split the air. From the south! I jumped to my feet and drew my Colt. The rest of the Sioux, still mounted, charged past, their own screams of fury in reply. A gunshot rang out. Brody started running after the Sioux.

More gunshots!

I didn't want to leave my pony. I turned away from the commotion and—

—watched one of the dwarves slowly fall off his pony, an arrow in his chest.

The other dwarf yelled and turned just in time for an arrow to slam into his shoulder. He tumbled from his horse with another cry.

I dashed forward to my own pony, keeping low to the ground. I couldn't see the archers. Could they see me?

I reached my pony without any arrows coming at me. I peered around it, toward the dwarves and beyond.

The one that'd been hit in the shoulder rolled to his hands and knees, cursing the entire time. He scuttled on all fours toward a short, fat tree, still using the arm that'd been hit. I didn't see the arrow—it must not have penetrated his armor.

But where were the bowmen? Had they seen me?

I had to chance it.

"Brody!" I yelled as loud as I could. "Brody!"

No reply.

The dwarf had gotten behind the low tree. He'd climbed to his feet and drawn a long knife. He stared north, through the trees and up a small slope. My eyes followed his.

Four black-clad figures carrying bows with nocked arrows slowly crept toward us. They were tall and thin—definitely not dwarves. Their heads were covered with hoods, so I couldn't tell if they were Indians, but no Indians had ever dressed like that.

They walked slowly, and then I realized only two moved at a time —the other two stood still and watched, covering them.

With a loud, guttural yell, the dwarf jumped out from behind his tree and threw his knife at the nearest figure. The knife flew true and sank into the figure's chest, just before two arrows hit the dwarf and he went down as well.

Another dark figure ran to the fallen one's side. It knelt and touched its downed comrade's chest. Then it bent closer, brushing its hood back.

I sucked in my breath. The being had a long, thin face, deep black skin, and pointed ears.

Whatever it was, it wasn't human.

TWENTY-FIVE

I STAYED AS STILL as I could. The gunfire to the south had faded, but I didn't dare call out again. I didn't know what these creatures were, but I didn't think I could get all three of them before one of them got me.

"Lieutenant!" It was Brody's voice, behind me, to the south. "Lieutenant!"

Oh, God. I hoped he wasn't running back.

The kneeling figure quickly stood and brought his bow up. All three figures looked forward, toward where Brody had to be. Then one glanced over my direction.

"Human, behind the horse! Come out now!"

Well, at least they spoke English.

I carefully slid my Colt into one of the horse's saddlebags, one that they couldn't see from their side. Then I raised my hands and stepped out from behind the pony. The nearest robed figure—well, I'd call them Dark Ones—lowered his bow and strode forward.

"Your gun," he growled. "On the ground."

"Don't have one." I nodded toward my empty holster.

His eyes narrowed, but his face was too lean to form the sneer that Otaktay wore like war paint.

"Your knife."

I glanced at my waist. I'd forgotten about it, since it was more of a tool than a weapon. Still, I slowly reached down, unsheathed it, and dropped it in the dirt.

As the Dark One approached me, I looked him over more carefully. He wore thin black boots that ended just below his knee and hugged his calf. His cloak hung open, revealing a black leather jerkin and trousers. He had a short sword sheathed at his waist in addition to the bow, which he'd lowered as he walked. When he got about ten feet away, he shouldered the bow and drew his sword.

His sword had the same bright sheen as the one Zeke now carried. I couldn't help but shudder. I was sure it had the "rift fog" that Maria had seen and that same amazing sharp edge.

"Who are you?" I asked. "*What* are you?"

"We are Svartálfr. From Svartalfheim."

"Where the dwarves are from."

He spat. "We are the true rulers of Svartalfheim. The dwarves are mud that walks."

"And what are you doing here?"

He didn't answer. Instead, he closed the distance until his sword hovered a few inches from my chest. He thrust slowly, just enough to make me step back. Then, he waved the sword toward the south, where the others had gone.

I glanced behind him. The other two still had their bows pointed my direction. Even if I somehow got away from this one, they'd shoot me down in no time.

I didn't see any choice. I turned and started marching south. After a few dozen yards, I glanced back to see the two bowmen loading their fallen comrade's body onto one of the dwarves' ponies.

The swordsman snarled, "Keep walking."

So I did.

After about three hundred yards of walking through the trees and going up over one rise and down another, we joined another group of the Dark Ones. I decided I'd have to keep calling them that because I couldn't remember exactly how the one had pronounced their name. There were four new ones scattered along the thin trees. Two stood while the third laid on the ground and the last tended a wound in the downed one's side.

My heart sickened. The first thing I saw were dead horses—the corpses lay everywhere. Then I saw the Sioux that'd come with us lay sprawled all around. From their awkward positions, they had to be dead. Finally, I spotted Brody. He sat cross-legged in the dirt pressing a handkerchief to his nose. His eyes widened when he saw me.

Then one of the Sioux groaned and rolled to his side. They weren't all dead!

"Keep walking," the swordsman behind me said. I hadn't realized I'd stopped, but I did as I was told. I headed straight toward Brody.

"Are you all right?" I asked him as I knelt by his side.

"Tripped." He grimaced. "One of 'em was on me before I could get up."

"Well, you're lucky to be alive."

The wounded Sioux moaned again. I glanced around. The two Dark Ones that'd been trailing behind with the ponies had joined us and were conferring with the swordsman and one of the newer Dark Ones. I realized only one was actively watching us. I stood, stared directly at him, and walked over to the wounded Sioux. I didn't say anything, but my glare dared him to stop me.

The Sioux's eyes widened as I knelt by his side. His face was pale and his breathing shallow. He clutched his gut and his hands and clothes were covered in blood. I reached out, slowly and gently. He shook his head.

"I want to help," I said quietly.

I knew he wouldn't understand the words, but he got the gist. He slid his fingers apart so I could see the wound. I recoiled in shock—it was hideous! I struggled to keep from vomiting as he moved his hand back into place.

"I'm… I'm sorry." I put a comforting hand on his shoulder. My own heart raced as I did so and I tried to keep my breath steady.

I'd been with Ma when she died. I'd held her hand. I'd seen the look in her eyes. The fear as she knew what was coming. It'd shaken me bad, even as I knew there was nothing I could do.

And now I was watching this Indian do the same. And I didn't even know his name.

Old pine needles crunched nearby and I glanced over to see Brody joining me. The Sioux's eyes darted to him and then back to me. Brody's mouth hung open in horror as he knelt by my side.

"This…" He shook his head in disbelief. "This is…"

"Evil," I said flatly. "Letting him die like this is evil."

Brody nervously glanced around, but I was confident none of the Dark Ones had heard us.

"What do we do?" His own breathing had turned shallow, panting.

"We don't panic," I said. I gave the Sioux the best comforting smile I could manage. His eyes were fluttering closed. It wouldn't be long.

But he surprised me. He moved one hand toward his waist. Toward the hilt of his knife. He couldn't reach it, but his eyes pleaded.

"For me?" I asked. I pointed at my chest.

He nodded.

"Stand up," I hissed to Brody. "Distract them."

Brody nodded and then stood. He stretched and waved his arms in a circle. I grabbed the Sioux's knife and slipped it into my boot. Brody waved at the Dark One watching us and then crouched back down.

"Now what?" Brody asked.

I focused back on the Sioux. "What do you want?"

His eyes narrowed. Then they darted toward the Dark Ones. His face turned into a sneer and, after a struggle, he spat.

I was surprised he'd understood me, but I understood him. He wanted revenge.

And a minute later, he died.

The clouds rolled in while the Dark Ones herded Brody and me along. One now rode a Sioux horse, though poorly. He was the injured one and I couldn't tell if his poor horsemanship was due to his injuries or to lack of skill. The rest of the Dark Ones walked, with one in the rear leading the remaining surviving ponies. Seven of them, two of us. The odds were not good.

We trudged about an hour until we came to a small creek flowing down from the east. Then we turned and followed it upstream. The sides of this small crevice stretched steeply up, so that walking was less sure-footed. The trees grew thicker, too—more lodgepole pines that shot straight up. Shade blanketed the whole area and, with the clouds blocking the sun, it was downright chilly.

The Dark Ones didn't seem bothered. They strode on, always far enough away that neither Brody nor I dared lunge for them. They didn't speak but they didn't ignore us. The one behind us kept his sword out and raised it each time I looked back.

Me, I was tired and thirsty. Brody looked the worse for wear. He'd started favoring one leg as they walked.

"You hurt?" I gestured at the leg.

"Banged my knee when I fell. It's starting to ache."

I nodded. Since he could walk on it, he'd be fine, eventually. It clearly hurt, though.

But at least it gave him focus. Me, the dread in my gut had started to grow. The Dark Ones had just left the bodies of the fallen Sioux for the scavengers. Would I find Zeke's body in a similar state? And would they do that to me and Brody?

We approached a tumble of rocks on the hillside and I glanced up and saw another Dark One standing at the highest point. It wasn't much of a vantage point, being lower than the nearby trees, but he still had his bow out. He watched as we approached, and then I saw more.

A small fire burned at the base of the rocks. The light flickered and I let out a relieved breath. Zeke hunched between the flame and the stone. Next to him were the two Sioux who'd ridden out with him all those hours before. They looked tired but unharmed. When they saw us, one tapped Zeke, who looked up.

I couldn't tell if he was happy to see me or not. He smiled, but his shoulders and neck tensed.

"Sit with the others," The swordsman said. His voice was cold and sharp.

Brody and I walked around the fire to Zeke. As we did, I tried to count the Dark Ones. To my surprise, there were only four new ones. One prepared food at the fire while another lay on blankets opposite where Zeke and the Sioux huddled. That Dark One looked injured, too.

The Sioux shifted and I sat next to Zeke. "Are you okay?" I asked.

He slowly nodded. "We couldn't fight 'em. They was all around us before we knew they was there."

"Where?"

"Back in a clearing, that-a-way." He nodded toward the south.

"Ah. We couldn't find your tracks."

"They musta covered 'em."

And done a good job, if the Sioux with me couldn't find them.

The Sioux that were now all dead. Along with the dwarves. Whatever these Dark Ones were, I'd grown to loathe them. Even the Jotun weren't as ruthless about taking life. Maybe not even trolls were as ruthless, just hungry.

The swordsman had sheathed his weapon and stood a few feet away.

"You are Army," he said. "How many of you are there?"

"Here or all together?" I did my best to glare at him, using the practice I'd had with Otaktay and Cheéte.

"Both." He clenched his hands into fists and tried to stare me down. That wasn't going to work.

"Here? Just a few more." No need to give him an exact number. "All together? Millions."

He snorted in obvious disbelief.

"How many are there of you?" I shot back.

"Can you open a rift?"

"Why would I do that?"

"Because if you cannot, you are of no use to us. Like them." He pointed at the Sioux, who just gave him an impassive look in return.

"And if we're of no use, you'll kill us, right? But then the army will come looking for you."

He gave me an evil grin and chuckled. Then he gestured at the lieutenant's bar on my shoulders.

"We have already killed one who wore that," he said. "The army did not come. They will not come if we kill you."

My stomach lurched. I was sure he meant Lieutenant Caldwell.

"On the plains? You killed a man with a brown beard and wavy hair?" I hoped that was a good enough description of the lieutenant.

He acknowledged my accusation with a nod and a thin-lipped grin.

Rage flared. I wanted to kill him. My hand drifted down to my boot. I didn't want to make it too obvious, so I shifted my leg a bit. That'd make it easy to grab the knife. I probably couldn't throw it well enough to matter, but there was no way I was going down without a fight.

"Can you open a rift?" His tone was more forceful. His hand drifted back to the pommel of his sword.

"No." I inched my hand closer to the knife. I figured I had one chance, and it wasn't going to be a good one.

The swordsman snorted and drew his blade.

"Wait!" It was Brody's trembling voice. He gave me a quick sideways glance full of terror before pleading with the Dark One. "He's lying. He can open a rift!"

The swordsman looked from Brody to me and back again.

"He's lying!" Brody repeated. "And I can prove it."

TWENTY-SIX

MY HEART FROZE, and for a moment it seemed like everything else had frozen, too. The Dark Ones stared at Brody. Zeke had started to rise, but remained on his knees. Even the birds and bugs fell quiet.

"I can prove it." Brody's voice cracked. He quickly wiped the sweat off his brow.

"How?" the swordsman asked.

"The book! It's in the book." Brody stumbled to his feet. "Let me show you."

The swordsman scowled. The tip of his blade wavered as he turned his attention to Brody.

My heart raced. "No, Brody!" I scrambled up, letting the knife slide back into my boot against my ankle. "No!"

"We gotta, sir." He trembled as he spoke. "They'll kill us all otherwise. They'll kill us," he repeated. "Please, sir. At least this way one of them dies, too."

"What?" The swordsman had his full attention on Brody now.

"You have to kill one of your own people to open a rift." Brody looked at me, his eyes pleading. "Just like when Billy killed Cassidy to open a rift."

My chin nearly dropped, but I recovered before it did. That was a complete lie! I hadn't killed Cassidy to *open* a rift. I'd killed him to *close* one! Any determined soul could close a rift, I'd been told. But *opening* a rift required the sacrifice of a human witch, which is why there weren't many rifts. Witches were rare enough. Maria was the only one I'd ever met. Witches that were willing to die were even harder to find. Maria did not qualify.

And Brody knew that! It was in the book, too. He was bluffing!

"Brody!" I cried. "No! Don't help them!"

The swordsman now looked from Brody to me and back again.

"I can prove it," Brody pleaded. "It's in the book. Let me show you. It's in the book."

"What book?" the swordsman asked.

"In my saddlebags." Brody gestured toward the ponies. "I can get it."

"No." The swordsman waved his blade at me. "You get this book."

I let out a deep breath. I thought of my Colt. Did the Dark One know which pony was Brody's? I figured he probably did. Besides… I looked around and counted. Five, eight, nine, the tenth Dark One up on the rock, and that didn't count the two wounded. My Colt only held six bullets. I'd have to think of something else.

I had to buy time, so I marched to Brody's horse. I searched through his bags and made a show of doing it. I kind of remembered him putting the book in the front right one, so I went through it last. Then I pulled it out and tapped it.

"Here it is!" I started riffing through the pages. I fervently hoped the Dark Ones couldn't read, but I didn't want to take a chance. I slowed down and looked for the chapters in the back where I'd…

…where I'd killed Cassidy.

My gut twinged, but only a twinge. I didn't have time for more.

I found the chapter and bent the cover back to the exact page. Then I strode back toward the swordsman. When I got close, he sheathed his weapon and held out his hand for the book. I passed it to him and clasped my hands behind my back, which was as non-threatening as I thought I could be.

He bent and squinted in the low light. His lips moved, and then he looked up at me. After I shrugged, he bent his head over the book again.

"I do not understand what this says."

I couldn't help but let out a deep breath. He couldn't read! He could speak English, but not read it!

"Is that the part where you killed Cassidy on the altar?" Brody called.

"Altar?" The Dark One asked.

I nodded. "You have to do a ritual on an altar. It's not well described in the book…" I shrugged.

"You will do this ritual."

"Only if you let my men go." I gestured toward Zeke and the Sioux.

"No."

"You can't sacrifice us," Brody said. "That won't open the rift you want."

I was impressed. That was both clever and true.

"If you kill the Sioux," I said, "you'll open a rift to their heaven. The same with Zeke. You'll need to use one of your own men." I gave him a satisfied smirk.

He studied me. I couldn't tell from his face if he bought it. His features were still too angular and his expressions unfamiliar.

He lowered the book. "It does not matter. We have wounded we can sacrifice."

"You still need an altar."

"We will build one. That is not hard, is it?"

I decided that answering was a bit too dangerous, so I just stood there.

"Join them." He pointed at Zeke and the Sioux. Then he called to two of the other Dark Ones in a language I didn't understand.

I went over to our men, but made a point of sitting as far from Brody as I could. I gave him my best evil glare, which I hoped he realized was fake. He only looked at me once before looking away.

"You really gonna help 'em?" Zeke whispered.

"We're buying time."

"I… suppose so. But we will be saved, I'm sure. I will keep the faith."

"You do that, Zeke." I patted his arm. "You do that."

***

We huddled by the fire well into the night. The Dark Ones didn't feed us, and when I asked if we could get food from our own saddlebags, the swordsman refused. To my relief, they basically left our horses and stuff alone. They were too busy. While one continued to tend to their wounded, and another archer kept a loose watch on us, the rest chopped down two trees and began trimming off their branches. I had little doubt what they were building as they whittled wooden pegs that could fasten their newly felled logs together.

At the rate they were going, they'd have a crude wooden altar by dawn.

I watched them work as best I could. The dim firelight didn't show me much of what they were doing, but they worked steadily. That told me that they could see in the dark as well as the dwarves. I suppose that made sense, if they were from the same world.

But they also seemed to be in a terrible hurry, whereas the dwarves were not. They had the same swords, though. They sliced through the tree limbs like they were carving butter instead of pine.

And as I watched, I began to get real worried. What would they do when a rift didn't open?

***

Hours passed. The night had turned cold, so we were almost freezing unless we were close to the fire. Brody and I had given up any pretense of feuding. The five of us clustered as close as we could to the flames. Despite the worn faces and occasional yawn, it was clear that none of us were going to sleep.

The more we just sat and did nothing, the more the Dark One that was supposed to be guarding us paid more attention to the growing altar than to us. I used one of his distracted moments to pull the hilt of the knife out of my boot and show it to Zeke and Brody. One of the Sioux spotted us and pointed to his own boot. Then he pointed to his friend's.

So… there were five us of us, with three knives between us. And ten of them, armed with bows and those god-awful swords.

Yeah, the odds still weren't good, even if I could get to my Colt.

But, I realized, there had to be other guns around. Zeke, Brody, and the Sioux had all been armed when they'd been captured. Those weapons weren't being used by the Dark Ones. Maybe they didn't know how to use a rifle, but I doubted they'd have just left them in the woods.

I leaned over to Zeke again. "Where'd they put your guns?"

"Bottom of that tree." He nodded with his head. "Behind the guard."

I nodded. That was a good twenty yards, but it could've been worse. They'd moved the ponies even further behind the guard into the woods, so there was actually a chance of escaping if we could get past the guard without getting shot by any of the others. I was acutely aware of the archer atop the rocks that I couldn't see.

Which got me wondering about how well he could see. The darkness of night didn't seem to bother them. The ones working on the altar managed just fine, as far as I could tell. Their silhouettes moved with purpose as they continued cutting the pegs and logs and putting the structure together. But even the best guard couldn't see through trees.

But from the altar's growing height, I was running out of time.

My saving grace was that these Dark Ones really didn't know anything about opening a rift. They wouldn't kill me as long as they thought I could do it. My men… those were expendable to them.

And that's who I needed to save.

The question was when and how. The longer I waited, the more I suspected they'd be watching for me to do something. They knew I'd try. So sooner made more sense.

Besides, I didn't think I could really keep sitting around much longer. Better to do something on purpose than on impulse.

As for what, I had an idea. I leaned into Zeke again. "I'm gonna try something. When I flash my fingers at you, give me a long count of twenty and then distract them."

He slowly nodded.

I took a deep breath and stood. Our guard noticed and called to the others. I walked around the fire toward the altar and the swordsman came to meet me.

"You're gonna need my help," I said. "And I'm not gonna help unless you let my men go."

"If we let them go, you won't help us," he replied. "If you don't help, we will kill them. Slowly. While you watch."

I nodded. I'd been expecting that threat. "You're going to kill us all anyway. What difference does that make?"

"We can make it a swift death."

"If you kill us, the army will come."

He scoffed. "The army did not come last time."

That chilled me. I was even more certain Lieutenant Caldwell was dead.

"But we are here." I gestured at myself and then back at Zeke. "And we are just the beginning."

He stared at me. His nostrils flared and then he slowly shook his head.

"Well, at least let me get my supplies for the ritual. And some food. I can't do it if I'm hungry."

He continued to stare at me. Scowled, really, but his mouth was too pursed. His disdain was all in his eyes. Then he called something to our guard, who walked over.

The swordsman switched to English for my benefit. "Take him to the horses. If he tries anything, cut off his ear."

The guard nodded and drew his sword. Then he gestured for me to lead the way. The ground crunched under my feet and I had to step sideways when we reached the trees to avoid a low branch.

When I did, I flashed my fingers at Zeke.

Then I sped up my pace and started counting myself. I ducked under some branches as I went, which slowed the taller Dark One behind me.

I reached my pony at eighteen. The guard was a full step behind. Nineteen. I undid the flap on my saddlebag. Twenty.

Yells came from behind me.

The guard turned toward the noise.

I thrust my hand into the bag and grabbed my Colt.

He turned back.

I fired, straight at his face.

He dropped immediately. I was already scrambling for his sword before he hit the ground. Shouts came from the camp. With a quick flick of my wrist, I cut the leads tying my pony to a nearby pine. Then I vaulted onto his back. He bucked and shifted—the Dark Ones hadn't bothered to take his saddle off all night, which meant they didn't know how to take care of horses—but he settled and let me spur him into riding away.

I heard shouts—how close were they behind me?

TWENTY-SEVEN

WITH ALL THE TREES, I figured the Dark Ones would have a hard time seeing me in the moonlight. I couldn't see the one on top of the rocks, which gave me a bit of comfort. I rode uphill instead of directly away. After a minute or two, it got too steep, so I slid off and grabbed my sword and the ammunition bag out of my pouch. Then I slapped my pony. It ran ahead—I figured let them track it instead of me. On foot, I started slowly circling around to the top of the rock outcrop.

Despite the cold, sweat beaded on my brow. My heart raced and I kept staring ahead through the gloom, hoping, hoping, hoping, the sentry wouldn't try to come down my way. I was actually relieved when I saw his silhouette against the lighter sky. He appeared to be staring down at the camp. He held his bow, but hadn't aimed it at anything.

He was also at the edge of my range. I leveled my revolver at him and slowly crept forward.

I went slowly, ever so slowly. I lowered each foot as if I was stepping on dried leaves. I didn't know how good his sense of smell was, but I was downwind, which was a relief. As long as he didn't hear me.

I made it to about fifteen yards away when he turned toward me. I fired immediately. Twice.

The gun's bang echoed off the hills as he dropped, but I was already running. I almost fell to the ground when I reached his body. I wanted to stay away, well away, from the edge of the rock.

I didn't have much time to look at the fallen Dark One. His head was a bloody mess—one of my bullets had hit his skull. He'd mangled his bow when he'd fallen, but that wasn't what I was looking for. I rolled him over and found his sword, still in its sheath. I used the sword I'd taken from the other Dark One to slice the cords that held the sheath to his waist.

My heart pounded. I wondered how long I had before another Dark One climbed the ridge.

But with the Dark One's sheathed sword in one hand and my Colt in the other, I crawled forward. It pained me to leave the first sword behind, but I could barely manage as it was. When I got close to the edge of the rock, I peeked just my head over. I'd done no more than spot where the fire was when an arrow whizzed past. I scrambled back as fast as I could.

No second arrow followed, thank God, but yells now went up from the camp.

Seeing the fire had been enough to get oriented. I knew where Zeke and the others were, and I knew they'd be alert after the gunshots. What I needed was a distraction for the Dark Ones.

I felt around for a rock, but didn't find one. Then I snorted to myself. If I needed something to throw, the dead Dark One had plenty of things. I sliced a pouch off his waist—no idea what what was in it— and crawled back to the edge.

This time I stayed back a few feet so I could get on my knees. I hefted the pouch in one hand and the sword in the other. Then I heaved the pouch as far as I could in one direction and quickly tossed the sheathed sword toward where Zeke and the others would be.

I hoped they got it. I didn't think we'd have a lot of time.

There had to be a Dark One working his way up to me, so I took off at a run back down the slope. I picked up the first sword and ran toward where I guessed my pony was. I mentally cursed myself for spurring him on, but I couldn't change that now. I dodged branches and rocks but missed a step and tumbled. My shoulder slammed to the ground and I dropped my Colt. I rolled a couple of times and the sword was jarred out of my other hand. Grass whipped my face. More rocks banged my sides. I finally sprawled on my back against a spiny bush that dug into my leg. The wind had been knocked out of me and I lay there, gasping for breath.

As I did, I heard voices above me, at the top of the ridge. Two deep voices, with words I didn't understand. Which meant that at least two Dark Ones had climbed up from the other side looking for me.

And I'd dropped my weapons.

I looked around for them, doing my best to stare into the dark shadows without moving much. I didn't want to draw attention to myself. I didn't see a thing. I quietly cursed. Why hadn't I waited until morning? When I could see as well as them?

Maybe my impatience had won out after all.

My gun had to be up the hill from me. I'd dropped it when I first fell, and it wouldn't have rolled as far as I had. I was going to have to risk it. Slowly, as quietly as I could, I got to my hands and knees. I kept my eyes up the hill toward where the Dark Ones had to be.

And then I heard something shuffling through the bushes off to my right.

My heart froze and I immediately dropped flat. What else was out here? Of course. My pony! It hadn't gone far in the dark either. Except the Dark Ones had to have heard it, too.

I couldn't hear their voices anymore. I slowly eased myself up the slope on my belly. As I did, I ran my hand back and forth into every shadow, every dark spot.

Then I saw them—two dark figures slowly gliding down the hill—toward my pony. My pulse raced. They'd figure it out in a few minutes. Where was my gun?

I sent up a small prayer. It had to be close. It couldn't have gone far. All I had to—

—the moonlight glinted off something not more than three feet away.

I scrambled that way, but not as quietly as I should've. One of the Dark Ones yelled just as I grabbed my gun.

I rose up and fired. Twice at him, twice at the other. Then my gun clicked on an empty chamber. But to my relief, both Dark Ones were down. With nervous, fumbling hands, I reloaded. I kept watching the spots where they'd fallen as I did.

I got the first bullet into the chamber, dropped the second, and then pulled a third one out of my ammunition pouch. I looked down to make sure I could load it correctly.

When I glanced up, I froze.

One of the Dark Ones was back on his feet.

With a ferocious yell, he raised his sword high and charged. He came at me fast, like a spring storm. I slapped the Colt's cylinder back in, raised it, and fired.

The gun clicked on an empty chamber.

The Dark One roared and lowered his sword in front of him as he ran.

I squeezed the trigger. Nothing. Another empty chamber.

He'd fallen quiet, but there was no doubt he'd seen me. And I was still on my knees. I pulled the trigger again.

Another click!

I threw myself sideways—intentionally rolling down the hill, but with my gun cradled to my chest this time. I briefly lost sight of him, but when I stopped rolling, he was picking his way down the steep slope toward me. Meanwhile, I was flat on my back.

But that meant I just had to raise my arm and fire.

A bullet this time!

My arm kicked back since I hadn't braced it, wrenching my shoulder, but the shot went straight.

The Dark One jerked back as the bullet hit him. Then he wobbled and fell forward. I scuttled sideways as he slid down the slope toward me. When he stopped, he let out a low groan. Then he went still.

I sat up and quickly reloaded all the chambers in my Colt this time. My shoulder ached as I did. I kept looking at both Dark Ones, but neither stirred. I did a quick count—I'd taken out four of them, which meant six more to go. Not counting their wounded.

And not counting Zeke, Brody, and the Sioux. I fervently hoped they were okay.

Once I had the Colt loaded, I lurched to my feet. My ankle

screamed at me—somehow I'd twisted it, and shots of pain went up my leg every time I put weight on it.

I somehow made my way over to the fallen Dark One. I could already smell that his bowels had released, which strangely comforted me. Still, I nudged his body to confirm he was dead.

I had to drop back to my hands and knees to clamber up the slope to the other one's body. This time, I tucked my gun away in its holster so I'd know where it was.

I tried to stand and hop for a bit, but I gave up and went back to crawling. I started to sweat. What if I couldn't walk again? What if this Dark One got up like the other one?

Thankfully, he was dead. Now I just needed to figure out how to not be a sitting duck if more came up.

My pony! If I could get on my pony, it wouldn't matter that I'd hurt my ankle.

But I didn't want to crawl back down that steep slope. It'd take too long. I flexed my foot—it hurt, but not like I'd broken it. I'd probably be fine in a day or two. A day or two that I didn't have.

I needed a crutch. None of the nearby trees had good limbs, even if I used one of the really sharp swords to cut one. But then I snorted.

Just use the sword itself!

I'd lost the one I'd been carrying, but this Dark One had his own, still strapped to his waist. With a bit of wrestling, I managed to roll the corpse over enough to draw the sword and use it to slice the sheath free. It was messy—blood covered most everything and the rank smell had already started. But it worked.

I put the sword back in its sheath and plunged the point in the ground. That was good enough for me to stand. Then, using it as a short cane, I hobbled toward where I'd heard my pony.

Somehow, I made it down to the trees where the animal was. It loomed, a dark shadow among the branches, and snorted and tried to pull away as I approached. Then I realized what the problem was. The reins had gotten tangled on a pine tree branch. Fortunately, it was easy to unwind them without cutting them.

I kept looking around and listening, but I couldn't hear anyone coming. Had the Dark Ones given up? Or were they around and I didn't know it?

It didn't matter. My gun was loaded, and I needed to get on the move.

I opened one of my saddlebags and wedged the sheathed sword into it. It wasn't great, but it'd have to do. Then I pulled myself up on my pony.

And banged my ankle in the process. I clamped my jaw tight to avoid yelling out. I really, really, wished I had some of the dwarves' medicine. Then I cursed myself. I hadn't even checked what the Dark Ones had been carrying. For all I knew, that pouch I'd thrown over the rim had been full of medicine.

I could go back to the other bodies. Search them. I stared through the darkness. A breeze had started to pick up—still light, but enough to make the tree branches I could see shake. I could do it, but it'd take some time.

Which I really didn't have. The longer it took for the two Dark Ones I'd just killed to report to the others, the more likely there'd be trouble for Zeke and Brody and the Sioux. I decided to ride the long way around. It'd take more time, but they'd surely be watching the way I'd fled. That'd be delay enough without me crawling back for something that might not be there.

I snapped the reins and rode into the night. I hoped I wouldn't be too late.

TWENTY-EIGHT

I MADE the big loop around the Dark Ones' camp without trouble. A few night critters scampered away from me as I rode, but I never saw them, and more important, I never saw any Dark Ones. The night air chilled me, but I did my best to ignore it, just like I ignored my ankle as much as I could.

The campfire still flickered, which I took as a good sign. By the stars, I figured we had a few more hours until dawn, and the fire gave me just enough light to navigate by. I'd kept it in the distance, a mere candle between the trees, until I'd circled all the way around from the rock ledge, back to the steep little stream we'd climbed up when we arrived.

Except it was really too steep. I was yards and yards away and the pony was already laboring on the slope. I knew he could make it, but I didn't think he could do so quietly. Which meant I'd have to dismount and go on foot, which I wasn't sure I could do, either.

I flexed my ankle. It still hurt. But maybe it'd been a bad twist and I could still walk? There was only one way to find out.

I found a scraggly bush where I could tie up the pony's reins. If he pulled hard, he could get free, but none of the trees nearby looked much better. Then I slowly slid to the ground.

I winced when my foot hit. It wasn't as bad as before, though. I put a little weight on it, and it held. So a bad twist or maybe a sprain, but that was it.

Not that it still wouldn't slow me down. But with the sword as a crutch again, I could at least walk.

I began slowly working my way toward the distant flame. "Slowly" was an understatement. I suspected I could crawl faster, but this way I at least had my Colt drawn. It was step, plant the tip of the sword in the dirt, take the next step, repeat. At least I was quiet, unless they could hear the labor of my breath. My chest ached, my legs ached, and my arm sometimes shook from holding the Colt out for so long.

Finally, I got close enough to see more than the flickers of firelight. Dark shapes moved ahead of me, past the trees. I paused and checked the wind. The breeze was still very light, but I was now upwind. I hoped the Dark Ones didn't have a dog's sense of smell, but I'd have to chance it. I needed to get closer.

I worked my way past a few more trees so there were only two or three left. It looked like the altar was finished, or at least a dark lump the right height loomed in the darkness. The upright figures were closer to the fire, but I still couldn't make out individuals. I'd have to continue to get closer still. I idly wished I had my rifle. I mentally kicked myself. Why hadn't I taken Brody's rifle off his horse when I'd run? Some hero I was…

…and now, staring at the Dark Ones, I wondered just how stupid I was. I should've gone for help. I should've run while I had the chance. Captain Mercer said the mission came first, and I'd botched the mission by not fleeing when I could. The army and the dwarves both needed to know about these Dark Ones. If they opened a rift, it'd be a disaster!

"Come out, Lieutenant!" It was the swordsman's voice.

I froze. I couldn't believe I'd been seen. And if I had, why hadn't they attacked?

I could still run. I could get away and get help and get rid of these Dark Ones before they opened a rift…

"Come out, Lieutenant," the swordsman repeated. "Come out or your men die."

…but I couldn't leave my men.

A cry pierced the air. Brody's. It continued—full-throated pain, before suddenly stopping.

"That was his ear, Lieutenant. Shall we cut off the other one?"

I couldn't—I couldn't. I was sweating so hard I had to wipe my brow, but both hands were full. I started to tuck my Colt back into my holster and then thought better of it. Instead, I jammed it into my waistband behind my back. After I'd wiped the sweat away, I hobbled forward.

One of the Dark Ones held Brody close on the far side of the fire, the dark one's arms wrapped around Brody's chest. Enough light flickered off Brody's face to show him pale and in pain. Blood covered the side of his head. His eyes found me and he sighed.

I quickly spotted Zeke and the other two Sioux sitting on the ground behind Brody. Two more of the Dark Ones stood on either side of them with swords drawn. The swordsman and another were in front if the fire, facing me. I looked around until I saw the last Dark One, who still knelt by the wounded.

The swordsman strode toward me and I whipped my Colt out. He froze as I leveled it at him.

"Not a step closer," I growled.

"You shoot me, they die." His face was too shadowed to see if he was smiling, but I sure felt the gloat in his voice.

"You're going to kill them anyway." Then I added, "You'll die with them, if you come closer."

He paused, and the tip of his sword wavered.

"If you want me to open the rift, you let them go." I raised my Colt just enough to point at his heart.

"You won't open the rift if we let them go." He gestured behind him and the Dark One holding Brody started shoving him forward. Brody stumbled, but let himself be brought around the fire.

"Then we have a standoff." I fought to keep my eyes on the swordsman, but my eyes kept being drawn to the one bringing Brody up. Worse, my ankle throbbed and I kept wanting to peek down at it.

Brody was in worse shape. He stumbled several times. Behind him, Zeke and the Sioux jumped to their feet when Brody moaned. But the

Dark One didn't let go of him. Finally, Brody and his captor stood right next to the swordsman.

My heart raced. Brody's captor was using him as a shield. I'd be hard pressed to shoot him and not hit Brody. Maybe with my rifle…

"Billy," Brody gasped. "I don't wanna die."

"I don't want you to die either," I replied, "but if I open the rift, they'll kill us all. They can't let us warn the dwarves." I stared at the swordsman. "Can they?"

His shoulders and arms tensed, but he didn't reply.

Brody's captor shifted his grip to Brody's upper arms. As he did, he put himself squarely behind Brody's back. The Dark Ones in the back were moving, too.

And then I realized what they were going to do. They were going to shove Brody forward to distract me and then hit me with arrows. I quickly checked by the fire—yes, the two Dark Ones there were moving to the side so they'd have clear shots.

"Well…," Brody said, "remember what Caesar said about stand-offs. Ivegay ethay ignalsay."

My eyes widened. Pig Latin again. *Give the signal.* As hurt as he was, Brody still had his wits about him.

There was only one thing to do: "Now!"

I fired twice at the swordsman.

Brody dropped low, grabbed his captor's shoulders, and flipped the bigger Dark One over him.

I shot that Dark One, too.

Then I dropped to my knees. Arrows flew through the air, but over my head. A moment later, there were shouts from the fire.

I checked the fight. Brody was repeatedly punching his previous captor in the face, but neither he nor the swordsman I'd shot were moving. By the fire—the ringing clang of metal on metal.

I let out a relieved breath. Zeke had a sword. The big man dueled with one of the Dark Ones—thrusts and slashes were driving the Dark One back. I couldn't see the others.

Brody rocked back on his haunches. I hurried to his side, as best I could. My ankle screamed every step of the way.

"You okay?" I asked. He'd smashed the Dark One's face in. He grinned maniacally in the firelight.

"No." He started to sway unsteadily. "But help Zeke."

I squeezed his shoulder. Then I limped toward the fire.

I didn't see the other Dark Ones. Nor did I see the Sioux—no, I did. One of them was crouched over the wounded Dark Ones. I didn't see the won that'd been caring for them earlier. Meanwhile, the screech of metal on metal echoed off the rocks.

Zeke pressed his foe hard. His arm swung, back and forth, back and forth, with a rhythm that was almost hypnotic. The Dark One parried each time, but with less and less strength.

My heart seized. We'd been taught not to fall into a pattern. A decent opponent would use it against you. So I aimed my Colt at the Dark One. But he and Zeke were too close. I couldn't risk the shot.

Zeke swung back and forth again. The Dark One shifted to a crouch. He'd spotted the pattern!

The Dark One thrust his sword forward, perfectly timed with the pattern—and got it knocked from his hand. Zeke flipped his sword around and sliced into the Dark One's neck. He'd suckered him!

The Dark One dropped. And I couldn't see another one standing. We'd won.

It didn't take long for the somber reality to settle in. One of the Sioux had been killed in the fight. The other had a nasty cut on his upper left arm, which we bandaged as best we could. It'd gone all the way to the bone, though, which made me fear he'd lose the whole arm.

Besides losing his ear, with all the blood covering him, Brody had bruises all over his face and body. The Dark Ones had beaten him, trying to get me to come back. But I'd never heard his cries, and they'd eventually given up.

Zeke had shallow cuts on his forearms and the back of one hand. "Good thing I had reach on him," he'd mumbled as we bound those up.

We were a sorry, wounded lot. But we'd survived. Most of us.

We decided to take the Sioux's body with us. It wasn't easy, strapping it across the horse's back, and it certainly wasn't dignified, but none of us had the heart to let any scavengers get to it. He'd been a hero, even if I'd never known his name.

We also gathered up the swords of the Dark Ones, and I grabbed the swordsman's waist pouch. I briefly thought about searching the bodies more thoroughly, but I was exhausted, and so was everyone else. We put out the fire, got on our ponies, and rode back toward the dwarvish town. We could return in the morning. Or better than that, Jeremiah could return in the morning.

My one worry was running into the Crow. They'd turned up at the gates to the dwarven town twice. Would they be there again?

I guessed they would be, eventually. If they hadn't already tangled with Otaktay and Jeremiah. That seemed like years ago instead of just earlier in the day.

Yesterday. It was almost dawn, which meant it was tomorrow. Or it was today. Or something. I was too weary to think straight. With luck, we'd be okay.

TWENTY-NINE

THE FIRST STREAKS of dawn lit the eastern sky as the walls of the dwarven town came into view. Deadwood. I didn't care what the dwarves called it. The name fit. All stone and rock and no plants. It was a dead, sterile place. I couldn't believe the dwarves wanted to live there.

We wearily rode toward the gate. We didn't see any Crow, for which I was grateful. I didn't think we could race our ponies if we'd tried. Brody barely hung on to his mount. The bandage on the side of his head was crusted with dried blood. Zeke wasn't much better, though he at least sat up straight.

The gates creaked open as we approached. Four dwarves, on foot this time, stood in the entryway. They waited until we were close and then beckoned for us to follow them.

Eira met us in the courtyard behind the gate. She looked anxious and wary, but she was a welcome sight.

"Take us to the hospital," I said. I struggled to not fall off my pony. "We killed the Dark Ones for you."

"Dark Ones?"

"Yeah. They called themselves Svartal-something. They said they were the real rulers of your land."

Her eyes went wide with shock.

"Hospital," I repeated. "Now." I tried to dismount, but stumbled and fell on my rear end. *That* hurt.

Two dwarves rushed to my side. They pulled me to my feet. Eira started giving orders, and after a minute we were all headed down the street. The dwarves let me lean on them, since my ankle was still a mess. The energy that had kept me going started to drain away. I felt like fatigue had slugged me in the head.

Still, we made it to the hospital and into the front room. The dwarves hustled me over to a bed and Brody to another, and I kind of lost track of Zeke and the Sioux. A few minutes later, Maria appeared.

I'd never been happier to see her in my life.

"Where are you hurt?" she asked.

"Sprained ankle." I pointed to it. "The usual cuts and scrapes. And I'm really tired."

She nodded. "I know just what you need."

She stepped back to be replaced by Jeremiah. His dark face was lined with worry, but I smiled with relief.

"You're alive," I said.

"We are," he said. "We had a nasty fight with the Crow, though. I'll tell you about it later. What happened to you?"

"Dark Ones. That's what I call them. They're from the same place as the dwarves. They killed the dwarves and three of the Sioux with us, but we got 'em all in the end." At least I thought so.

He sucked in his breath.

"We left the bodies. You need to go north. There's a rock outcropping up a narrow ravine. Look for an altar."

"They had a rift?"

I shook my head. "Tried to make one, though." I gave him a brief description of what had happened, from when they'd attacked the dwarves all the way through to Brody's Pig Latin. Jeremiah glanced over at another bed where several dwarves clustered around a patient that I couldn't see.

"That was courageous of him," Jeremiah said. "We need to make sure he gets a commendation."

"Yeah." We were gonna have to do a lot of things. But before I could start to plan with Jeremiah, Maria came back with a bottle and a spoon. She gave Jeremiah a look that said "step aside" and he did.

"Take this," she said as she undid the bottle cap and poured a white liquid into the spoon. "We'll work on your ankle while you sleep."

I nodded and accepted the spoon.

"Is that dwarf medicine?" Jeremiah asked.

As I expected, she nodded. The medicine tasted chalky and coated my tongue. It took a couple of tries to swallow it before Maria passed me a glass of water.

"Anything urgent you need to tell us?" Maria asked.

I shook my head.

"Then lie down."

I kicked my boots off and stretched out on the bed. My eyelids already felt heavy, and my mind began to float. It must've been the medicine, but it didn't matter. I was asleep within a minute.

I slowly drifted back to consciousness. The pillow felt too soft against my cheek, I didn't want to open my eyes. Warm and comfortable, I briefly tried to burrow deeper under my blanket. But then the memories of where I was started to surface. I smelled blood and soap. Then I heard the rustle of clothing close by. Reluctantly, I opened my eyes.

Maria sat on a chair a foot from my bed. She smiled at me and smoothed out the top of her nurse's skirt. Her eyes found mine, and hers were steady and calm.

"How do you feel?"

"Better." I flexed my ankle. It didn't hurt. "Maybe a lot better."

"Good. Alviss wishes to speak with you."

I nodded. I wanted to talk with him, too. "How long have I been out?"

"A few hours. You didn't miss anything."

"Is Jeremiah back?"

She shook her head. "But McNab is here, and Otaktay."

Good. I'd want to talk to both of them before Alviss. "How's

Brody? And Zeke?"

"Brody is asleep." She gestured toward a distant bed. "He will recover, except for his ear. Zeke is also asleep, but in the next room. The cut on his arm has been treated."

"Cut?" I sat up in alarm. "His arm? He didn't look wounded."

"His left arm. It was not deep, but it may be infected. However, the dwarves have a medicine that can kill infections."

I let out a relieved breath and sagged back. I became aware of the low hubbub in the rest of the room. All the beds were occupied this time. I could see Washta in the next bed over. She lay on her back, with Anoki in a chair next to her. Their heads were bent close in deep conversation.

"The dwarves do not think they can cure her," Maria said softly. "Not without some special plants they do not have."

I nodded. "What else have you learned?"

"There is a rift," she said quietly. "Their wounded come from it. Whomever they're fighting is on the other side."

"The Dark Ones." I started to fill her in on what had happened, but she held up a hand.

"Let me get McNab so you only have to tell it once."

That made sense. While she headed off, I swung my legs off the bed. I stayed sitting, but I put a little weight on my ankle to test it. It felt fine.

I stood. It still felt fine.

I marveled at how I couldn't really tell that I'd been hurt just a couple of hours before. Well, maybe several hours. I had no idea how long I'd slept.

I sat back down and pulled up my pants leg. The room wasn't as bright as I'd liked, but I slid my sock off and looked more closely at my ankle. Purple and blue bruises covered it, and it was clearly swollen. The dwarf medicine hadn't cured it after all. It'd only stopped the pain.

Maria returned a minute later with McNab. He actually looked rested and refreshed. If his shoulder was still bandaged, it was under his shirt. He smiled and brought up another chair.

"So what happened?" he asked.

I told them the full story, from finding the dwarves' mine to the final fight with the Dark Ones. McNab nodded and asked few questions. As I went on, his expression grew grimmer and grimmer. In contrast, Maria, just nodded her head knowingly.

"Jeremiah and I talked about these Dark Ones before he left," McNab said. "He said that there were two words in that book of his."

"The Edda," I supplied.

"Anyway, he thought they were both names for the dwarves. Guess he was wrong."

"No, but how did they get here? For the matter, how did the dwarves get here?"

"I may know," McNab said. "One of the dwarf guards knows a little English. He let some things slip."

"Like what?"

"Well, there's two groups here, the founders and the rest. Alviss, he's one of the founders. There's maybe a dozen of them. They've been here for a while. Jeremiah thinks they came through the original rift from Jotunheim."

"That makes sense," I said. "A dozen dwarves could've easily avoided us finding them."

"Yeah. Anyway, they wandered around. It seems they don't get along with trolls. We swapped stories about fighting 'em. Then they crossed 'the big river' and came here."

"But why here?" I asked. "I mean, if they were after gold, why not go to California?"

McNab shrugged. "But they didn't build this town until their wizard—that was the word he used—died."

"Ah," Maria interjected. "I was wondering."

"Wondering how they opened the rift?" I blinked. "I just assumed they opened it from their side."

She shook her head. "They can't. Or at least the Jotun can't."

"Why not?" I realized I hadn't thought about it before.

"Dunno," McNab said. "But if they could, we'd have been overwhelmed years ago."

"Which reminds me." I turned to Maria. "The Dark Ones didn't know that I can't open a rift. But can you?"

"Only if I die doing so." She actually smiled. "Something I do not wish to happen."

"No," I quickly agreed. "None of us want that."

Her cheeks actually dimpled when she smiled.

"But what I don't get," McNab said, "is where the Dark Ones came from. Why are they here?"

"We should ask Alviss," I answered. "Or Eira. She was shocked when I mentioned them."

"And speak of the devil," Jeremiah muttered. He gestured toward the door.

The dwarf woman stood in the entryway. When she spotted us, she marched on over. The bright sun spilled through the doorway behind her, which made her look like she was surrounded with white fire. I actually had to blink and let my eyes adjust. Eira didn't slow down. She only came to a stop a short, respectful distance away.

"Alviss wants you," she stated. "Now."

"Is Jeremiah back?" I asked. I made no effort to stand.

Her eyes flashed. "Now."

Her tone grated on me. It got my back up, but I forced myself to take a deep breath and calm my heart. After all, I wanted to see Alviss. It was about time he gave us some answers.

I looked for my boots, found them, and started putting them on. I moved slowly since my ankle was still swollen, despite not hurting. My foot hit the Sioux knife that had been in there earlier, which made me start with surprise. I decided that having a hidden weapon might not be a bad idea, so I shifted it to the side and finished sliding my foot in.

Eira crossed her arms and tapped her fingers on her sleeve. I kept waiting for McNab or Maria to tell me to hurry up but neither of them did. McNab had his arms crossed and was coolly watching the dwarf. Maria had pasted on her calm, unflappable expression. Both seemed happy to wait for me.

Once I had my boots on, I stood. Then I found my Colt and slid it into my holster. I still missed my rifle. McNab wasn't carrying his, but he too had his revolver. He gave me a hardened nod.

I turned to Eira, who looked like she was ready to chew nails.

"Let's go," I said. I gestured for McNab and Maria to follow.

THIRTY

FOR ONCE, light filled Alviss's hall. Apparently it did have windows, or at least the next best thing. Openings high up the walls had been uncovered, which made the room bright. I'd gotten so used to the dim torchlight inside that I was momentarily stunned.

Then I realized that the hall wasn't filled with its usual bustle. Instead, the table was lined with sitting dwarves. To my relief, I spotted Jeremiah, Otaktay, and Anoki all near the head of the table. Alviss himself sat at the end, with two empty seats to his right. When he saw me, he gestured for me to take the one further away.

I took a deep breath. Whatever this was, it was serious.

I headed for the chair that Alviss had indicated. Eira took the chair in between. I relaxed at that—better to have our translator where I could watch her and Alviss at the same time.

As I was seated, a dwarf appeared and placed a small silver goblet in front of me, filled with a dark liquid. I quickly realized that similar goblets sat in front of Alviss and Jeremiah and the Sioux, who were across the table from me. None of them were drinking from them, whatever they might contain. Smart.

Alviss cleared his throat. Then he said something which Eira relayed. She did so quickly and clearly enough that I could remain focused on him.

"We thank you for killing the Svartálfr," Eira relayed. "We deeply regret that they are here in this world, and are grateful to you for what you did."

I nodded slowly. I had too many questions to know where to begin, but it didn't matter. Alviss only paused a moment.

"Your actions have shown that we must have a close alliance with you and the Sioux," Alvis said through Eira. He nodded at Otaktay and Anoki. "We wish to discuss how that may happen."

I nodded again. I wasn't sure what an 'alliance' would mean. They'd already offered to trade, and I didn't see them giving us medicines and swords for free.

"We will reduce our claim." Eira looked directly at Otaktay. "Our town, the mine, all the gold under the ground, and enough land for wood and farming."

Otaktay scowled.

"Washta has already agreed," Eira continued. "In exchange, we give you medicine for two hundred."

I nearly choked in surprise. I looked over at Maria, who was down the table to my left a few seats. Her eyes were just wide enough for me to know this was a surprise to her, too.

"Will they cure Washta?" Otaktay asked.

"No," Eira replied.

To my surprise, Anoki had started shaking his head before Otaktay had even finished the question. He'd already known, which meant we needed to talk.

Otaktay crossed his arms across his chest.

Alviss frowned at him and then said something to Eira in Dwarvish, who listened intently before turning back to the Sioux.

"We know Washta cannot speak for all the Sioux," Eira said, "but we believe this is fair. And this is before trade. We will also trade with you. More medicine and knives for meat and ponies."

"I thought you were getting your ponies from the Crow," I said.

Eira looked at me. Without breaking eye contact, she said something in Dwarvish. When Alviss replied, a small smile crossed her face.

"We do not trade with the Crow anymore," she said. "We believe they work with the Svartálfr."

This caused a round of gasps, from both my team and the Sioux.

But as Eira's words sank in, I realized they kind of made sense. When I was their prisoner, the Crow had said they were taking me to the town, which I'd thought meant the dwarves. But what if they'd been taking me to the Dark Ones instead?

But at the same time, I didn't fully trust the dwarves. They'd lied plenty themselves, and they had their secrets. Eira's words were weaselly, I realized. They *believed*, but they didn't *know*. And as if on cue, Eira continued.

"We wish your help against the Crow," she said. "We believe one of them killed Hilldingr when you arrived."

"The battle at the gate?" Jeremiah asked.

"Yes." Her tone was emphatic.

"The one where I lost my rifle." I'd been thinking about that off and on. If the Sioux had it, they'd've had returned it by now. Cheéte had returned the books, though I suspected Brody's was finally long gone, since we'd left it with the dead Dark Ones. But if Cheéte had my rifle, he'd have had no reason to keep it when he returned the books.

Eira and Alviss exchanged a look. He said a few words and then something to a dwarf next to him, who hurried out of the room.

"We apologize," Eira said to me. "We have found your weapon. One of our soldiers claimed it as his own. He has been disciplined. We are sorry."

Her words were too practiced, too smooth. I didn't believe her for a minute.

But the dwarf who'd left came back in, carrying my rifle. He brought it to me and bowed as he handed it over.

I took a long look at it. They'd cleaned it. I popped it open. It also didn't have any bullets. I wondered if they'd tried to take it apart.

"What about the Army of the West?" Jeremiah asked while I was inspecting my gun. "You've made your offer to the Sioux. Is the offer for the Army of the West still the same?"

Eira frowned.

"Do you want our help with the Crow, too?" he continued. He

shot me a look that said "trust me" before I could object. "That must be worth a great deal more than a handful of swords."

Eira's frown turned into a near sneer. She turned back and exchanged a few words with Alviss before looking back at Jeremiah.

"We will need to confer."

Jeremiah gave me a nod. Apparently we would, too.

"What about Washta?" Otaktay asked.

"We can take away her pain," Eira said, "but we cannot stop the disease within her. We are sorry."

Maria shifted in her seat. She kept her eyes on Eira and her face blank, but it was enough to tell me what Maria thought. I instantly didn't believe the dwarf.

"No help Washta, no deal," Otaktay. He crossed his arms across his chest and pointedly stared into space away from Eira.

But then Anoki leaned forward. He placed one hand on Otaktay's shoulder, who flinched, but didn't pull away.

"We will deal with the Crow," he said. "I am sure you can come up with something more for Washta while we do."

"Excuse me, Private," I gave Anoki a flat stare. "We haven't yet determined if we'll deal with the Crow."

He met my stare without blinking or changing his expression. Then the corners of his mouth quirked up, as if he was holding back some pointed words. The moping man I'd seen hanging around Washta's side was gone. The outspoken gravedigger was back.

"It appears we must both confer," Eira said. "We will provide you with what we know about the Crow's locations and their intent. We will also provide some swords and warriors once you are ready to depart."

"Swords yes, warriors no." I stood. "Send them to our barracks."

A small company of dwarvish warriors accompanied us back to the barracks. The dwarves were clearly unhappy, but I didn't care. They hadn't played straight with us, and I was sick of it. I kind of wanted them to attack us so I'd have an excuse to call them the enemy, like the

Dark Ones. It was always easy in the books. The hero and his team were the good guys and the trolls and Jotun were the bad guys. The good guys killed the bad guys, and it was simple.

This was anything but simple. The only clear bad guys were the Dark Ones. Even the Crow weren't clearly our enemies. Maybe they were Otaktay's, but not mine. Well, not the Army's. Otaktay had said they'd wanted to attack us when the Jotun came, but they hadn't. And could I really trust Otaktay's word on that?

I didn't *like* the Crow, but that didn't make them our enemies. I suspected they had killed the dwarf at the gate simply because they'd been closest. I also figured they had traded with the dwarves in the past. If so, something had gone wrong, and I didn't know what.

Would something go wrong with us?

I hoped not, but the more I thought about it, the more I realized I hadn't gotten very many of my questions answered. The big ones that bothered me were that I didn't know where the Dark Ones had come from or how many more there were still out there. I should've asked Alviss but it'd slipped my mind.

I snorted softly. That was something else that got left out of the books.

When we reached the side road to the hospital, we paused. Maria's dwarvish doctor shadow had turned up somewhere and now stood by her side, along with two armed soldiers, who carried their bows over their shoulders.

"I'll go to the hospital," Maria said. "I don't think Brody should go with you."

I snorted in surprise. "You know where we're going?"

"Yes. You have questions that only the Crow can answer."

I managed to not roll my eyes. Of course she knew that. It was the only logical thing to do. The real question was how.

"Send Brody and Zeke to the barracks if they're healthy enough to travel," I said, "and keep doing what you've been doing." Which mean finding out more about the dwarvish rift.

Maria nodded. Her dwarvish shadow only blinked, which made me suspicious. The Dark Ones had spoken English just fine. Why didn't more of the dwarves?

But maybe they did, and were just hiding it to see what we'd say in front of them.

The Pig Latin was still the way to go. I was pretty sure they couldn't understand that. But I was also looking forward to not having them around at all. Thankfully, once we got to the barracks, our dwarvish escort stayed outside.

I took a few minutes to get re-oriented. It seemed like ages since I'd slept here, but my gear was untouched, tucked under the bed I'd last used. The room had been swept, and the beds on the army side of the room made. I detected McNab's hand in that, keeping things all orderly.

The Sioux had similarly straightened up their side of the barracks, though not with the military precision of the army side. Except they now had notably fewer warriors. They'd lost all but a handful, it appeared. The three survivors huddled around Otaktay and Anoki. All of them looked grim and a bit forlorn.

I grimaced. Anoki was army.

"Anoki!" I called. "Join us!"

He looked over at me and frowned. I glared back.

"Come on, Private!" I waved him over.

His frown turned even more sour and he lumbered over. Instead of sitting on one of the beds like McNab, Jeremiah, and me, he continued to stand.

"Time to compare notes," I said. "Jeremiah, what happened when you and Otaktay rode south?"

He sighed softly and shook his head. He glanced over at Otaktay. Then he lowered his head and spoke softly.

"We found the Crow camp about an hour south, in a little valley with a stream," he said. "They were doing nothing, just resting more or less, but Otaktay charged anyway. He and his men went riding down, firing their rifles. They shot several of them before the Crow could react. Otaktay himself killed two."

"Sounds like him," Anoki said with a frown.

"Yes, but he charged before scouting around. That was stupid, if you ask me."

Anoki snorted. "That's him all right."

"It turned out there was a Crow hunting party nearby. They came riding to the rescue and surprised us. They killed several Sioux before we pulled back."

"How many?" I asked before I thought about it.

Jeremiah pointed behind me. "That's all that's left."

"Stupid." Anoki glared at Otaktay. "He never should have stayed war leader."

"Okay." I glared at him. "What *is* going on with you two? I know you both love Washta, but why'd you leave her?"

"It was the only way to save her life."

THIRTY-ONE

THE FOLLOWING SILENCE STRETCHED ON, with only a few low words from the Sioux on the other side of the room occasionally breaking the stillness. McNab and Jeremiah patiently waited, only shifting a little bit in their seats. Meanwhile, Anoki sat tense, his muscles coiled. His breathing grew shallow. But while I saw the worry in his eyes, I also saw the steel underneath. He silently pleaded with me not to ask.

I did anyway. "How did you save her life?"

He let out a long deep breath and stared at the floor. It took him a minute before he looked up.

"Washta hated the war with the Crow," he said. "She hated that we lost men. Even with Otaktay killing so many of them, we lost many of ours."

"Just like yesterday," McNab murmured.

Anoki nodded. "Even when we won, we lost too many." He looked at me. "She wanted it stopped. So I stopped it."

"How?" I asked.

The scratch of a pencil told me that Jeremiah was now taking notes, as fast as he could write.

"I rode to their camp by myself," Anoki said. "I told them the Sioux wanted peace so that the Crow would be free to fight the trolls."

"Who'd attacked them," I said.

He shook his head. "They attacked the trolls."

"But—"

"They'd heard about Memphis," he said. "I just pointed out that they'd be next once the trolls crossed the river. But the trolls were already across."

"Hit them before they hit you," McNab muttered.

"You must've been very persuasive." Jeremiah tapped his notebook with the end of his pencil.

"No." Anoki hung his head for a moment, but then looked Jeremiah right in the eye. "I bribed the Crow."

"With what?" Jeremiah asked.

"With a stone." Anoki spoke slowly. He looked pained, like every word hurt. "We... the Sioux found some trespassers here. American prospectors. They'd found gold. One of them wrote where on a stone. I knew it'd be valuable to the American government and said they should trade it for guns."

"But they gave it to the dwarves instead." Jeremiah snorted and shook his head.

"We didn't know about the dwarves," Anoki said.

"What happened to the prospectors?" McNab asked.

Anoki clamped his jaw and didn't answer.

"I thought so." McNab leaned back with a scowl.

"Anoki wasn't a soldier then," I interjected. It wasn't hard to figure out what had happened to the prospectors, if the Sioux called them trespassers. But now wasn't the time to hash out old sins.

"So why did you leave?" Jeremiah asked.

"I took the stone," he said with a shrug. "It was the tribe's. I chose exile to end the war."

I blinked. That was... noble. Especially if he was leaving his wife behind, whom he clearly loved.

"So the Crow gave the dwarves the stone, which is why the dwarves are here." Jeremiah furiously wrote it down. "And then they had a falling out."

"I wouldn't put it past the dwarves to have cheated the Crow," McNab said.

"Me neither," I said, "but what do we do? I don't want to fight the Crow." I nodded toward the Sioux. "As much as Otaktay might want to."

"Yeah," McNab agreed. "We don't want war with the Crow or the Sioux."

"We might not have a choice," Jeremiah said. "We've fought alongside the Sioux, how many times now? Three? The Crow might already consider us their enemies."

McNab shrugged in acknowledgement.

"What do you think, Billy?" Jeremiah asked.

"We need to know if the Crow are working with the Dark Ones," I said. "I don't trust the dwarves, but I know the Dark Ones are evil."

"So how do we find that out?" McNab asked.

"We talk to them. Without the Sioux or the dwarves."

"You think that's safe?" McNab asked.

"Even when they had me as a prisoner, they didn't hurt me." I leaned back. "I don't think they want to. Yeah, that's what we need to do. We need to talk to them."

"But how?" Jeremiah asked. "You know the dwarves will assign 'escorts' if we go out, and that splitting up trick won't work again."

He had a point. If I counted Anoki there were six of us. I figured Maria was still best off where she was, and we couldn't count on the Sioux this time. The dwarves could easily spare six warriors to keep us company.

But even then, was it fair to include Zeke and Brody? I didn't know how serious Zeke's wounds were, but Brody'd lost an ear. If it got infected, it could kill him.

I snorted softly. With Maria and the dwarves' medicine, I didn't think an infection was likely.

"I've been thinking about one other thing," Jeremiah said. "The Dark Ones killed Lieutenant Caldwell and his men."

"At least that's what they told me," I replied.

"If the Crow had a part in that," he continued, "then they're already effectively at war with us."

"I… I think they did," I said. "They borrowed my uniform jacket for a while when Zeke and I were prisoners."

"So they may not have done it themselves," Jeremiah said, "but they know about it."

"Yeah… I didn't see much more. But maybe Zeke did."

"Well," McNab said, "let's go find out."

The dwarves were happy to escort us to the hospital. Low clouds had blown in, which made it a tad unpleasant as we walked through the sterile streets. I couldn't help wondering how they managed this. No plants? No decoration? Even Fort Chicago had paint and flags and color. So I felt a little relieved to see the small garden in front of the hospital. In the daylight, the green shoots looked like splashes of life.

Both Zeke and Brody were awake. Zeke was sitting on his bed with his Bible in his lap. Brody still lay on his back, but he turned his head when we approached. The large bandage covering his ear was clean and unbloodied, at least on the outside, which I took as a good sign.

I stopped by Brody's bed first. "How are you feeling?"

"Maria says I'll live." She hovered a discreet distance away and he gave her a familiar admiring smile. Familiar, because I'd smiled that way myself, in awe of her skill.

"You were a hero, you know," I said. "Your quick thinking kept us alive. Both with the book and later."

"I wish I hadn't lost my ear." He blushed as he said it.

"Better your ear than your life. Or all our lives."

Jeremiah coughed. He'd somehow come up behind me without me hearing him.

"What?" I asked him.

He shook his head and then said to Brody, "He's right. You were a hero. When you're ready, I want you to tell me all about it for my next book.

"I'm ready now!" Brody's eyes brightened and he struggled to sit up.

"Well," Jeremiah chuckled. He looked at me for confirmation and, when I nodded, he continued, "Let me get my notebook."

I chuckled, but a part of me actually winced. Would he really write the next book about Brody instead of me?

But then what I'd thought sank in. Did it matter? Before I'd met Cassidy, I'd wanted to be in the books, and now I was. I'd even read the books, and it was like reading about someone else. I'd been there, and I knew I hadn't been half the hero that Jeremiah had made me out to be.

But Brody had believed that, even when I'd tried to dissuade him. And then he'd gone and been a hero himself.

"Um, sir?"

I shook myself out of my thoughts to see Brody looking curiously at me.

"Sorry," I said. "Just thinking. I've got another task for you, and it's a tough one." I bent close, so I could keep my voice low.

His eyes widened. "Yes, sir?"

"We're gonna go look for the Crow," I said. "I need you to stay here and learn what you can. Especially about the rift."

"But how, sir?"

"I've been thinking about that. I'll tell Alviss I need you to go through the things we recovered from the Dark Ones' camp to see if there are any clues about what happened to Lieutenant Caldwell. That'll get you doing more than just lying around in a hospital bed."

"Thank you, sir." Brody smiled. But the blood had been slowly draining from his face and he lay back down.

"One other thing," I said. "You're a hero now. I'm ordering you to live long enough to get your medal, you hear? You don't get to die out here."

That just made him blush more.

"Okay," I said. "We're gonna talk to Zeke."

McNab had already joined Zeke, sitting on the side of the big man's bed. Zeke had closed his Bible but still had his finger in it, marking his place.

"Zeke says the Crow didn't talk about Lieutenant Caldwell," McNab said, "or the Dark Ones."

"They didn't talk," Zeke said. "Not in English. Except that one. The one you was talkin' to."

"Did they understand English?"

"Don't think so. When I was in that fight, I called him a bad name and he did nothing. Like he didn't hear me."

"A bad name?" McNab fought to keep the smirk off his face. "What was it?"

"Not gonna say. But he shoulda fought harder. Or done somethin'."

"So just the leader." Jeremiah nodded knowingly. "That fits."

"What do you mean?" I asked.

"Eira's fluent," he said. "None of the others are. Some of the 'first ones' have learned, but they're worse than the Sioux." He nodded toward Washta's bed, where she sat talking with Anoki, their heads close together. "It takes time and practice to learn a language, and none of them seem to have had either one."

"But Eira's fluent," I said.

"Exactly. How did she learn English so well? And how did your Dark One learn it at all? They couldn't have been here long."

"How do you figure that?" McNab asked.

"They'd've learned how rifts are made," Jeremiah said. "It's not common knowledge, but it's not exactly a secret. The dwarves knew, but the Dark Ones didn't."

"Maybe they know, but they don't have a witch, or… wizard I guess. That's what the dwarves had, right?"

"Hmm." McNab grimaced. "Their camp was pretty crude. If they'd been here for more than a few weeks, they would've done more, like build a permanent latrine or dug a garbage pit."

"They could've just been moving around a lot," I said.

McNab shrugged acknowledgement.

"They're new devils," Zeke said. "They're meaner and nastier than the Jotun. They're more evil than trolls. We gotta fight 'em."

"He's right," I said. I looked at McNab. "My orders were to make sure there was no threat in the army's rear. The Dark Ones are a threat."

"No question," he agreed. "But are there any left?"

"There have to be." I gestured toward the hospital. "Who else would be fighting the dwarves? They're not getting this many wounded from accidents."

"The bigger question is *where* are they getting wounded?" Jeremiah said. "It's not inside the town. I'd have heard or seen something, but I didn't."

Suddenly, realization struck home.

"The battle's on the other side of the rift!" I caught my excitement before I got too loud. "It has to be!"

"Mmm hmm," Jeremiah said. "That's the way I figure it, too. We're behind the lines."

"So why are they here?" Zeke asked. "On this side?"

I nodded. That was the question. And I only saw one way to find out.

"We have to talk to the Crow," I said. "Without the Sioux or the dwarves. That's the missing piece."

"Good thinking to leave the Sioux behind," Jeremiah said. "When we rode off after the Crow earlier, Otaktay made it clear he wanted to kill all of them. He's angry, really angry."

"They attacked a Sioux village," McNab retorted. "He's got a right to be mad."

"But if he attacks the Crow," I said, "we won't get answers."

"Nor will we if the dwarves come along."

"Yeah." McNab snorted. "So how do we keep them away? If Brody and Maria stay here, there's only five of us." He was counting Anoki, which I wasn't sure we could. "The dwarves can spare five men to go with us."

"I know," I said. "So… we just ask them not to come."

THIRTY-TWO

MCNAB and Jeremiah both stared at me like they didn't believe me one bit. The hubbub from the hospital behind me suddenly filled my ears, as I wondered if I'd said something stupid. Both of them were older and more experienced. Both of them had been in more dire straits. But for ridiculous reasons, I was in command.

Maybe they were right. Maybe just telling the dwarves to leave us alone was a bad idea.

But then I caught sight of Zeke's face. Calm. Serene.

"We can't trust 'em," McNab growled. "Just look at your rifle. It's been fired, hasn't it?"

I nodded.

"And they're still hiding things from us," Jeremiah added. "That's not how allies behave."

I sighed. If I asked the dwarves to let us go alone, they'd probably just have us followed. But I didn't see any other way.

"They must choose," Zeke said. "They cannot get in the way of us stopping evil."

I blinked at his words. *They cannot get in the way.*

Yeah. We had a mission. I'd lost sight of that. Our mission was to make sure this town wasn't a threat to Americans. We'd investigated the town and we knew what the danger was. Back when I'd been given my orders, Captain Mercer had worried about a rift to our rear. Now we had one, and if the Dark Ones had their way, we'd have two.

The dwarves had amazing medicines, and those incredible swords, and probably more. I knew that'd help in the war with the Jotun. But at what cost?

"Well…," McNab drawled. "I suppose it won't hurt to ask."

"Let's do it." I stood, and the others did the same. I waved at Anoki, who nodded in reply, said a final word to Washta, and then stood. As he walked over to us. I looked around and, to no surprise, spotted Eira hovering by the door. I strode over to her.

"Take me to Alviss." My tone was firm, and I stared hard at her eyes.

She didn't blink, but then nodded and turned. I gestured for McNab, Jeremiah, Anoki, and Zeke to follow me. A couple of dwarven warriors fell in behind them as we walked out the door.

———

They'd returned Alviss's hall to its previous gloom. One of the upper windows was open, which cast a column of light down onto the far end of the table. The sunlight diffused enough through the room for us to see, but that was all. Clusters of dwarves once again huddled here and there. Smoke from the torches filled the room and made it feel like night instead of day.

Eira marched us right over to Alviss, who was in a conference with two fully armed dwarf soldiers, one of whom had dried blood in his beard from a split lip. Alviss broke away and turned to face us. He himself looked exhausted, but his eyes were still filled with steel as he regarded me.

"The five of us leave now to look for the Crow," I said. "Just us. No Sioux. No dwarves."

As Eira relayed my words, his eyes narrowed. He shook his head and said a few words.

"We will send our soldiers with you," she conveyed.

"No." I crossed my arms over my chest. "You need our help against the Dark Ones. We go alone, or we will not help you."

"We do not need your help," Eira retorted. Alviss hadn't said anything, so she was speaking for herself.

"Then we will go back to Fort Chicago. The Army of the West will not protect you from the Sioux or Crow then."

"We don't need your protection!" Eira shouted, which took Alviss back a bit, and he said a few words to her.

I looked at Jeremiah and McNab. "Let's go." Then I turned on my heel and strode toward the door.

"Stop!" Alviss's voice boomed out, and I blinked. He knew English after all?

But I did stop, and slowly turned. Alviss said something to Eira, but the fury was clear in his eyes.

"You will stay," she said.

I shook my head. "The only way you can make us stay is by force, and if you do that, the army will destroy this town."

"He's right," McNab said. He nodded at me. "If Billy doesn't report back by the end of summer, they'll send a few thousand men here."

"With cannons that can beat down your walls," Jeremiah added.

"The Sioux will help," Anoki said.

"Do you really want to stop us?" I asked. "We go. Alone."

Eira glared at us as she translated our words, but she didn't need to. Alviss understood.

The dwarf leader sneered and then turned and stomped off.

"Let's go," I said quietly to my men. "Before he changes his mind."

It was just the five of us when we rode out of the town gates. I basked in the warm sun on my face and just reveled in seeing the pine trees. It was bright, it was warm, and we were out of the town.

Jeremiah guided us south, toward where he and the Sioux had found the Crow before. He figured they'd have moved their camp, but not too far, unless they'd abandoned the area entirely. I was sure they hadn't. They weren't going to abandon things after everything they'd done so far. The question was whether we could find them.

Which turned out to not be much of a question at all. About an hour before dusk, they found us.

As we rode along a ridge, three Crow on horseback emerged from the trees to our left, about twenty yards away. They stopped as soon as we saw them and leveled rifles at us.

I pulled up on the reins and raised my hands above my head. With some hesitation, McNab and the others did the same.

"We want to talk!" I called in Arapaho.

The three remained still, and a minute or so later, Cheéte rode up behind them.

"We want to talk!" I repeated.

"Why you here?" Cheéte said. His men lowered their rifles, so I lowered my arms. He gestured at Anoki, and then Jeremiah. "Kill us? Kill us all?"

"No," I said. "No kill. Talk."

"They kill us." He pointed at Anoki and Jeremiah again.

"You kill Sioux. You kill dwarves. You not kill us, we not kill you."

He sagged in his seat. "Then why you here?"

"Talk. We don't trust dwarves. Dwarves lie. Want truth." I leaned back in my seat as well and did my best to smile.

"Dwarves lie," he agreed. "Why help you?"

"We not lie. We give you…" I couldn't think of anything we *could* give them. "What do you want?"

"Revenge."

"Against us?" No, that didn't make sense, and he was already shaking his head.

"Dwarves."

"Dwarves?" I couldn't help but snort in surprise. Not the Sioux.

"Dwarves betray us." He looked at Anoki. "We find them. We want knives. We give them rock from Sioux. We lead them here. They promise more knives. Many more. Promise help against Sioux. Ask our shaman to help get more knives. Then shaman gone. Dwarves attack when we seek shaman."

"Oh, God," Jeremiah murmured.

"What?" I said quietly.

"The dwarves didn't open their rift," he said. "The Crow shaman did. Which means they killed him."

Oh, God. He was right. The Dark Ones hadn't known how to open a rift. How would the dwarves? Maria'd said rifts couldn't be opened from the other side, so the dwarves wouldn't have known how before they came here. Even if they'd had a wizard, he would've had to learn somehow, once he was here.

"You work with dwarves," Cheéte said. "Bad. You help us against dwarves."

They'd betrayed the Crow and probably murdered their shaman.

"What about the others?" McNab asked. It was in English, so Cheéte just stared at him impassively.

"What about Dark Ones?" I asked in Arapaho. "Tall. Dark. Pointed ears." I pulled the tips of my own. "What about them?"

He scowled, but wasn't as annoyed as I expected.

"Those ones say they help," Cheéte said, "if we bring you to them. Now?" He shrugged. I didn't know if that meant he knew they were dead.

"Where'd they come from?"

"Inside." He gestured in the direction of the dwarvish town. "They scouts. Surprise dwarves. Enter our world through dwarf door. Want to get back. That why they want you. Offer us much if we help."

Well, that explained a lot. It also confirmed that the dwarves had a rift. And if the Dark Ones were on the other side, I didn't think we could leave it open.

I relayed what he'd said to my team.

"What about Lieutenant Caldwell?" McNab asked. "Do they have any idea what happened to him and his men?"

I turned back to Cheéte. "When we run, back at river. Other army run, too. You know where?"

"They run toward Dark One scouts, so we chase you. We never see them again."

My gut lurched. That just confirmed what I'd feared.

"The Dark Ones had scouts at river?" I couldn't keep the shock out of my voice.

"They look for help with way to their world. We avoid them."

"What'd he say?" Jeremiah asked.

I quickly summarized. As I did, McNab started cursing. The others' faces grew hard.

"I wish we hadn't split up," Jeremiah said, "but we didn't know."

"No," McNab agreed. "I'm glad you killed them, Billy."

Cheéte's horse snuffled and pawed the ground. I couldn't help thinking—the Crow hadn't killed me and Zeke when they'd had the chance. Were they really our enemies, or just the Dark Ones?

"You not help against the dwarves," Cheéte said. From his tone, it wasn't a question.

"No," I said, "but we not help them against you. We not help Sioux against you. We not help you against Sioux."

"Then you get out of way."

"Yes." I gave him a final nod, and then turned my horse.

"What'd he say?" Jeremiah asked as we rode away.

"We're gonna stay out of each other's way."

"Good," Zeke said. "Vengeance belongs to the Lord."

I wasn't quite sure what the Crow had to do with the Lord, but I just snapped my reins and shifted to a canter.

And that's when all hell broke loose.

Gunshots erupted from the trees to our left, along with Sioux war cries. One of the Crow fell from his horse, and the others immediately began firing back into the trees. I whirled around on my horse to see that my team had their guns out, but no one was firing.

Otaktay and his remaining Sioux rode hard out of the trees. One slowed up and fired his rifle and brought down another Crow. The third Crow warrior raced away, leaving just Cheéte.

Who calmly drew a revolver from behind his back and fired at Otaktay.

The big Sioux ducked low on his horse, but then a second bullet slammed into him and he tumbled to the ground.

A gunshot rang nearby. I turned to see Anoki with his pistol out, his eyes fierce.

Cheéte was down.

The remaining mounted Sioux chased after the fleeing Crow into the trees, and like that, the battle was over as quickly as it had begun.

I dismounted and raced over to the Indians. Cheéte was closer, but his eyes were already glassy as he gasped and vomited blood. A moment later, he closed his eyes and went still.

Anoki and Jeremiah were already at Otaktay. The Sioux warrior lay on his back, gasping for breath. Anoki pressed down on a wound in his gut, but the blood flowed around his fingers. Otaktay's eyes were wide.

"It's not good," Jeremiah said.

A shadow fell across us. I looked up to see McNab behind us, a grim expression on his face.

Otaktay said something in Sioux to Anoki, whose eyes opened wide for a moment, but then he let out a long breath and nodded.

"He cannot move his feet," Anoki told us.

"The bullet may have hit his spine," Jeremiah said.

"He does not wish to live like this," Anoki said. He and Otaktay exchanged another deep look, and then Otaktay closed his eyes.

Before I could do anything, Anoki drew his knife and slashed it across Otaktay's throat.

"What!?" I shouted.

Otaktay convulsed and then fell still. Anoki wiped his knife on his now-dead cousin's shirt.

"Better to die than live a cripple," Anoki said as he stood.

"Amen," McNab muttered.

I looked from one to the other, not quite able to believe what I'd heard.

We rode to the town well after dark. We'd taken the time to lay the bodies out on platforms, as was the Sioux custom, according to Anoki. The last surviving Sioux had come back and helped. I'd insisted on laying out Cheéte as well as Otaktay. Somehow it seemed fitting that their final resting places were so close.

We didn't talk much as we worked. Mostly, I was still shocked at what'd happened. I couldn't believe Anoki, but I also couldn't fault him either. The others were somber, but kept their thoughts to themselves.

I hadn't really liked Otaktay, but I'd respected him. He'd been fierce, and as stubborn as me. But around Washta…

…well, that was where I really respected him. He would have given his life for her. And instead, he'd just given his life for Cheéte's.

That felt like a horrible waste. It wouldn't end the war with the Crow. It wouldn't even turn the battle. If I were gonna die before my time, I'd want it to make a difference.

Like Cassidy. My mind couldn't help but drift there. His death had stopped a huge monster from coming into our world.

And then I caught myself. How would we close the dwarves' rift?

Someone would have to die, which was horrible. At least Cassidy had been dying anyway.

I hated the idea. It was horrible. But I couldn't think of anything else. I thought about it the entire ride back.

When we arrived at the gates, the dwarves opened them without a fuss, but as we dismounted, Eira hustled down the street. She had a troop of guards with her, and her glare could've melted steel.

"Did you find the Crow?" she demanded.

"Yes." I touched the hilt of my Colt. "They won't be helping the Dark Ones anymore."

"You took care of them." Her tone still dripped with accusation.

I didn't answer, and my team held their silence too, but one look at the Sioux, who'd ridden out after us, gave her all the answers she needed.

"Good." She crossed her arms across her chest.

"We want to see our wounded," I said. "And then we need to rest. We will meet with Alviss in the morning."

She nodded and then stalked off without another word.

Brody and Washta were both on the beds under blankets when we entered the hospital. Brody snored loudly. I was surprised, because the low buzz of conversation would've kept me awake. Most of the beds that had been empty before were now filled with dwarves. Some moaned or cried softly. Others talked with dwarves standing nearby. Only a few seemed like doctors or nurses. Most were other warriors, perhaps friends.

Maria stood talking with two dwarves in white. She looked haggard and worn. When she saw us, she broke off with a few words and came over. From her stride, I wondered when she'd last slept.

"How's Brody and Washta?" I asked quietly.

"She's a little worse." Maria nodded toward Washta's bed. "She's awake, but resting, if you want to talk to her. Brody is better. He figured something out."

She furtively glanced around. My eyes followed hers, and I realized that the dwarf shadowing Maria lurked against one of the walls.

"The rift?" I quietly asked.

"The wounded come from the direction of the main hall," she quietly said. "The rift must be nearby."

"So what are we gonna do?" McNab asked.

"We're gonna talk to Washta," I said. "She needs to know about Otaktay. And after that… we're gonna do what we should've our first night," I said. "We're gonna march down to that rift and see if the dwarves are bold enough to stop us."

"Or foolish." Zeke said.

When I looked at him, he only grinned.

THIRTY-THREE

I NEEDED to talk to Washta before we left the hospital. Without the dwarves hearing. The dwarvish doctors bustled from patient to patient, but they largely left her alone. Only Maria's watchful shadow and the guards that had brought us here paid us any attention.

"Distract them," I said to Maria, with a nod toward the watchers. "I need a few minutes with Washta." I turned to Anoki. "Join me."

We approached her bed, and she opened her eyes but did not sit up. She looked even more worn than she had the last time I'd seen her.

"How are you doing?" I asked.

"Dying." She gave Anoki a warm smile. He reached down and took her hand.

"They can't cure you?"

"No." She smiled at Anoki again. "I've had a good life."

"I don't know how to say this… Otaktay's dead." I briefly described the battle. She grew somber.

"He died as he would have wished," she said when I came to the end of the story. "He was a good man. A hard man, but a good one." She exchanged a look with Anoki that was deep and full of meaning I couldn't comprehend. Obviously something private.

I nodded. "So… um…" It was harder to find the words than I thought. "You know the dwarves have a rift, right?"

"Yes."

"We need to close it. Do you know what it takes to close one?"

"I've heard the tales."

"Well, um, they're probably true."

"You want me to close the rift."

I let out a deep breath and struggled to find the words.

"What does that take?" Anoki asked.

I didn't want to say it, but I had to. He had to know. I struggled with the words.

"She has to be sacrificed," I finally said. "Then her soul can close the rift."

"I'm going to die anyway." She squeezed Anoki's hand and looked into his eyes. "What are a few days?"

"You could have more than a few days." His tone was fierce, but his voice trembled.

She shook her head and turned to me.

"When the time comes," she said.

"Thank you." I stood. I ached, out of fear and sadness and necessity. I couldn't believe I'd just asked Washta to die. But she was right—she was dying anyway. And we had to close the rift before more Dark Ones came through.

My gut twinged. I wanted those swords and that medicine, but I couldn't let those distract me. They were poisonous bribes. We couldn't trust the dwarves, and if the Dark Ones came through…

I shuddered.

I had my orders, though. This is what I'd been sent out to do. To end any threat to the army's rear. And the Dark Ones coming through was certainly a threat.

"But there is a price," she said.

I shook myself. I'd been lost in my thoughts, but Washta just smiled.

"Tell the dwarves," she said, "that the Sioux require two hundred doses of their special medicine in exchange for the land their town sits on."

"That's it?" I said "Just two hundred?"

"I suspect that is all they can afford to give," she said. Her eyes flicked toward the other wounded in the hospital. "We will give half that to the Crow to end the war."

"But they attacked us!" Anoki protested.

"And they have lost a great number of their warriors," Washta said smoothly. "It will work."

I nodded. This woman had ended a war once. Somehow I was sure she could do it again.

Next was Alviss. I tried to get one of the dwarves, the one that appeared to be in charge of the room, to understand that I wanted to be taken to Alviss, but he didn't seem to understand me. He nodded when I said Alviss's name, but otherwise just stared at me blankly. Eventually, he said something to another dwarf, who took off at a run.

It looked like we'd have to wait.

Maria kept tending patients while Zeke found an out-of-the-way patch of floor and stretched out for a nap.

To my surprise, about a half hour later, Alviss and Eira appeared. I hadn't honestly expected them to come to us. He'd always wanted to meet in his hall, so it was disconcerting to see him here.

I didn't give him or Eira a chance to speak before I approached them.

"The Sioux will grant your claim to the town on one condition. They get two hundred doses of your medicine right now."

They both blinked at me in surprise. Which confirmed Alviss did indeed understand English just fine.

We definitely couldn't trust these dwarves.

"Right now," I repeated.

Eira started to object, but Alviss cut her off with a gesture. Then he said a few words to her. She began to argue, but again he cut her off. With one last grumble, she turned back to me.

"So the army also agrees," she said.

"Yes." If the Sioux agreed, the only thing the Army of the West would care about was the rift, and Washta would take care of that, once we knew where it was.

"We will deliver it to the barracks." She exchanged another few words with Alviss, and then they strode off together without a word.

I motioned for my team, except for Maria and Brody, since he was still asleep. We walked back to the barracks while I thought about what we'd do next. And what the dwarves would do next.

We couldn't trust them. The more I thought about it, the more my gut tightened at the thought of what they might do once we closed the rift. We knew the Dark Ones had killed Lieutenant Caldwell and his patrol, but we didn't know about the first patrol, the one that had gone out before and just disappeared. I wouldn't've been surprised at all if the dwarves had done it.

If we closed the rift, I was sure they could do the same to us.

I shuddered. We needed a hole card.

We arrived back at the barracks to find the remaining Sioux in a small circle talking quietly. They looked up when we entered. I gestured for Anoki and Jeremiah to follow and we headed over.

"Tell them we need them to take the medicine to their village as soon as it gets here," I told Anoki, "and to keep it safe. They also need to take Jeremiah with them." Next to me, Jeremiah stiffened.

"Why?" Anoki asked.

"The Crow have been working with the Dark Ones because the dwarves double-crossed them. If they double-cross us and we're all inside the town walls…"

Anoki's expression turned grim.

"But why do you want me to go?" Jeremiah quietly asked.

"Because you're the writer. You can write down everything that's happened and give letters to some of the Sioux. That way if something happens to you, we can still get word to the army."

"And what do you want me to write?"

I let out a deep breath. "Tell the army there's a rift here and to send as many men as they can spare to tear this place to the ground." I looked at Anoki. "If we're not in the Sioux village by the lone butte in two days, tell them to deliver the letters."

He nodded and conveyed my words to the Sioux warriors. Then they all started to hurriedly pack.

My team gathered on the far side of the room near our own beds. The mood was somber. Even Zeke looked grim. McNab cleared his throat.

"You think it'll come to that, Billy?" he asked.

"Them double-crossing us? Do you trust them?"

He slowly shook his head.

For a moment, as they looked at me, the certainty in my gut gave way to nerves. We could easily all die here. And this time, it'd be my fault. My choice. We could just ride back and report ourselves, save ourselves. Ensure that we all lived.

But that didn't feel like the right thing to do at all. It'd take months for us to report back and return with a sizable force. If the Dark Ones had come through the rift once, how long would it take for them to do it again?

I didn't think we had months.

The men looked at me and waited. I briefly wondered what they were waiting for, and then I snorted softly. They were waiting for orders. I was in charge.

I wondered if Cassidy had found leading a team this hard.

"Get some rest," I quietly told them. "We'll keep a watch, but we'll be watching the dwarf guards. Is there a shift change during the night?"

"There is," McNab said. "Around two in the morning."

"So if we don't get a better chance, we leave around one-thirty and go find the rift. Let's see if they'll stop us."

I was pretty confident they'd try, but I didn't know how far they'd go. They'd generally kept only one or two guards at the barrack doors. If they didn't block the door itself, we could just shove on by them. They'd have to draw weapons to stop us, and I wasn't sure they'd do that.

McNab let out a tired sigh. "Then we're done, right?"

I nodded. I was looking forward to this being over as much as he was, I suspected. Still, I could use some rest. After a long day of riding, I was asleep moments after my head hit my makeshift pillow.

I awoke to McNab gently shaking me. He had his Colt in one hand and his rifle slung over his shoulder. He stepped back from my bed and motioned toward the door. While I put my boots on, he quietly crept over to the entrance. My eyes were adjusting to the dimness and it looked like we were the only ones awake. Jeremiah and the Sioux had long since departed.

I stole to Zeke and gently woke him. Anoki snored on his side but snapped up before I got to him. They all gathered their things while I crept over to McNab. He'd pulled the door open an inch, and he turned at my approach. His eyes were wide and he gestured for me to look through the door

The street outside the barracks stood empty. I'd expected the guards to be on watch there, but I didn't see any. I looked carefully, too.

"Where'd they go?" I whispered.

"Dunno. They were going to accompany Jeremiah and the Sioux to the gate, but they never came back."

Well, now was the time. I took a deep breath, opened the door all the way, and headed out.

I kept to the balls of my feet as much as I could. McNab moved quietly, too. I glanced back to see Zeke a few feet behind McNab and Anoki bringing up the rear. We reached the main street and looked up and down it, but didn't see a single other soul.

A chill hit me. The lack of dwarves was foreboding.

We quietly crept down the street toward the plaza and Alviss's hall. The air was cold, but without a breeze. In the low light, we went slowly. I kept glancing right and left and even behind as I wondered where the dwarves were. I half wished for a lamp or torch, even if it'd give us away.

Just before we reached the plaza, we heard shouts and calls. They sounded alarmed, with notes of panic, though of course I had no idea what they said. We slowed before we turned the last corner, just in case anyone was looking our way, but no one was.

Instead, there was a steady stream of dwarves running between Alviss's hall and a smaller building with double doors to the hall's left. The dwarves running toward the building carried armfuls of arrows and other bundles. The ones stumbling back… carried wounded dwarves.

"There must be a shorter way to the hospital through there," McNab murmured. He pointed at Alviss's hall.

I remembered Maria and the doctor had come down a side hall earlier, and nodded.

We watched for a couple of minutes. There were a lot more dwarves running back and forth than I'd even expected to be in the town. I even saw more female dwarves. I had to look close for the lack of beards, but they were there, helping.

Fortunately, none noticed us, but I suspected that wouldn't last.

"We gotta get in there," I said. "That's where the rift is."

"But there's a lot of them," McNab pointed out. "It'd be a bear to fight our way in."

"So we'll offer to help. They're obviously fighting the Dark Ones in there, somehow."

"Yeah… that could work," McNab said, "but they haven't exactly wanted help before."

"Let's not give 'em the choice." I pulled my rifle off my shoulder and held it across my chest. Then I stepped out into the plaza proper. I gestured for McNab and the others to join me.

We walked slowly, out in the open, and it didn't take long for one of the dwarves to spot us. He let up a cry and ran into the main hall. A few minutes later, Eira, Alviss, and a small bodyguard cohort came out. These dwarves had swords at their waists instead of bows. None were drawn, which I took to be a good sign.

We were about two thirds of the way to the building that had to host the rift when the dwarves moved to intercept us.

"Stop!" Eira held up her hand, palm out, to reinforce her words.

"We've come to help," I said. "We know you have a rift." I gestured toward the building the wounded had been coming out of. "We know you're fighting the Dark Ones. We can help."

Eira relayed my words to Alviss, who scowled.

"We can help." I pointed at myself, McNab, and the others. "We're good fighters."

Alviss's scowl lasted way too long before he finally nodded. He called to a passing dwarf warrior in chain armor and carrying a sword and then said something to Eira.

"Follow Nár," she said to us. "Do what he tells you."

Nár nodded, and from the look in his eyes, I didn't think he understood what Eira said in English, but he gestured for us to come with him as he strode toward what I now thought of as the rift building.

Double doors—smaller than the ones into Alviss's hall—opened up into a small hall with multiple little doors and shuttered windows along its length. I glanced up and saw similar shutters above us, as if trap doors hovered above our heads. The walls were plain smooth stone and ended in another set of double doors. The room was too dim to make out much else.

The room beyond was even darker. I slowed my pace, as did McNab beside me and the others behind. Nár noticed and turned to me. I pointed to my eyes and then the room. He appeared to understand, because after a few words to another dwarf, one of them lit a torch.

I had to blink at the sudden light, but my eyes quickly adjusted. Then I sucked in my breath.

In the middle of the room, maybe ten feet away, a dark grey disk about my own size hovered in the air. Two dwarves with raised swords stood to either side, facing it. As I watched, the grey disk rippled, and then something stepped through. The dwarves tensed and pulled their swords back, but relaxed when an emerging dwarf tumbled to the ground. He was bloody and obviously hurt, but two other dwarves in grey robes were quickly at his side and helping him up.

I glanced around. As expected, a small, low stone table stood off to one side, with unlit sconces on either side. It appeared the altar hadn't been used in some time.

My gut tightened as my eyes returned to the rift. It looked almost identical to the rift I'd seen back in Colorado, but much smaller. The same grey. The same sheen. The same in just about every way except for the size.

Part of me was relieved. No Jotun could get through this rift. As it was, us humans would have to duck to make it through.

Still, the rift existed. Where there shouldn't be one. And the dwarves were obviously in a battle on the other side.

But there were too many dwarves around for us to do anything about the rift. We needed Washta for that, and I wasn't sure how long I could stall while someone ran to get her.

Not long at all, it turned out. Nár said something guttural and pointed to the rift. I quietly cursed the language barrier. Then he pulled a sword from his belt and pointed toward the rift with its tip.

I stared wide-eyed at him, feigning ignorance, but he raised his sword just enough to be threatening. I heard other dwarf warriors draw their blades behind me.

I took a deep breath. We needed a better opportunity. We needed the dwarves to trust us just a bit more.

"Let's go kill some Dark Ones," I snarled as convincingly as I could. I drew my Colt. The others fell in behind me as I followed Nár to the rift.

We paused, just a couple of feet in front. I briefly wondered if that was so someone could come out, but then Nár lowered his sword and stepped through.

I ducked my head and did the same.

The cold struck me first. Not bone cold, but the chill of the morning after a Colorado snowstorm. It was dark, too, but not pitch black. I took a few steps forward, following Nár's general outline as my eyes adjusted. We were in some small stone cavern with dim light from what looked like lichen growing in seams in the wall. At least the footing was even.

There were other beings here, I realized. More dwarves. I looked around, but I didn't stop following Nár. I didn't want to block the way for the others.

After walking about twenty feet, Nár approached a narrow passage. Two fully armored dwarves looked out of it. One turned his head as Nár approached and they exchanged a few words. Then Nár stopped and turned around. He stood as if waiting.

I did the same. Now that my eyes were used to the gloom, I could see that the entire room wasn't particularly large and only a few dwarves were in it. Besides the two guards, three others stood at the ready, weapons drawn. They looked worn but unwounded.

McNab came through the rift, and then Zeke. They both paused to look around and then headed to join me. The sitting dwarves shifted to the walls as Anoki entered as well.

When McNab got close, I asked, "Where do you think we are?"

"Svartalfheim, I'd guess. Jeremiah said it was the home of the dwarves."

That made sense, and that just confirmed my belief that they were fighting Dark Ones.

Nár peered around until he seemed satisfied we were all through the rift. Then he led us down the passageway. It, too, was lit by the strange lichen, which made the tunnel feel more like a vein or an artery of rock than a simple passageway.

We had to walk single file and duck most of the way. Zeke was almost bent double in places. I found myself breathing hard. The air was thicker and far wetter than I was used to, though still incredibly cold. When I breathed out, the cloud of fog was so thick it almost made it hard to see.

We walked for several minutes. We passed some side passages but kept to the main one, which slowly sloped up. Finally, a different grey-ness appeared ahead. It looked like dawn on a cloudy winter day, which I guessed it was as we finally emerged from the cave.

We stood on the edge of a small shaded valley. If there was a sun above, I couldn't see it through the clouds. Not much grew here. Rocks and dirt were everywhere and I saw what looked like it might've been an orchard at one point, but the trees were all burnt husks. Off to the right, smoke rose from what must've been a field of wheat or a similar grain.

Closer by, hunks of rocks and dirt formed a low palisade. dwarvish archers manned it, though they were spaced further apart than I reckoned good. At the moment, they weren't firing arrows, though they had their bows at the ready.

And facing them, in that small valley? Just beyond the range of the dwarvish arrows?

An army of Dark Ones.

THIRTY-FOUR

I GAPED at the army ahead. Hundreds, if not thousands of fully armored Dark Ones stood in ranks with a dozen banners arrayed behind them. In the dim light, they looked like a black wall. A black wall with teeth.

The ones in front held swords and shields. I wondered if there were bowmen behind and figured there had to be. They easily outnumbered the dwarves five or ten to one. The only question was why they hadn't charged.

The answer came a moment later. A distant drum banged, and then the air above them filled with black needles—arrows—arcing high above.

Oh, God! That many arrows couldn't all miss!

"Back!" I yelled. Some of the dwarves around us raised small bucklers over their heads. We humans didn't have any!

We raced toward the cave entrance. Only Anoki, who'd been in the rear, made it.

The arrows slammed down all around us. McNab cried out. One arrow narrowly missed my head—

—and then another sliced through the side of my lower leg.

I stumbled and collapsed, but then Zeke was there. He grabbed me under the armpits and pulled me up. Then he slung me over his back and ran toward the cave. Once we made it inside that narrow entrance, he lowered me back to the ground.

I clutched my leg. The arrow had cut through my trousers—a grazing hit barely more than a scratch, but enough to draw blood. I slammed my hand on the cut to slow the bleeding and then Zeke pulled a cloth strip from somewhere and started tying a bandage around it. I leaned back against the rough stone wall and looked around.

Anoki had his Colt drawn, his back against the wall. His eyes darted from me and Zeke to the entrance. Then he moved to join Zeke.

Where was McNab? Where was he?

I looked around frantically and couldn't see him. There were only a couple of dwarves still in the cave entrance and they were looking out.

Where was McNab?

A dwarf ran up from the depths—one of the robed ones. He handed a small bottle to Anoki and then turned to me and Zeke. He waved again and again for us to head back into the tunnel. It had to be more defensible.

Not without McNab.

"Here!" Anoki held out the bottle to Zeke, who took it and handed it to me.

The liquid tasted bitter and chalky, but it went down smoothly. I took several deep swallows. I was breathing too hard—I had to catch my breath.

Zeke finished binding my leg and I tucked the bottle into a pouch at my waist.

"Get McNab!" I ordered.

"Yes, sir!" He stood, took a deep breath and headed toward the entrance, Anoki at his back.

I could hear more cries from outside. The dwarves in robes started carrying wounded past us.

Then the drums started. Low at first, but they grew in volume as more and more began to pound.

Then chanting. I didn't understand the words, but I understood the tone.

The Dark Ones were about to charge.

And the dwarves would get slaughtered.

I checked my leg. The makeshift bandage was stained with blood, but the pain was gone. Carefully, I eased my way to my feet. I could stand, and even put weight on my leg, but it didn't feel too strong. It didn't hurt, though. That must've been the medicine.

I unslung my rifle and tried to walk slowly toward the cave entrance. I could do it, as long as I stutter-stepped and didn't put any real weight on my injured leg.

I met Zeke and Anoki at the entrance carrying McNab, his arms around their shoulders. My mouth dropped open in shock.

McNab bled heavily from his lower chest. With blood on his back as well, it appeared the arrow had gone clean through him. He looked at me, wild-eyed and delirious, before Zeke and Anoki yanked him past me.

"Save him!" I called back.

"Gotta stop the bleeding!" Zeke called back. Then he carried him back toward the rift.

I didn't have time to watch. I turned back and stumped my way to the entrance. I wondered if I should use a crutch and snorted softly to myself. I didn't have any Dark One swords like last time.

I reached the cave entrance and stared out. The drums had become deafening and the chant crescendoed. The Dark Ones beat their swords against their shields while the remaining dwarves readied their bows.

I didn't know what good it would do, but I shouldered my rifle and took aim at the nearest Dark One. He was at the edge of my range, but he was big.

So… why wait for their attack?

I took a deep breath and steadied by breathing. Then I pulled the trigger and… nothing happened.

I pulled the trigger again. It clicked. Desperate, I flipped the rifle up to look at the breech. It didn't look like a misfire.

And then with a roar, the Dark Ones charged.

They ran screaming toward the dwarves behind their embankment. Some fell to archers as they came, but they didn't stop.

I tried firing again, but just got more clicks. The dwarvish archers ahead of me didn't let up, though. As they ran out of arrows, they stood and ran back toward the cave.

The first few ran past me, but then two stopped and turned. They drew swords and braced themselves and then looked at me. I could sense their question even without words. Was I going to join them?

But what could I do? My rifle didn't work!

I shouldered it and then drew my Colt. The Dark Ones were beyond its range, but I didn't care. I pulled the trigger anyway.

And got another click.

Before I could figure it out, Zeke appeared at my side.

"He's hurt bad," Zeke said. He nodded back down the tunnel. "Anoki's trying to stop the bleeding. Dunno if he can."

"We have to get him out." I pointed toward the dwarves at the cave entrance. "They might hold the entrance for a while, but they'll be overwhelmed."

Zeke looked at them. His eyes narrowed and he set his jaw.

"No they won't." He gave me a quick glance. "You get the Sergeant-Major out." Then he drew his sword and strode toward the entrance.

I hurried down the tunnel toward McNab. Anoki was pressing bandages against his chest, but the blood kept soaking them. McNab was pale and gasping for breath. He looked like he was about to pass out.

We needed to get him to a hospital. We needed Maria!

"Let's carry him the hard way," I said. "I'll get his feet."

"Yes, sir." Anoki shifted behind McNab and took ahold of his shoulders. I grabbed his feet. Then we hurried as fast as we could back down the tunnel.

It took ages. A million heartbeats. A million pulses of McNab's blood, spilling across his chest. I started panting myself and sweat ran down my forehead. Finally, finally, we reached the rift chamber.

To my shock, Eira had come through. She wore burnished chainmail and had a short sword at her belt, but in her hands was a short wooden stick.

I blinked. *No, it was a wand!*

"You're a witch!" I proclaimed.

She glared at me. "Only in this world."

Of course, I realized. Magic didn't work in ours.

"Cure him!" I pointed at McNab. "Use your magic."

"My magic cannot heal." She turned her head as two more warriors strode through the portal.

But they had healing magic! I knew they did!

I did! How could I have been so stupid!

I gestured to Anoki for us to lay McNab down on the rocky floor. I fumbled for the medicine bottle I'd just tucked into my pouch. His eyes had gone glassy and his tongue lolled in his mouth. I wasn't sure he could swallow, but I put the bottle to his lips anyway.

"Drink!" I ordered.

He didn't respond.

I urged him again and tipped the bottle. Then I poured a little into his mouth.

He didn't swallow, so I tilted his head back. I could only hope some of it would trickle down his throat.

He coughed then, and I pulled him close. Anoki had switched places with me and now held McNab's feet, waiting for us to lift him again. I paused to catch my breath. My leg didn't hurt, though I felt weak. I couldn't help shivering. The cave was cold. So cold, I could only hope McNab wasn't freezing.

I checked the bottle again. Nothing else came out.

McNab started to cough, and it wasn't pretty. Blood splattered out with every hack. He had to be bleeding inside, into his lungs.

My own heart raced. How long? How long until someone got here? We needed Maria! We needed her now!

But even as I thought that, I was too afraid to look down. I didn't want to see his face. Couldn't. I'd looked into Cassidy's eyes when he'd died. I couldn't look into McNab's.

Because he was dying. I knew that. Maybe there'd be a miracle in the dwarvish medicine, but I couldn't believe it. Didn't believe it. Not if they couldn't cure Washta. No way they could heal McNab.

McNab stirred and then coughed some more.

"Too…," McNab gasped. "…stubborn…" He sucked in his breath in pain.

"Too stubborn to die," I said. "You keep being stubborn, you hear?"

He tried to laugh, but it turned into a cough. When he recovered, he closed his eyes again.

"You can't die," I told McNab. "You can't die."

"Might… not… have… choice." Then he closed his eyes again.

I held him. Tears filled my eyes and ran down my cheeks. Some probably fell on his head, but I didn't care. Instead, I rocked back and forth, holding him.

Anoki sat patiently, somber. Dwarves scurried back and forth. More rushed into the tunnel than returned, but that was about all the attention I paid.

Instead, memories rushed through my vision. McNab's gruff greeting the first time I'd met him. The time In Louisville when I knew I'd won his respect, because he'd cleaned my gun while I was in the hospital. The way he'd been so excited to be on the road with me, just a short few weeks ago.

I held McNab until he coughed and opened his eyes again. Blood spittled out, which made mine run cold.

"Didn't…," he gasped, "…didn't think I'd go like Cassidy."

"You're not gonna die!"

He tried to laugh, but it just turned into a hard cough. Tears filled my eyes.

"You…" His breathing had gotten more labored. "Stay… stubborn. I'll… close the rift."

Then he fell unconscious again.

I was breathing hard myself. But I knew it. I knew he was right. He wasn't going to make it. And we *had* to close the rift. A few dwarves could protect the tunnel entrance for a while, but there were just too many Dark Ones. Sooner or later, they'd win.

My tears slowly stopped as my mind worked. Finally I took a deep breath. Maybe we could save him and Washta could close the rift. Either way, we had to get McNab out of here.

"Let's get him through the rift," I said to Anoki. "We've got work to do."

THIRTY-FIVE

WE EMERGED BACK into the world, our world, and I let out a deep breath. The rift room felt like a summer day after the cold of the cavern on the other side. Anoki carried most of McNab's weight, with me just supporting his legs. My own leg ached miserably, though it took my weight. I glanced down to see the bandage spotting with blood.

That was bad. Not as bad as McNab, though.

I steered us toward the disused altar I'd seen earlier. We halted a few feet short of it—didn't want to raise suspicions yet—and set McNab down. Anoki crouched by his side. I took the opportunity to check my own wound. It wasn't as bad as I'd thought. I'd just ripped the budding scab off and the pain was back. I retied the bandage tighter and turned to Anoki.

"Keep him alive," I told him. He nodded and fished in a pouch at his waist for another bandage. While he did, I looked for one of the brown-robed dwarves.

I spotted an older one with grey streaks in his long beard and thick hair watching from several feet away. I strode over and he shifted his stance, bracing himself as if expecting a confrontation.

"Maria," I said. "We need Maria!" I pointed at McNab and then toward the door. "Maria," I repeated. "You get Maria."

He furrowed his brow and I repeated my words. He seemed to get it the second time and scurried out. I returned to Anoki.

"We can't close the rift yet," he said quietly. "Zeke's still over there."

I nodded. My commanding officer, Captain Mercer, would've done it in a heartbeat. The mission before the men.

But I wasn't Captain Mercer.

"He took care of me," Anoki said. He started to rise. "I'll get him."

"No," I said. "You could get trapped there, too. We have to close this before McNab dies on his own." Or before any Dark Ones came through, but that was a given. "I'll go. If it starts to look like McNab's not going to make it any longer, you do it."

"But—"

"That's an order."

He frowned but didn't argue. Instead, "How?"

"Put him on the altar. Stab him in the heart." That's all I'd had to do with Cassidy. We could do it again. I rolled my eyes at my own words. I knew it wasn't that easy.

He looked uncertain, so I added, "Maria will help. I'll get Zeke."

I turned before he could object again and strode toward the rift. The dwarf guards just stared at me, but didn't stop me from stepping through.

<hr>

The cold struck me again. I stood and let my eyes adjust. I realized my leg had stopped hurting again, and a shiver went up my spine as I considered the implications. Whatever the dwarf medicine was, it behaved differently in the two worlds. What if taking McNab out of this world had made things worse for him?

I didn't have time to worry. I marched up the tunnel toward the battle as fast as I could. Running was out of the question. Between the low ceilings and the slick stone floor, I had to pay attention to every step. That was good. It kept my mind from wandering to what I'd just ordered.

I had to find Zeke.

Maybe we could save McNab. Maybe Washta would close the rift. Maybe, maybe, maybe.

The one thing that mattered was saving Zeke. I couldn't leave the big man on this side of the rift. I wouldn't be able to live with myself. It'd be too much.

The walk to the tunnel entrance took forever and no time at all. I realized the battle had actually moved inside, short of the exit by a good fifty feet. That portion of the tunnel had a high ceiling, which had allowed Zeke to stand.

Which he did, with a dwarf on either side of him, peeking around him. One fired arrows and the other—the other was Eira pointing her wand past Zeke's ribs.

Zeke himself wasn't actually fighting. His sword was out but he wasn't swinging his arms. When I got close enough to see around him, I realized why. The tunnel ahead of him was nearly clogged with Dark One corpses, from a few feet in front of him to a small bend that obscured any view beyond it.

"C'mon, Zeke!" I shouted. "We gotta go!"

He looked back over his shoulder, as did Eira.

"Let's go!"

"Can't." He tilted his head toward the ceiling. "Too big. Can't duck and fight back there."

"Then duck! Don't fight!"

"No!" Eira screamed. "We can't hold them without him."

"You can't hold them anyway! There's too many." I gestured toward the bodies. "Zeke has to kill every single one that comes around that bend. They only have to get lucky once."

She whipped her wand around and pointed it in my face with a sneer. I sneered back.

Just then something moved up the tunnel. The dwarf archer fired and then cursed. His target had ducked back in time. That distracted Eira.

"Go," I told Zeke. "Give me your sword. I'll cover for you."

"You sure?" He gestured up the tunnel. "They're devils. We gotta stop 'em."

"Yeah," I said. "But do you think God wants you to die here when we can just close the rift?"

"No!" Eira had heard my words.

She turned on me, but I was ready. I batted her wand arm aside, lowered my shoulder, and smashed into her. We slammed into the tunnel wall and her head hit the stone with a loud crack. She slumped to the ground, stunned.

"Grab her and go," I ordered Zeke. I gestured at the dwarf archer, who just stared at me. "We'll hold 'em."

Zeke blinked, but then extended his sword, hilt first. Once I had a good grip on it, he scooped Eira up and ran down the tunnel, carrying her like a sack of potatoes. He'd been right—he was almost bent double as he ran.

With a curse, the archer fired another arrow up the tunnel. This one was rewarded with a yowl of pain. I glanced at the quiver on his back. He had maybe five more arrows left.

But where were the other dwarves? Was he the only one left?

I looked more closely at the corpses filling the passageway ahead and my stomach sickened. Dead dwarves mixed in with dead Dark Ones. The archer might just be the last one.

I moved Zeke's sword to guard position. The blade was light and easy to swing, but I fervently hoped I wouldn't have to. Instead, I motioned to the archer and started backpedaling down the tunnel. His eyes went wide, but he quickly caught on and fell in beside me.

Another Dark One tried his luck peeking around the bend. He quickly ducked back to avoid an arrow. I quickened my pace, the archer with me step for step. Then the tunnel jogged and we lost sight of the bend.

"Let's go!" I turned to run, and made sure the archer was on my heels. I figured we had a minute, maybe two, before the Dark Ones figured out we were gone and picked their way past the carnage Zeke had left behind.

We ran as fast as we could keep our footing, which was agonizingly slow. We heard a yell about the two minute mark, and I judged we were about a third of the way back to the rift. We'd make it with not much time to spare. As long as we didn't trip or fall.

Which I did, turning another bend.

I hit a slick spot of stone and my foot skidded. My momentum carried me forward and I banged into the wall. I dropped the sword and lucked out when it didn't slice into my foot. But in dodging the falling blade, I lost my balance and banged to the ground.

The archer didn't slow down. By the time I'd climbed back to my knees, he was gone. I grabbed the sword, climbed to my feet, and glanced up the tunnel. The bend obscured my view, but I could hear loud voices.

I ran.

I focused on my footing, so I didn't go quite as fast as I wanted. The tunnel somehow seemed longer than it had on the climb up. Still, it had just enough jogs and turns that I never saw anyone behind me in the few times I glanced back. I still heard the yells and calls, but couldn't tell if they were closing or receding. I just needed to get to the rift.

So I kept running. The voices got louder and more excited. They were closing! They had to be!

And then I was in the rift chamber. The two dwarf guards were gone, leaving just the grey disk and me. I skidded to a stop and took one last glance up the tunnel. My heart froze.

Two Dark Ones with drawn swords ran toward me. They moved silently and swiftly and they raised their blades when they saw me.

I was no match for them. I raced to the rift and dived through.

I slammed into the stone floor with more force than I'd expected. I'd expected to tuck and roll, but apparently the floors weren't at the same level on both sides of the rift. Instead, I bellyflopped and banged my chin. One of my teeth caught the underside of my lip and the tang of blood seeped into my mouth. The butt of my rifle strapped across my back banged my hip. I sat up and stared back at the rift.

It hadn't changed. The Dark Ones hadn't followed me through.

I looked all around. The room was crowded with dwarves. I spotted Zeke looming above them, back by the altar. Only the dwarves nearest me gave me more than a glance. Most kept their eyes on the rift.

I scrambled to my feet. I'd dropped my sword again, so I hurriedly picked it up. As I did, I realized that there were fewer dwarves than I'd first thought. Only a dozen or so, because the room wasn't big enough for many more. The ones in front bore swords and shields. The ones behind held raised bows. They seemed to quiver with anticipation.

But the Dark Ones didn't come through.

I worked my way among the dwarves over to Zeke. I blinked when I realized he was by himself, other than McNab, who now lay on top of the altar. McNab's chest rose and fell slightly, but his eyes were closed.

"Where's Maria?" I hissed.

Zeke shrugged. "Dunno. Anoki left a while ago."

This was not good. I turned back toward the rift just in time to see something small and round fly out of it.

And explode.

The blast blinded me, I ducked and twisted around, covering my head with my arms. Dwarvish screams filled the air. I blinked several times until the afterimages faded and I could see again.

Zeke wasn't moving. He'd thrown himself on top of McNab, shielding the older man from the blast. Then he stirred and his arm moved. He was alive!

Most of the dwarves weren't so lucky. Those close to the rift lay shattered on the floor. The ones further back were on their knees. None stood.

The first of the Dark Ones stepped through the rift. He stood tall, and his long cloak made him seem even taller. He scowled in a way that looked like a sneer. His blade shone in the low light. He quickly stepped away from the rift.

I reached for my own sword, but paused. We were on *my* side of the rift now.

I drew my Colt and shot him. Twice.

The bullet caught him in his shoulder, but it was good enough to throw him back. My second shot hit him square in the chest.

Another Dark One stepped through the rift. I didn't even let him get both feet planted. He dropped without a word. Another came through right after him. He spotted me an instant before I fired, but it did him no good. I shot him right in the heart.

As he fell, he flipped backwards and his body disappeared back through the rift.

I waited three heartbeats but no more stepped through. As I did, Zeke stirred and stood up. Blood smeared his face, but the gleam in his eyes told me he wasn't hurt bad.

And then another bomb came through the rift.

I caught it out of the corner of my eye and yanked Zeke to the ground. Small pieces of metal shot over our heads, and one hit McNab's side. He gasped and started convulsing.

Oh, God. We couldn't wait for Maria!

I climbed to my feet just as another Dark One strode through the rift, immediately followed by a second one, and then a third.

Zeke had stood as well. He looked shaken, but his eyes filled with fire. He'd picked up my sword, well, his sword from where I'd dropped it again.

"Hold 'em off!" I told him. Then I turned to McNab.

McNab's eyes were open but crazed and his eyes pale. Battle shock, I guess, along with blood loss. McNab closed his eyes again. I realized his bandages were soaked.

I took a deep breath. He wasn't going to make it more than a few minutes.

We just couldn't wait for Maria. I fished the knife the Sioux had given me out of my boot. It seemed fitting, somehow to use it. But how?

I hadn't needed a ritual when I killed Cassidy. His soul had closed the rift. I had to trust that McNab's would do the same.

It had to be done.

Yells and the clang of sword on sword came from behind me. I ignored them and raised the knife.

I did what had to be done.

I killed my friend.

THIRTY-SIX

A CRY SOUNDED BEHIND ME. I turned to see the rift shifting from grey to a swirl of black and white. The colors mixed and whirled and slowly the white overcame the black. It spread until it filled the disk, and then the entire rift winked out.

Only then did I see Zeke, standing and gasping for breath. The three Dark Ones that had entered lay dead at his feet. We were the only two people upright in the room.

Which didn't last. Two dwarves in doctor robes rushed in from the outer room. They immediately went among the fallen, moving from one to another quickly. One stopped by a dwarf that was only injured instead of dead. Neither of them gave me or Zeke more than a glance.

I sagged against the side of the altar. Every bone in my body felt weary, but there was one thing left to do. I turned back to McNab.

His eyes were closed, which helped. I kept my gaze on his face, so I didn't have to see all the blood on his chest. I'd dropped the knife without realizing it. Not that I wanted it again. Whoever found it could keep it.

I sensed Zeke at my side. I didn't turn. After a bit, he put one hand on my shoulder.

"Time to go, sir," he said. "Maria's here."

I grimaced at the "sir" but let it go. Instead, I turned to see Maria, her face grim, standing in the doorway. She nodded and stepped back, an obvious invitation to join her. Just seeing her made every bruise and cut on my body scream reminders that they were there.

We picked our way among the dead dwarves. As we did, more of the robed ones pushed past Maria and moved to their fallen comrades. There would be much mourning later, I suspected. For everyone.

Though to my surprise, I wasn't as torn up about McNab as I'd expected to be. Or as I thought I should be. His soul had closed the rift. He'd done what had to be done, as did I. I missed him, and grief had already found a home in my chest.

But without guilt. Not like it'd been with Cassidy.

I couldn't help shaking my head with irony. Captain Mercer had once called me the most dangerous man in the army. Yet I'd only killed two humans. And both had been my friends.

Maria led us back to the hospital building. For once, we didn't have an escort, and she didn't have her shadow of a spy. We just walked through the town as if we were welcome, which I knew we weren't.

All the beds in the hospital were full when we arrived, but Brody saw us and sat up. He scooted to the foot of his bed. Maria shepherded both me and Zeke to the head of the bed and had us sit down.

"Where are you hurt?" she asked.

"My arm." Zeke pointed to a bloody spot on his shirt just below his left shoulder. I hadn't even noticed it before.

"You?" she asked me.

I did a quick check. I ached in dozens of places and my leg hurt, but that seemed to be all it was. I couldn't see any blood anywhere beyond some scrapes. I slowly shook my head.

"Let me see that," she said to Zeke. "Please take off your shirt." Then to me, "Go wash up. Use soap." She pointed toward a door on the far wall.

I nodded and headed to where she'd indicated. Inside, I found a small toilet and a sink. I marveled at the toilet. It was indoors and it didn't stink. I lifted the lid and saw what looked like a big hole or pipe. I closed it and shook my head in wonder.

The dwarves had built an entire city in a few months. They'd mined hundreds of acres for gold. They'd even managed a privy that didn't smell. They'd done marvels.

Yet they'd been slaughtered by the Dark Ones. Even Eira's magic on the other side of the rift hadn't protected them.

We'd basically saved them by closing the rift. But somehow, I suspected they'd still be mad.

It didn't take long for me find out and I wasn't disappointed. I walked back from the privy into the main room to find Alviss already there. He glared at me with the fury of a mountain lion and the disgust of someone who's swallowed a dung beetle. He actually strode toward me, with two angry dwarf warriors in his wake.

"What did you do?" he snarled.

"So you can speak English." I glared back at him as hard as I could. Even though I was a bit taller, he outweighed me by quite a bit, and every muscle in his body was coiled for a strike.

"I can now." He dismissed it with a wave. "You closed the rift. Open it."

"Nope," I said. "Can't. How'd you learn English?"

He almost snarled in frustration at me changing the subject.

"Open it!"

I squared my shoulders and looked him right in the eye.

"I. Can't. You know what it takes to open a rift. We don't have someone here who can do it."

This time he did snarl and he looked around wildly. When he spotted Maria, he barked an order to his two guards, who then strode toward her.

My Colt was out of my holster in a flash. I stepped back so I could level it at his face.

"Touch her and die." I cocked the hammer back.

He smirked "If I die, you die."

"And if I don't report to the Sioux village in two days, the army will tear this place to the ground. You all die."

His jaw tightened even more as he worked it out.

"That's right," I added. "You can't catch Jeremiah. It's too late."

We glared at each other. I didn't dare look to see what was happening with Maria. I wasn't going to blink first.

Alviss did. He said something loud and curt in dwarvish and the room around us went quiet.

"We cannot make medicines or blades here," he said. "We need the rift opened."

"Last time I checked, the Dark Ones had taken over. They were even coming through."

"We could fight them."

"You'd already lost."

His gaze flicked to my gun and then his eyebrows rose in a silent question. I lowered my Colt.

"We have not lost as long as we live," he said.

"And you'll stay alive on this side of the rift. As long as you don't do something stupid."

That seemed to strike home. For the first time, his shoulders sagged.

"We will trade with you," I said. "For your gold if nothing else."

He snorted and shook his head. "Not gold."

"Then the other things you mine. The Army could use iron. We'd pay well for that."

He stared at me, but it was more like he was thinking hard than glaring at me. I decided to press the point.

"The Sioux have accepted your claim. The Crow who fought you are dead. The Army will leave you alone as long as you don't cause trouble." I almost said, "As long as you don't try to open another rift," but I knew that was pointless. They were going to try no matter what. We'd just have to make sure they couldn't get a human witch to do it.

Alviss frowned and then slowly turned and looked over the hospital room. His eyes moved from wounded dwarf to wounded dwarf. Finally, he turned back to me.

"Get out," he said. "Before I change my mind."

We were on horseback within an hour. Once Brody and Zeke were awake and moving, neither needed much time to gather his things. Washta didn't have much to begin with. Maria had already packed, once she'd known we were headed for the rift. She retrieved McNab's things and wrangled a promise out of the dwarves to bury his body. Anoki found some food, we filled our canteens, and were off.

We rode hard through the cool night until we reached the east end of the road at the timber cutting spot. We had to slow down then, given the darkness and the lack of a clear path. Except it wasn't as dark as I'd expected. In fact, it was close to sunrise.

Suddenly, I felt bone tired. All the rush of the past few days wore off in one great whoosh. I could barely hang on to my pony. Somehow I did, at least until Zeke nearly fell from his horse. He'd started to doze in the saddle and just barely caught himself in time.

"We need a break," I said. As much as I wanted to push on, I knew we had a ways to go.

"I'll keep watch, sir!" Brody volunteered.

"All yours, Private." Grateful, I found a soft spot of dirt near a pine and nodded off.

I awoke to the fleeting memories of a dream about McNab, but it'd faded by the time I'd sat up. I snorted softly. I'd expected a nightmare after what'd happened, but whatever the dream was, it wasn't that.

To my mild surprise, Washta sat a few feet away with her face toward the risen sun. I judged it to be an hour or so past dawn, which meant I hadn't slept long. Brody slowly circled our little camp, his rifle held across his chest. He glanced my way and smiled before turning his eyes outward again.

Even in guard duty, missing an ear, the kid had a dogged determination I couldn't help but admire.

Especially because that ear had to still hurt. Which made me wonder if he'd taken any of the dwarf medicine.

The others were still asleep, and I figured I should give them a little longer. So I decided to join Washta. She didn't move when I walked up next to her, but looked at me as I sat down beside her.

"Good morning," I said. "How are you feeling?"

"Strange." Her voice felt far away. "Yesterday, I did not expect to feel the sun on my face again, yet now..." She closed her eyes and turned back to the dawn.

"But you're still gonna die." It might've been rude to say, but it just slipped out. "I mean, they didn't cure you."

A small pursed grin crossed her lips. "No, they did not."

"Well..." I didn't know how to say it so I just decided to be direct. "I still appreciate what you would've done. That was pretty brave."

"No braver than your McNab. Anoki told me about his injury." She looked over at the sleeping Indian and smiled affectionately.

I let out a heavy sigh.

"I'm... I'm not sure I did the right thing." Yet even as I said the words, I knew they weren't true.

"Would your McNab have done it? If he could?"

I thought about that. I thought long and hard. McNab had once told me he was too stubborn to die. But he'd also made it clear he was done with being in the army, done with the missions. He'd just wanted one last ride.

For me.

That's when the guilt hit. Not that I'd stabbed him, but that he'd come on this mission at all. He'd still be alive if I'd left him back in Fort Chicago. Instead, I'd gotten him shot by the Crow and then by the Dark Ones, until my knife was a mercy.

My stomach tightened so bad I thought I'd be sick.

"It is not bravery," Washta said, "when death is certain. There is no fear to overcome. I was ready, last night. I will be ready when it comes."

"You could still recover."

She slowly shook her head. "I will be gone by winter. But at least Anoki will be home."

She looked fondly at him, just as he started to stir.

THIRTY-SEVEN

WE RODE as hard as we dared through the warm day. All the bruises and cuts and other injuries seemed to hurt even more than they had the day before. A bouncing horse just made them worse. It didn't help that Maria had run out of dwarf medicine. She had some of her willow bark powder, but it didn't work nearly as well.

We didn't talk much as we rode. Mostly we all seemed to be eager to be as far from the town as we could get. From time to time, Zeke or Brody would look back, but we were never followed.

Dusk fell just as the Sioux village came into view. The first camp-fires served as our beacons, guiding us in. Several warriors and, surprisingly, a large number of children, came out to meet us. They hailed us and started talking to Washta and Anoki in excited tones. When we reached the center of camp, I dismounted and almost fell to the ground from exhaustion. The ride and the day before had taken more out of me than I'd thought.

Instead, Zeke caught me. He eased us toward the nearest fire, where some large rocks gave us makeshift seats. I'd barely sunk to the ground when Jeremiah appeared.

"You're alive," he said. "How'd it go?"

"We closed the rift. Well, McNab did." I started to explain what happened but he interrupted me.

"Let me get my notebook."

I nodded, and while I waited, a Sioux boy cautiously approached and handed me some still-warm buffalo meat with some berries. My stomach reminded me we'd skipped dinner during our hurried ride, and so I tore into the food. Zeke ate with similar gusto. He actually grinned at me when I looked his way.

I wondered about Brody, but didn't see him in the crowd of Sioux milling around. Nor Maria or Anoki. I figured they'd manage fine, though.

When Jeremiah returned, he sank to the ground beside me. His face was more somber.

"So McNab closed the rift," he said.

"Yeah." I described McNab's horrible injury and how it'd been a struggle to keep him alive even long enough to get to the altar.

"He was a good man," Jeremiah said. "We will miss him terribly."

The grief grabbed my heart at those words, and I choked up. I managed to nod and then swallowed my sob. He'd been a hero. I could hold onto that thought.

"So… tell me what happened," Jeremiah said, "and please start at the beginning."

"Where's that?"

"Right after I left."

So I did. I told him about my plan with Washta to close the rift once we found it, and then how I demanded that Alviss let us help. He asked a lot of questions about the world on the other side of the rift—I still couldn't pronounce its name correctly. I kind of skipped through McNab's death. I didn't want to relive it, and he didn't press me. Instead, he laughed when I told him about Alviss speaking English.

"What?" I asked. "It was strange."

"I can imagine," he said, "but I'm surprised he didn't do it earlier."

"He wanted to hide it from us," I grumbled.

"I'm sure he did, but that wasn't the only reason." When I raised a questioning eyebrow, he continued, "Apparently there's some magic that will allow them to understand all spoken languages, but, obviously, it can only be cast in their world and not ours."

"But they can still understand everything when they come back to ours?"

"That's what the dwarf I'd sort of made friends with said. He was trying to learn English and was upset that he wasn't given a chance to go through the rift and get the spell cast on him."

"I wonder why."

Jeremiah shrugged. "We don't know how their magic works since it doesn't work here."

"Yeah," I conceded. "Good thing it doesn't work here. Those bombs they threw were bad enough."

"You got lucky there."

"I get lucky all the time."

Jeremiah laughed at that. I'd meant it seriously, and my face heated as I first thought he was making fun of me.

"You are so, so right," Jeremiah said once he'd stopped chuckling. "The Lord must be looking out for you."

"He is." Zeke had somehow come up behind without us hearing him. "Billy does the work of the Lord. He may not know he does the Lord's work, but we do."

I was about to disagree, when Zeke casually rested one hand on the hilt of his sword. The only dwarvish sword we'd come away with. If a huge colored man could be the Angel of Vengeance, then that was Zeke. I wasn't about to argue with him.

Zeke sat cross-legged on the ground next to us, after first undoing his sword belt so the sword wouldn't stab the dirt. He held it tenderly before setting it beside him when one of the Indian boys appeared with more food. We all just ate quietly for a while.

Maria found us about the time we were finished. Somewhere along the way, she'd washed her face, combed her hair, and changed into a new brown Sioux-style dress. She looked almost refreshed compared to how doggone tired I felt.

She also looked smug.

"You know something. What?"

"Washta has told the tribal leaders that they will give the Crow half of the dwarf medicine to stop the war. They are arguing now."

I rolled my eyes. If the tribal leaders were anything like the army, there was no way they wanted to give up the medicine. But I also was sure Washta would get her way.

Which reminded me, she wanted Anoki back with the tribe. She'd made me promise to get him discharged. Of course, that'd been if she'd closed the rift, and she hadn't.

But it still didn't feel right to make him go back to digging graves in Fort Chicago.

The problem was, I didn't know if I could discharge him. I was pretty sure a lowly lieutenant didn't have that authority. There was probably a lot of paperwork to do as well, and I hated paperwork.

I couldn't encourage him to desert, either. If he got labeled a deserter, there'd be a reward on his head. One of the "Dead or Alive" ones. Besides, he wasn't a coward, like the men who deserted were. He didn't deserve to be labeled like that.

He was just a man who needed to be home.

I snorted softly. He wasn't the only one. The army wasn't my home either. I thought of the people I knew back in Golden City and felt my chest tighten. I missed some of them. Not all of them, but definitely some of them.

And Anoki had left Washta. His wife. That was almost hard to imagine.

He needed to stay with the Sioux. If I ordered him to come back to Fort Chicago, he'd do it, but he'd be miserable.

That's when the idea hit me. I needed to talk to him. Since I didn't see him nearby, I excused myself to the others and went in search of him.

The Sioux camp bubbled with excitement. Children ran everywhere, laughing and throwing little clods of dirt at each other, and stealing bits of meat from the cooking fires. The adults didn't stop them, as most were too caught up in their own conversations or storytelling.

The few warriors who'd survived the trip each had a cluster of people around them, listening to them talk or boast or whatever they were saying in Sioux.

To my complete lack of surprise, I found Anoki with Washta in front of her tipi. For once, he looked relaxed instead of worried, though he drew himself up when he saw me and started to stand.

"At ease, Private," I said.

He blinked at me using his rank, but sat back down.

"We need to report back," I said, "but our mission isn't quite done."

"What do you mean, sir?"

"Our orders were to investigate the town and ensure there was no threat to the Army. There's still a threat, though it's small. We can't have the dwarves opening another rift, and I'm sure they'll try."

"They don't have a witch," Washta said.

"No," I agreed, "but we still need to keep an eye on them." I turned back to Anoki. "So I'm assigning you to do so. Your orders are to stay here in the Black Hills and watch the dwarves. If you see anything suspicious or dangerous, you're to send word to General Sanborn and myself immediately."

He blinked as it sunk in, but Washta was already grinning by the time he turned to her.

"I can stay!" His eyes were wide with excitement.

I chuckled. Somehow, Fort Chicago was going to have to find another gravedigger.

We began the long trek back the next morning. The Sioux gave us what food they could spare and promised to have some warriors ride with us for a day, but I knew we'd be hunting for our meals before long. I didn't care, though. I was tired and sore and ready for everything to be over.

In the evenings, Jeremiah, Brody, and I talked around the campfire. Jeremiah mostly asked questions and probed for details for the book he was writing. Brody was more philosophical.

"I understand why you leave the boring parts out," he said to Jeremiah one night after we'd been riding for a week. "But why do you leave the bad stuff out?"

"I don't leave the bad stuff out," Jeremiah said. He pointed at Brody's ear, which, while still bandaged, no longer pained him. "That's going in the book."

"But you leave out the blood and the bodies and stuff like that."

"True," Jeremiah conceded, "but no one wants to read that. Why put it in?"

"So... um... people can know what it's *really* like."

I chuckled. "If you'd known what it was really like, would you have wanted to be a hero?"

"I... um..." He stammered to a stop as the blush overtook his face.

"You are, you know," Jeremiah said.

When Brody looked at me, I nodded.

"You saved our lives back in the Dark Ones' camp," I said. "I promise you'll get a medal for it."

"I, uh... okay."

"And... if you're willing," I continued, "I'll ask to have you transferred to my command."

Brody didn't stop beaming for the rest of the night.

THIRTY-EIGHT

SEVERAL MILES outside of Fort Chicago, we spotted a small patrol riding toward us. I couldn't help grinning. As tired as we all were, and as much as Fort Chicago wasn't home, it was good to be back.

As the patrol approached, I looked for members of my former team. I didn't recognize anyone. The officer in charge appeared to be in his sixties, with a grey-white beard and hair and more wrinkles in his face than I'd seen in an army officer. He wore a sergeant's insignia on his crisp uniform. Ours weren't nearly as nice, though we had washed them at Fort Randall a few weeks before.

That had been quite a melancholic visit. Captain Logan had been very upset to learn about the deaths of Lieutenant Caldwell and his team. He gave the impression that he would've ridden out himself in revenge if there'd been any Dark Ones left. He'd thanked us again and again for stopping what would've been a disaster. He'd promised to help the Sioux keep an eye on the dwarves.

Of course, he did suggest he'd be able to do a better job with more men and more supplies, if I could find a moment to suggest that to General Sanborn. That was the way of the army. Even in the middle of grief, ask for more provisions. I'd said I'd do my best and we'd set out for the rest of the long journey home. Well, back to Fort Chicago.

The patrol was only four men, instead of the usual six. Their horses were also on the bony side. Apparently, supplies were already short near the Fort. Even though we outnumbered them, they stopped a respectful distance away and waited for us to approach. The sergeant saluted when we were close.

"Sergeant MacIntyre, Fort Chicago, western patrol."

I returned his salute. "Lieutenant McCarty, returning from special assignment. We've been gone for months. What's the news?"

"The army's in Indiana, sir. The Jotun didn't go for New England. They crossed the river at Louisville and came for us."

I winced. That was unexpected.

"How's the fighting going?" Jeremiah asked.

"We stopped 'em," MacIntyre said, "but casualties were high. General Sanborn himself was wounded. He's back at the fort."

"Ah," I said. "Who's in charge at the front?"

"General Mosby, sir. General Sanborn promoted him."

I nodded. That was good. Mosby was very clever and known for sneak attacks. As long as he had the men, I was sure he'd push the Jotun back.

Jeremiah cleared his throat and looked pointedly at me. I rolled my eyes. We were back in the army all right.

"Please take us to General Sanborn," I told MacIntyre. "It's not an emergency, but he'll want to see us right away."

MacIntyre saluted, and only then did his eyes widen. He hadn't said anything, but I couldn't help wondering if he recognized some of us and just had the good sense to keep it to himself.

***

We headed straight for Sanborn's headquarters. I didn't see any reason to delay, and I figured we should all be present when we reported. It was probably my best chance to get medals for my team, after Sanborn saw us all there together. MacIntyre agreed to take care of our horses and so we all walked into the building together.

In the reception room, the general's aide's eyes widened as we filed in. He stood and I spotted his captain bars. I quickly saluted.

"Lieutenant McCarty and team," I said. "Reporting to General Sanborn. We're back from the Black Hills."

"The General's at the hospital, Lieutenant. Why don't you and your team take a seat in the briefing room while I send someone for him?" He gestured toward the room where I'd first received my orders.

Inside, most of my team settled into the chairs around the long conference table. Jeremiah wandered over to the large map on the wall. After a moment I joined him.

"I think we're winning," he said. He gestured to little penciled squares on the map. "These should be our men." He pointed at some circles. "These should be the Jotun. Judging from these erasure marks, we've been pushing them back."

I nodded. The fighting was clearly in Ohio now, except for what looked like one small group in southern Indiana along the river. If those Jotun couldn't get back across the river, they'd certainly be destroyed.

I stepped back and looked at the Black Hills part of the map. Someone had drawn a thick question mark on it, a bit north of where the dwarves of Deadwood actually were. Well, that was one thing we could fix.

There wasn't much else of interest on the map, so I found my own seat. We waited about twenty minutes before General Sanborn arrived, trailed by his aide holding a notebook and pencil.

I blinked in surprise as we all rose to our feet and saluted. He didn't look as worn or as tired as when I'd seen him before we'd left, nor as gaunt.

But he was missing his left hand. His arm ended in a bandaged stump.

"At ease," he said, "and welcome back. Report, Lieutenant McCarty."

"Dwarves, sir," I answered. "The town was built by dwarves who came through the Andersonville rift, but then opened one of their own. We've closed it, though."

"This sounds like a long story. Be seated."

He took a chair at the head of the table as we all sat back down.

His aide sat at his right and flipped his notebook open. General Sanborn gestured for me to begin, so I did.

I started at the beginning and gave him the full report. He asked questions here and there, some to me and some to my team. He was impressed at Brody's quick thinking with the Dark Ones and nodded when I suggested a medal. He made me back up and describe McNab's injuries and even had Zeke describe them, too.

"So the Sergeant-Major was already dying," he murmured. "God rest his soul."

"Yes, and he closed the rift."

"Which was the right thing to do," General Sanborn said. "As much as I would love those swords and medicine, we cannot have an enemy in our rear."

"I'm not sure the dwarves are our allies, though."

"True. But there's no sense in making them enemies either. We'll keep an eye on them, along with the Sioux. That was good thinking, assigning a private with local knowledge to stay behind and watch."

That hadn't been why I'd left Anoki, but I didn't feel the need to correct the general.

"Anything more?"

I shook my head. The general's eyes went from person to person and when they all shook their heads too, he stood. We were all on our feet at the same time.

"Then dismissed," he said. "Get some rest. Take one of the barracks reserved for visitors. I'll send a messenger when we know what we're going to do with you."

My heart skipped. I hoped, hoped, hoped he'd remember his promise to let me have my own troubleshooting team. But given the way the war was going, I could see him sending us to the front. However, before I could muster the words, the general walked out.

I settled onto a bench in the mess hall and took a deep whiff of my coffee. Glorious, glorious coffee. The coloreds had driven the trolls far enough back from New Orleans that they'd been able to open the port again. The first shipment of coffee beans had made its way up the Mississippi to Fort Chicago the week before, and I was one of the lucky, lucky, recipients.

I slowly savored each sip.

As much as I'd loved being on the trail, I'd really missed some things. Coffee was near the top of the list. So was a bed. The ground got rough after a while. For that matter, a solid roof was a blessing.

I idly wondered how long we'd stay. With the fighting still going on in Ohio, I suspected it'd be days, at most. Not that I wanted to go fight the Jotun, but at least that was simple. I didn't have to figure out who was the enemy and who wasn't. There was something pleasant about that.

We'd already spent a few days at the Fort and none of us had been given any specific orders. Maria had returned to the hospital, but the rest of us remained in one of the guest quarters. Our units were still out fighting, and I suspected the Army wasn't quite sure where to reassign us.

That was fine by me. I had coffee and a bed and no need to rush anywhere.

After a bit, Jeremiah came into the mess hall. He carried his notebook and gave me a broad smile. I waved him over, and his eyebrows rose when he saw the steam from my mug.

"Coffee," I said. "There still might be some hot."

"I'm good." He chuckled at my expression of mock disbelief and sat down across from me. "I've been writing the next book all morning."

"About Deadwood?"

"Mmm hmm. I hope you won't object to reading it this time? I'm not sure I have all the details correct, particularly when you were fighting the Dark Ones in the woods."

I looked at him as I took another sip. He was gonna make me out as a hero again. It didn't bother me that much, though. He was right, the world needed heroes.

"Okay…," I said, "but only if you make Brody out to be a hero, too."

"Oh, I will."

That was good. Brody'd lost an ear, after all. He deserved to be a hero.

And speaking of him… Brody appeared in the mess hall doorway. My eyebrows went up. He wore his full dress uniform and had his new medal pinned to his chest. I had to chuckle. We'd had the ceremony the day before and I wondered if he'd ever taken it off. He looked around and, when he spotted us, hustled in our direction. As he reached our table, he came to attention and saluted.

"Sir! General Sanborn wishes to see us, sir!"

"Now?" I asked. I took another sip of coffee. Since it was still hot, I didn't want to leave any behind.

"Sir, yes sir!"

Jeremiah chuckled and stood with me. We didn't have to share an eye roll to know what the other thought. Sometimes army life was just silly.

General Sanborn met us in the conference room. To my surprise, Captain Mercer stood next to him. The Captain, whom I supposed was still my direct commander, looked worn and tired, though uninjured. The corners of his mouth turned up when he saw me, and then broke into a full smile when I saluted.

"Lieutenant McCarty, Sergeant Freeman, and Private Brody, reporting as ordered, sir!" I stood straight and tall.

"At ease." General Sanborn looked us all over before returning his gaze to me.

"We've been wondering what to do with you, Lieutenant. I know we promised you your own command of a troubleshooting team before you left for the Black Hills, but Captain Mercer makes a good argument that we'd be better with you at the front."

I glanced at the Captain. He pursed his lips and didn't look like he felt guilty at all. My blood started to heat.

"But as good as his argument is," General Sanborn continued, "we did make a promise to you. So we thought we'd phrase it as a request. Will you come assist Captain Mercer at the front?"

"I'd…" I swallowed hard. "I'd like my own troubleshooting team, sir. Like Captain Cassidy's."

General Sanborn gave Captain Mercer a sly smile. "Told you."

Mercer just shrugged in acknowledgement.

"So we have new orders for you," General Sanborn said. "There's been a giant sighting in the mountains south of Fort Laramie. It may be that one that went missing from your time in Colorado, or it may be something else. We want you to take a team and investigate. When you're done, report back to Golden City. We'll have orders for your next mission delivered there."

"Sir, yes sir!" This time I saluted with enthusiasm. I couldn't have kept the smile off my face if I'd tried.

"Dismissed."

Jeremiah, Brody, and I turned and marched out. Once outside, I relaxed and saw them grinning back at me.

"You know what this means, Billy?" Jeremiah asked.

"Yeah. We're going home."

AUTHOR'S NOTES

Scout rounds out Billy's growth from wanting to be a sidekick (in *Sidekick*), through his heroism as part of a bigger team (in *Sharpshooter*), to being a hero and leader in his own right.

As with *Sidekick and Sharpshooter*, my goal was to make the Mythic West Universe as realistic as possible. The history up through 1865 is identical to the actual history of the United States. All the history after the rift at Andersonville was opened is my best extrapolation of what was likely to have happened. This story centers on the dwarves, who were unexpected visitors from the other side of the rift. I wanted antagonists that weren't pure villains both to show the greys of the world and to make Billy's job a bit tougher. Too often, action stories are just "kill all the bad guys." That's harder to do if the hero doesn't really know who the bad guys are.

I set the story in Deadwood, South Dakota, partially for the name and reputation, and partially because the largest gold mine in North America is nearby in Lead, South Dakota. The Sioux and the Crow, who warred several times with each other, both contested the land at various times, which added to Billy's challenges in identifying who exactly were the enemies.

This story also let me explore magic, which does not exist on Billy's side of the rift. I'd already introduced elements of how magic changed into high technology in my novel *Gunslinger*. The obvious "magics" to add here were the technologies of monomolecular blades and highly effective painkillers.

Finally, I wanted to continue to explore what it means to be a hero. While Billy worked his way to accepting what he had to do in the end, he got to mentor his own wanna-be sidekick in Brody. This let me look at heroism from both a mentor and mentee perspective. Hopefully they both will have many adventures to come.

ABOUT THE AUTHOR

A fourth-generation Coloradoan, Edward J. Knight only left the Denver area long enough to learn how to put a satellite into orbit. Four satellites (and counting) later, he's returned to both the mountains and writing fantastical fiction. Along the way, he met the love of his life and became the father of two amazingly curious kids. He's a huge fan of tightly constructed universes and smart plots. He hopes his own Mythic West stories hold up to those standards. More of his work can be found at www.edwardjknight.com.

Want to keep up on Ed's writing and get notified when new books are released? Sign up at www.edwardjknight.com/mailing-list/.

www.edwardjknight.com

ACKNOWLEDGMENTS

This novel turned out to be a challenge and I couldn't have finished it without a great deal of support. First, my wife, Sarah's, continued support has been critical for my continued sanity and productivity. I also want to thank Griffin and Gwyneth for their patience with Daddy being off writing. I'd also like to thank Marcia Knight, Elizabeth Knight, Griffin Knight, Gwyneth Knight, and Steve Hartmeyer for proofreading. I'd also like to express my appreciation to Terry Mixon and Sam Sheddan for their ongoing encouragement.

ALSO BY EDWARD J. KNIGHT

Sidekick

Sharpshooter

Gunslinger

PREVIEW OF GUNSLINGER: THE DRAGON OF YELLOWSTONE

The Fourth Novel in the Mythic West

THEY SAY girls can't be gunslingers. Beth's gonna prove 'em wrong.

Even if she has to fight a dragon to do it.

It won't be easy to prove her worth while working as a hotel chambermaid in Golden City, Colorado. The famous battle that defeated the giants was fought thirteen years ago. The trolls remain confined east of the Mississippi. No one's spotted a harpy since 1875.

But Beth trained with legends: the ghost of Calamity Jane gave her the gun, Wild Bill Hickok taught her to shoot.

And at sixteen, she's ready to make a name of her own.

So, when strange assailants murder a visiting Arapaho Indian shaman, Beth straps on her Colt .45. Without waiting for help, she must find the killers, defeat their dragon, and prevent the destruction of the Western world.